OUT DAMNED SPOT!

OUT
DAMNED
SPOT!

F.J.McQueen

URBANE
Publications

First published in Great Britain in 2016 by Urbane Publications Ltd
Suite 3, Brown Europe House, 33/34 Gleaming Wood Drive, Chatham, Kent
ME5 8RZ
Copyright ©F.J.McQueen, 2016

A CIP catalogue record for this book is available from the British Library.

ISBN 978-1-910692-42-4
EPUB 978-1-910692-43-1
MOBI 978-1-910692-44-8

Design and Typeset by The Invisible Man
Cover by The Invisible Man

Printed in Great Britain by
CPI Group (UK) Ltd, Croydon, CR0 4YY

urbanepublications.com

This book is dedicated to
Anne Bow, carrion crow, for noises off.

ACKNOWLEDGEMENTS

Thank you and huzzah to Matthew Smith, non pareil, sine qua non, rooty toot toot, magnanimous seer and independent publisher supremo.

And a big shout-out to William and Anne Shakespeare and Lewis Carroll.

☙ CHAPTER 1 ❧

SHIRLEY

William was waiting for the Noise. He was sure it was about to kick off for the third night running, he could feel it collecting in the air, he could sense the little clicks and snaps as though it was being doodled from static. William's scalp prickled and the hair rose on his head like a reverse corn circle. Or maybe, William thought, I am about to be struck by lightning — didn't your barnet stand on end if you were in the crosshairs of a lightning bolt?

So he looked up, but the clouds over Balham were patchy, huffed like dandelion-clocks, with the sky mostly clear. Although lightning could fall out of a clear sky, well, it was unlikely, so why the fizz?

Ah ha! William realised he was anxiously bunching and mangling the polyester curtains, it was him inadvertently cranking up the voltage, so he let go of the fabric and tentatively reached down to touch the nylon carpet and release the charge. Before his hand could make contact with a tuft, the air thickened and lit, William recoiled from an almighty sting, and his hair wilted back against his skull.

But the Noise? Where was the Noise?

'Come on, come, get started!' William muttered, his stubbled cheek flat against the window, the view outside stretched by the innumerable times he'd wiped his breath from the pane until he was staring through a smeary magnifying glass. The Noise, when it came, sounded like the hubbub shed by traffic on the world's busiest motorways; metal, rubber and stone shaken through flesh and petrol and tipped onto William and Anne's compact corner house. For the last two nights the Noise had begun at midnight, coming from everywhere then breaking into three, sometimes four, directions. If William pointed to it, the Noise shot away like that gnat in the birdbath he'd tried to rescue with his index finger. When the Noise stopped, it stopped as abruptly as though sliced by a blade. The silence that replaced it, William thought, was the muteness of someone waking during surgery and unable to scream.

William checked his watch, twelve minutes past twelve — the Noise was late, perhaps it wasn't coming — and he turned to look at Anne, a bed-clothed heap with her back to him, night giving her all the definition of a speed bump. The Noise never bothered her. She slept right through it.

'Anne, are you awake?' he said loudly, but the Sleeping Policeman slept on and William went back to staring down at the tiny front garden. Lamplight and a faint London moon made the stunted privet, the erratic crab apple, and the weak-kneed rose bush resemble the cardboard-coloured husks in the dish of ancient potpourri on the hall table. Your eyes could dry out just staring at them, he thought. But then London Nature was desiccated; people scurried along the streets, bottle feeding themselves water because, if they didn't, their flesh would straddle their bones like so much pulled pork.

William listened. Ticktickticktick. Time being sliced like bread; a car engine that rang out as if it had been hoiked like an egg and cracked against a glass bowl; a group of male voices smeared beneath the heal of the wind; a police helicopter that beat like a milli-stranded stethoscope held to the hearts of all wrongdoers. Otherwise the silence, the silence, the puffed-up bags, the nubs and nodules of airy nothing pushed into the box of London to keep its residents in place as the night took them and shook them. Goodnight. Goodnight.

Bed, he thought, get into bed, it's not happening tonight, the novelty of scaring me has obviously worn thin. So William strode back, reapportioned his pillow — and the Noise irrupted! He shot back to the window, perhaps now he'd see the culprits? No, no he couldn't see anyone. No people. None. But what William *could* see made him scream. William screamed and screamed but all he could hear was the Noise — was he screaming the Noise out of his own throat? And he screamed because the Noise had fetched its horror props, its Grand Guignol spectacle, its monstrously cruel tableau - sweet Jesus, they must know I'm a vegan, he thought because ... look what they've done, look, look what they've done! Packed into the garden were the upright, skinned and headless carcasses of cows and bullocks, a horse, sheep, lambs, pigs, hens, even three standing ostriches resembling trunked pouffes balanced on rickety beanpoles. They shimmered. Light shone from their hollow anuses and from their slit bellies, rows of lit candles replacing entrails so that their flesh glowed a maudlin red, and the terrible Noise sang round them in death and bone, in twang and clack.

Hands shaking, William switched on his phone and began filming. Even now, with these meat lanterns only just lit, the stench was slinking through the double glazing, through the foam cavity insulation, and into William's nostrils. It'll smell just as bad outside, he thought, so he opened the latch, stuck the phone through the open window, suddenly aware that the noise sounded different tonight, frantic, louder, wilder. William scoped the phone this way and that, zoomed in and out, took a selfie with the horror clearly visible at his back and his face aghast. The Noise should have fetched the neighbours to their doors and windows, and the police whee-wahing in their squad cars, but it didn't. The street was empty. The houses dark. Mrs Tudor's opposite lay in a shadow that blotted out every feature that made it a home. Mrs Tudor's was a roofed cube on which a shape sat with a violin under its chin, the bow caught midway across the strings, like a paper cut-out flinching beneath someone's breath. The shape tilted and bent though the bow didn't move. It was stuck. Decorative. At least it wasn't a flayed corpse. The phone couldn't pick out the shape from the night sky above it, so William returned his gaze and phone camera to the garden.

'You know what — enough!?' Whoever they were, they weren't going to stop him getting into bed and shutting his eyes. So William climbed beneath the duvet with his shirt tied around his face against the stench, and for two hours sleep failed to ignite. For two hours William listened hard, his other senses switched off at the mains. For two hours William was just a pair of ears dripping fear directly onto his caged and fettered heart, his heartbeats pooling next to him on one side, his sleeping and unawares wife, Anne, on the other. Then the Noise stopped and Anne woke.

'Is that you shaking, William?'

'Of course it's me,' said William, deciding not to tell Anne about the slaughterhouse garden furniture. He doubted it would still be there. And he wasn't going to check.

'Was it that racket again?' Anne said, wiggling her elbow between William's ribs as she tried to turn over to face him. William felt the mole on Anne's crooked arm prodding him, a mole that was, in fact, a drifted nipple, and he tweaked it gently.

'Don't,' said Anne. 'You do that and you're being unfaithful.'

'Hardly,' said William.

'That's how I read it.'

'You should have it removed,' said William, glad of the distraction. The normality.

'I can't,' said Anne. 'You know I can't. I promised mum and dad.'

'You'll still have the ears,' said William.

'True,' said Anne. 'But if that's all that was left of your twin

4

would you be so quick to lop off a third of it?'

'I'm not sentimental.'

'That's because you're a doctor. To the rest of us there's a person involved.'

'You're hardly conjoined twins,' said William. 'Shirley consists of two partially formed ears and a nipple.'

'She's more than that,' said Anne. 'I dream her dreams.'

'How do you know they're not your dreams?'

'Because I know everyone in them and you always dream of strangers. That's how I know.'

'I'm too tired to work out if that makes any sense.'

'Dreams don't have logic. It's like saying that jelly has a sense of rhythm.'

'What?'

'Ignore the noise. It's gone now. Sleep whilst you can, love.'

'Still don't know how you manage.'

'Because I don't make anything of it. Do you still think it's connected to your whistleblowing?'

'If it is, they've gone to a lot of trouble,' William said, 'and after long shifts.'

'Well, you won't have to put up with a lot of nonsense after today. And maybe tonight was their swansong.'

'Bloody weird swan,' said William.

'People are bonkers,' said Anne and rolled over. William reached out and gently played with her ear. The one on Anne's back.

Anne had four ears. Two were where you'd suppose them to be. The other two were arranged on her torso, one a little below her left shoulder and the other above her left breast. They were tiny curls of flesh. They were Shirley. Almost completely absorbed in the womb, Shirley had fought bravely as each trimester gobbled her up. Yes, twin Shirley had been his wife's amniotic kebab log.

'Good night, Shirley,' William whispered into the ear.

'Night, night, Billy boy,' Anne muttered in her sleep.

* * *

Drowsy, with less than two hours before the alarm clock's death rattle, William heard a police helicopter dithering over the street, like a damsel fly with a blocked ovipositor over a puddle. Perhaps the police had arrived to check out the disturbance? Well, it didn't matter now. They'd see nothing. Hear nothing. Besides, today was William's final stint as a doctor attempting to heal the sick and save lives. From now on William would be following Violent Death around with a mop and bucket – he'd be a blue gloved, white masked, disposable overalled, wellington-booted henchman, expunging the unimaginable, rendering horrific crime scenes habitable again. He'd be a veritable Igor after the fact. William would be seeing far more terrible things, greater atrocities, than had populated his garden this night.

William Shakespeare slid into an uneasy and unhappy sleep.

❦ CHAPTER 2 ❦

OBERON OUT

Thirty metres above the ground at 5:30am in the late October darkness, a police helicopter spotlight turned the patch of Balham beneath it into an identikit ultrasound scan. Shifting the light to the East, the photofit foetus was female; appropriating the cowl of a pole-mounted cctv camera to the North, male. They shared a heartbeat — the tarpaulin hooked across a bulging skip which fluttered violently in the helicopter's downdraft. When pilot Inspector Benedicke Othello switched on the heat camera, the foetuses dissolved, replaced by a creeping blood spatter.

'Rats,' said Copilot, Sergeant Iago McDuff, 'I'd call that an infestation, sir.'

And an annealed clot.

'Dog fox or tom cat about to order from the menu,' said Pilot Inspector Benedicke Othello.

'Order what, sir?'

'The rat du jour.'

'Um. Right, sir.'

'But no sign of our missing Silver Surfer. You think you've seen everything then a new craze comes along and it's OAPs slithering about on car crawlers, whizzing to the shops beneath rows of parked cars. I blame it on fish oils and yoga. They bend when they didn't used to. Back in the day you could rely on the senior element seizing up. Have you seen them, McDuff?'

'No, sir. The wife has. One let her have a go and she slid the whole length of the high street beneath the parked cars. Said it's addictive.'

'Well don't let her make a habit of it — ha!'

'Ha ha. No, sir. Ha. Oh, and when she walked back to the precinct afterwards, she saw your new Mrs Othello with someone. My wife presumed it was her brother. They were about the same age. Obviously knew one another very well.'

'My wife doesn't have a brother.'

'Cousin, then. You could see they were close.'

'Quite likely. Anyway, car crawlers. You get convoys. Dozens of them head to toe. This is the oddest thing I've come across in twenty years in the force, McDuff. And the man we're looking for, well, he's the oddest of the odd. He's always accompanied by a crony in Pierrot costume.'

'Hercule Pierrot, sir?'

'No, McDuff. Pierrot. A type of morose clown not a fusspot Belgian sleuth.'

'Why the choice of companion, sir?'

'Haven't a clue. Probably a hanger on. Our man's titled. Had funds until he distributed them among his heirs to avoid inheritance tax or maybe to enjoy the squabbles caused by his decisions.'

'His family must be concerned.'

'Not in the slightest. His personal trainer reported him missing because he'd not been paid. There are doubts about the man's mental state, hence the flagrant use of police resources. But he's not here or he would have emerged by now. Better report back.'

'Wilco, Sir.' Sergeant Iago McDuff said, flicking the radio intercom. 'This is Sergeant Iago McDuff of Police Helicopter Unit 372. No sighting of missing IC1 male, Albert Lear, in the vicinity of the Prospero Estate. We're returning to base, over and out.' Sergeant Iago McDuff turned to his senior officer. 'I meant to say, sir, congratulations on your recent marriage. You surprised us all.'

'I hadn't expected to marry. An old warrior of the law such as myself, and so set in my ways, well, I thought no one would have me. But there you are. Love conquers all.'

'Apparently, sir'.

'And the helicopter jinked, rose and vanished.

* * *

William Shakespeare cornered the now unwatched and empty road as though he was riding an out-of-control jackhammer and not driving a car. As he slowed to avoid the speed camera, an elderly man wearing a crushed sombrero and lying on a car creeper slid from under a parked haulage truck and vanished with aplomb between the wheels of a darkened Hackney cab. A moment later he was followed by a sad, chalk-faced man in black swim-cap and baggy white costume. Volition made the material ripple like vibrating milk.

'Fancy that,' said William Shakespeare and sped on, mounting the pavement, his bumper thwacking a phalanx of steel shutters the colour of thin catering trays. The shutters fought back, cracking William's wing mirror. 'Typical,' William mouthed. Nothing seemed inert anymore. He sucked meditatively on his breakfast of Parma Violet sweet crumbs and thought about his wife's vendetta against these, his favourite confection. She'd bludgeoned his stash of fifty packets before tipping them into the council wheely bin. He'd had to drop the bin on its side and climb in, torch twitching, to rescue them, scooping the wreckage into a plastic bag which he'd then hidden in the glove compartment. The torn wrappers leaked mauve smidgens and William gathered them on his licked little finger. In a way it was more fun than popping an immaculate sweet.

A heavy rain began to fall from a pre-dawn violet sky. The spray rose in a doughy pall which looked, for all the world, like a ghost attempting to stroke cats, or a swarm of rats trying to make-off with the horizon. And on William wended, clipping the kerb, a buffoon behind the wheel, the fluffy dice, stuffed with his mother's ashes, swinging like incense censers. William glanced at himself in the rearview mirror above them. Yes, I look as grim as the man in the white rigmarole and swim cap, he thought. He scratched his tuppence-sized bald patch and considered that he'd soon have that swim-cap look himself. He stroked his soul patch, scratched the several transdermal patches on his arm (nicotine and a drug trialled male contraceptive) and tickled his left wrist from which a small eyepatch hung. His. He'd worn it for three glum childhood years to correct what his father had called 'a bleeding lazy eye like the bleeding rest of him'. Fawn-pink and pin-punctured, it was the miniature facsimile of the speaker on his Gran's circa 1970s transistor radio. Tied to his wrist by its perished elastic thread, it had served as a proxy lucky rabbit foot, and he'd biro-ed a full and obviously living lagamorph on it — a picture he had continued to refresh into adulthood, every time it attempted to delete itself. His ten year old peers had owned real rabbit paws dangling from key rings clipped to their schoolbags. They'd use them as weapons, scratching William's arms, and he'd wept because the rabbits had been murdered. If the rabbits had been alive he knew they wouldn't have hurt him, so he turned thief and rescued them. Twenty seven paws were hidden in his pockets and his socks and his satchel and nobody guessed it was him despite the lumps and bulges. Anyway, his Gran died the week of his thievery, and when William was marched into the funeral parlour to say goodbye to her, he tipped the lot down the side of the pink frilly, hairdresser's style gown his Gran was wrapped in — she looked as though she was having a nap after a particularly gruelling tint and perm. No one noticed. The adults were arguing about whose flowers could ride atop the coffin in the hearse and blows were being freely exchanged.

Ah the past. Such an appointment of contrary places to be visited by the heart and the long sword. Another dibdab of Parma Violet sweets.

I am a thing of patches, William thought as he cut across a narrow strip of wasteland, swerving to avoid several abandoned breeze blocks angled in the ground like bongo drums. He slid a CD into the player, his favourite album — Oberon Out. Yes, that was better. William hummed along to synthetic jazz from the Richard Burbage Band. Then he sang. 'Do dah dah, hawk from a handsaw, plywood, two-by-four, another hand, another jaw, takes a special drift to shut that door, dah doo doo.' Life, eh, what a palaver!

* * *

Twenty-three minutes later, William Shakespeare was roving the soft gradients and profligate leafiness of Hampstead. He was on his way to his last ever shift as a junior doctor at St. Largesse Cottage Hospital, his swan-song to prodding mostly docile strangers for a living. Now the road was lined with thin fencing. It swerved with the bends, holding back tubular hedges that pivoted as the rain struck them. And what had he to look forward to today? Ever since he'd admitted to being The Whistleblower, his locker had been filled with urine, harvested from the nearby urology ward, by a score of nurses poking the tube of a fat, mustard-bright catheter bag through the vents in his locker door and squeezing. On the few occasions William had caught a nurse mid-squirt they had passed it off as a good luck charm. As had the midwife. She'd carved his effigy into a fresh placenta, microwaved it in the staff kitchen, and was part way through the first smart-phone-filmed mouthful when William walked in on her.

The traffic was picking-up and now included the occasional articulated lorry, soiled-white transit van, and young career devils in low-key company cars, jackets on hooks, playing parental guidance rap on the way to morning huddles. William wondered if he could really hack it as a crime scene cleaner? Death was very different in hospital. Post mortems, the most violent, if legal, acts committed on a human body, were far more civilised than any aftermath of violent death. Would he be able to remove every species of heinous stain, could he obliterate the bloody spatters and spots sufficiently to earn his living in an increasingly competitive business? Crime scene cleaning was the new taxis, every Yvonne, Yoda and Yorick were setting up a crime scene cleaning business. William flipped open the glove compartment again, and retrieved a scrap of paper with a phone number on it. He re-read it. The Butcher had given it to him. The Butcher! William shuddered, a vegan since childhood, he had needed three brandies, two hours of self-hypnosis and a surgical face-mask impregnated with patchouli to enable him to enter the Butcher's shop. According to his wife's best friend and fellow water-birth specialist midwife, Helena, the Butcher had been insistent, he would not divulge the number unless it was a face-to-face transaction during business hours. William had watched till the shop was empty before going in. A bell tinkled above him like the signal for transubstantiation. Despite the patchouli, William smelled the smells he was almost on a social footing with from the mortuary. Unlike the mortuary, though, the Butcher's light had a candy-pink cast created by the blood, the white ceramic tiles, the white lightbulbs and the white trays cradling the unpicked bodies of guileless, murdered creatures. William gagged, choked back tears but couldn't blow his running nose without removing the face mask.

'Pickings from the internal fruit tree of the beast,' said the Butcher, rippling a rill of livers and slamming his chopper into a wooden board whose deep, fine cuts would render, if sliced thinly in transverse sections, William imagined, a great number of long wooden combs. The Butcher had hair like a centuries' deep ossuary of bluebottles, a face in which the ample fat had set so that his eyes were fixed slightly askance, his mouth damp and ruddy from baling out words. The Butcher's hands, though, were thin and tapered, ending in tiny shellac-bright nails. The finger tops, were deeply dented. Catching William's stare, the Butcher clenched and dropped his hands beneath the counter, rummaged round and returned them, clad in blue latex gloves. Twanging the cuffs, he brought them back into play.

'Now, these people, my contacts as it were, they know a thing or two about removing the extreme biological stains you'll be facing. Speak to them but, and I ask this as their friend, do not judge them.' The Butcher had then written down a phone number on a scrap of butcher paper, the loops of his 6s, 9s and 0s mimicking the tiny gelid eggs William noticed heaped alongside a headless, legless, ocarina-hollow chicken.

'Ring these people. Meet them. Do not fear them. They have the information that will see your business flourish. When you have spoken, burn the number.' William took the paper, wiping a tag of flesh from it before folding it into his pocket. 'Go,' said the Butcher, his laughter leaving his throat like slivers dropping from a bacon slicer. 'The Vegetables are worried where you are. Go. Shoo!' William fled.

* * *

The rain had stopped, the CD had ended. William dabbed a few morsels of Parma Violet, licked his fingers, closed the glove compartment. — and slammed on the brakes. A huge horse box was blocking the road ahead. It was painted some colour taken from a sci-fi inspired swatch, and its headlights burned with the strength to levitate a human of considerable poundage and carry them into the mothership. The driver, a woman, was out of the cab and waving at him. Her hair was as white and composite as a blob of poster paint, her nose so thin and sharp it could have borne a ridge of clothes pegs without pain, her mouth was small, oval and with the soft inward-suck of a kitten's arse. She began striding about, seemingly oblivious she was a traffic hazard, twirling a banana skin around her right index finger. Cautiously, William pulled over and climbed out. Her smell hit him. She stank like a room full of hot computers in which a banana festered. She shouted something but William couldn't make out what it was. He shook his head. She shouted again and twirled the banana skin like a gunslinger slinging a gun. William caught the word 'animal'. Was the animal inside the carrier injured? As he wondered if he'd be playing vet in a moment, the woman ran to the back of the vehicle and let down the ramp. William heard a growl. That horse must be in a lot of pain. The whole van shook as it lurched, still unseen, onto the road. The woman then began texting somebody, perhaps calling for extra help, and she stepped aside to let the horse past — and what a horse it was. Tiny legs were stuck on a large, flabby body. Its muzzle was too abrupt, the ears wrongly set and its mane was lost in a rough, pony-like pelt. It was, William thought, one of those spiteful caricatures that Nature sometimes made. Then the beast reared up. A small horse, certainly, but a very large bear. It was a bear. It was, quite incontrovertibly, a grizzly bear fizzing with ill will and outrage. Oughtn't it to be hibernating? Was this the grump of exhaustion? Whatever matter had contributed to its mood, the bear was taking its bearings and its bearings seemed to be William Shakespeare. It hurtled at him. Shocked, William staggered backwards, turned and fled. He tried to climb back into his car but realised the beast would be onto him before he was safely slammed inside. Play dead, play dead, and he saw his crimson organs twitching beneath the Butcher's nimble hands. A car drove by, passing the horse box with difficulty, but it didn't stop to help.

'Call it off! Help me!' William yelled as he threw himself over the hedge, kick-swimming himself clear of the sodden leaves and falling heavily onto his shoulder and into a leaf-plastered garden pond. The bear's head appeared above the greenery on the other side. It yawned. Roared. Yawned. It rifled through the leaves as though picking blackberries, then vanished. William, shivering, soaked to the rind in rank mud, bleeding from assorted cross hatched grazes, heard the bear pad docilely back up its ramp and the woman shut it in.

'Is it safe? Are you okay?' William peered tentatively above the twiggy parapet. 'Are you all right?' But the woman ignored him. Roaring with laughter she climbed back into the horse-box and sped away — her registration number obscured by mud. William, shivering, scratched, confused and shocked — retrieved his phone. 'Okay. I'm going to report you,' he said. A bird clacked and duttered above him. 'Yes, you too, matey.' The phone glowed for an instant, like the portal to the afterlife, and died. No amount of prodding, battery wiping and knocking could revive it. It had drowned in William's pocket.

It wasn't until he arrived, stinking and sodden, at the cottage hospital that William Shakespeare, pausing in front of his urine-dripping locker, realised that he had lost his talisman. His eyepatch had fallen from his wrist in the affray. His charm against the onslaughts of endemic NHS occultism was two miles up the road. William peeled off his filthy shirt, took a deep breath and ran his fingers through his hair, dislodging leaves and twigs. He felt something wending its way across his scalp, and sent his fingers after it. A withered man with what seemed to be fossilised dreadlocks since they clinked like wind chimes, teetered through the STAFF ONLY door towards William, steering a small oxygen canister on wheels.

'Can I help you, sir? Are you lost?' William said. The man nodded and lent into him as he drew alongside, and whispered, 'Not as lost as you are, sunshine. You don't know what they got for you the day, man. You don't know the weave of it.'

'I've got a pretty good idea, thanks,' said William.

'What's happened to your belly button? You come out of

an egg or something? Reptile? Ha ha, like the Queen and that. Illuminati. Unseelie never pinched their bellybuttons, though, so you must be very special. They've done the Fift Ceremony. Your belly button's gone. Good things will come.' William shielded his flesh.

'No. It's … Surgery. I had an operation…'

'What? To remove your bellybutton?' said the man, shuffling closer and bending to get a better look.

'I'd rather you didn't do that,' said William.

'Yeah, now you know what it feels like, peering right at a bit of person. Not nice, is it? Anyway, I can't see no scars.'

'Healed.'

'They don't go, not like that. Move your hand, Doctor.'

'I will not.'

'It's a spell, isn't it? Your belly button's been magicked away by the Unseelie Court.'

'Of course not. What Unseelie Court? What's that?'

'I seen them myself. The bellybuttons. They wear them on their fingertips. Put hazelnuts on a plate. Raisins. Pearls. Dib dab dob with their finger ends and the lot are snugged in the holes. It's a party trick. They have lots of parties. They do an awful lot of tricks. Go and see the Oracle. She'll tell you. Like I said, when they take a bellybutton they confer a certain power on the person they've filched it from. It amuses them. They like to think that if they take they give in return. They give more than you've lost.'

'Oracles aren't… look, superstition does nothing. It doesn't make people better. It doesn't make them worse. Superstition's just a string of nonsense.'

'Says you, the man with no bellybutton.'

'I have got a bellybutton.'

'Have not'

'Have'

'Look, Doctor, follow the green line.'

'What green line?' said William. There wasn't a green line,

only the grey floor and the blunt wall-mounted signs and the salutary smells drifting between them.

'The green line you can see only by not looking at it. Peripheripherererarily.'

'What-erily?' said William, and the man stared at nothing in particular. William followed his gaze and a wavy green line swung into focus, flowing away down the corridor. 'Ah... I haven't seen that before.'

'You wouldn't, you don't see it till someone tells you it's there. That'll take you to her. Mind, she's got friends staying. Two other Oracles. Their hospitals are beh beh beh being refurbish-sh-sh-ed...'the man had started to gasp. "S'all righ", I'm ill,' he said and doubled-up coughing, his body executing a series of sine waves. William put out his hand to steady the man, then stopped as he felt the something scuttling across his scalp again. This time it abseiled into his ear. William tilted his head, then shook it, slapping the opposite ear to dislodge the crawler. All the while the chiming-dreadlocked man coughed and wafted to and fro. William straightened his neck — he was sure whatever it was had fallen out onto the floor — and he was scanning the sleek grey vinyl around his feet when he felt the thing slip down his ear canal like a child into a cowled slide. For a moment William's jaw stung and his eyes watered, whilst the dreadlocked man's body continued to arc and contract as the coughs burst from it. Blearily, William watched a nurse clop towards them, her feet encased in shoes resembling vented rubber hoofs.

'You two dancing?' the Nurse said before doing a double-take at William's belly. 'Oh, Whistleblower, I see They've had their revenge.'

William straightened up, cupped his belly again and the thin, man gasped, linked arms with the Nurse. They set off walking.

'Follow the thin green line,' wheezed the man without turning round.

'This isn't the Wizard Oz!' said William.

'Yah, go and get a brain, Scarecrow!' called the Nurse.

'And a naval you can gaze into when you've got one,' said the man. 'And by the way,'— he shook the oxygen canister and his dreadlocks (rigid, white as icicles hung by the wall) and the corridor rang. 'Ding dong, your old patient's dead and may his demise impeticos thy gratillity. Tu wit to woo, always end on a merry note!'

'What? Who? Wait! Which old patient? Who's died?' said Shakespeare, but the pair had vanished onto a ward.

William was left with these circumstances: an empty corridor; a worried mind; a vanished naval; a death to pin on a patient like a tail on the Donkey of Mortality; day exceeding day.

* * *

William stared down at his vague bellybutton which had shrunk to the size of a match head. For the past six months, in fact, ever since he blew the whistle on the use of tarot packs in diagnostics, magic spells in theatre, and numerology on waiting lists, his bellybutton had begun to shrink. He kept it open with an earlobe plug. Without flesh tunnels his navel sealed over. When he swam unplugged, by the time he completed his first length, his bellybutton had closed up, trapping a thimbleful of chlorinated water under his skin — he could squish it with his fingertip. Then he'd had to pad to the changing room and extract the water with a syringe and hypodermic before making a small, painful incision and jamming the smallest sized lobe expander into it. Cultivating his belly hair and attempting a comb-over didn't hide the lack of naval. William had also tried wearing higher-waisted trunks but they'd drawn almost as much attention to his missing dent. Then Anne had bought him a sling swimsuit and William's stepbrother, Kit, had extended the height of the sling. 'I am not wearing any sort of mankini!'

'You're like Adam in the Garden of Eden.' Anne said. 'So am

I Lilith, Eve or God, or just the one evictee from Paradise?'

Grabbing a set of green theatre robes from stores and bagging-up his filthy clothes, William, in fart-mongering, dribble-squittering, sodden shoes, checked the time. Yes, ward rounds were about to begin but, hey, so what! After today Dr William Shakespeare would no longer participate in patient care. Why not bunk off? There was only William Kempe that he needed — or wanted — to see. Poor Mr Kempe, re-admitted after a sponsored, and massively publicised, one-hundred mile Morris dance from London to Norwich, he was back on I.C.U. — it'll be blisters and nipple friction, I bet, thought William. I'll rib him about it. So why not visit the Oracle first? Why not leave with my belief in the total inappropriateness of superstition in the NHS intact? William's mind was made up, he'd show them he was no fool. He could see right through their ruses, their con tricks, their connivances. He'd record the interlude on his phone. More proof. Yet more glorious, incontrovertible proof would be his to post on social media and flaunt at any tribunal. He'd add to the images he'd already uploaded, the life-sized corn dollies lining the walls of the fertility clinic and their moon-bathing suites, the taxidermied bats decorating Audiology, the seating in waiting rooms arranged into Minecraft®-chunked pentagrams. So William, dressed all in green, set off on the trail of the thin green line, a line so ethereal it was as difficult to see as a distant cluster of stars from the vantage point of a floodlit stadium.

A minute into his quest William remembered that his phone was dead. Whatever happened when he met the Oracle would be his word against theirs. Again. Evidence somehow managed to eat itself like the worm Oroberos. 'In for a penny, in for a pound,' William said and now continued following the line more out of resolute curiosity than point scoring and filling the evidence bag.

It was quite a trek. William lost the line several times, only finding it by backtracking. Close to windows it seemed to drift, becoming more visible as a reflection in the glass than on the wall. He was also aware that, with his flesh tunnel lost in a Hampstead garden, his navel had fused over pond water loaded with water-flees and mosquito larva. It lay like a twitchy, circular bruise. The snap-back of the elastic waistband set it swirling and he would need to extract the water splinter before it infected his body. Yes, William called them water splinters, called them his naval airtight tubs. A splosh pocket, a blunt blister: there was fun to be had in naming names. His bladder cartridge the colour of a dissolved eye.

On and on and on William plodded squeach squelch thurp. On and on and on in silt-slobbery footwear and a mantle all in green-io.

How much further would he have to walk before he reached the Oracle? Another five minutes and he'd turn back, he had better things to do on his last day, such as visit William Kemp on the HDU and box up the remains of his desiccated dissection cadaver and work out how to smuggle it into the boot of his car without being seen. On and on he went, the bare corridor echoing with the whistling farts from his shoes. William was now in a neglected-looking, dingy corridor. The floor slanted steeply downwards, a gradient impossible to negotiate with wheelchairs, beds or trolleys. Could he slide down it? William sat down, folded in his arms and scutched forward to encourage the floor to take him. He waited a moment. His weight settled. He felt his centre of gravity on the downward lift of his spine then thud, basement level, and William began to slide without having to help himself along. He picked-up speed and was soon sliding so fast that the vague green line became a bold, wide streak that broke away in offshoots, branches. Then it was like watching the bough of a great tree lunge and pummel at the sun. Speed drove the air out of William's lungs and he fell back, still sliding, slipping sideways, spinning uncontrollably in what now felt like a sheer drop, until he slammed into a wall. He lay crumpled and gasping against it in semi-darkness. To his right a dim light shone from a low, semicircular tunnel roughly hacked into the wall. William shuffled over and crawled inside. The floor felt and smelt and looked like partly composted garden waste. There were worms. Frogs. Several newts. The thing in his ear stirred and scuffled and William began to wonder if he was crawling inside his own ear. Then the tunnel widened and he emerged onto an old, abandoned ward (was the tunnel the same length as his body?). Beds stripped to their ironwork lay banked against a far wall and a draft fluttered the remains of drapes and swung a solitary, castor-footed chair with its back hanging off. A collection of partially deflated helium balloons (tarot designs sold in the hospital shop) were thronging above him and, as he watched, three more drifted in, walking on weakly curled satin ribbons that resembled decommissioned and deflated colons, before rising to join their kindred. The effect was spooky. William backed away.

'Hello?' William called out. 'Anyone there?' A door handle rattled in the shadows behind the blockade of stripped beds.

'Are you locked in?' said William, starting to scramble over bed springs that snagged at his trousers, and bent his ankles. Flitters of cloth lay screwed into their coils and someone had woven the hospital's old store of educational skeletons into the mesh. The door handle rattled again.

'Are you locked in?' William repeated. He heard whispered laughter.

'What do you think?' It was the kind of female voice that would sit on other voices.

'I'm not arsed about hearing his thoughts. We'll be here all day,' said a second female voice.

'Of course we're not locked in,' said a third woman's voice. 'Shall I open the door?'

'We're diabetic. We're just testing our blood sugar count. Pricking our thumbs. We're pricking our thumbs. By the pricking of our thumbs we'll know if we need to be a little more cautious with the chocolate. With the Parma Violet sweeties.'

'Oh, I like those. You can get sugar free,' said a second voice

'Don't taste the same though, do they?' said the first.

'By the pricking of our...' Another voice had joined them. 'I'm a bit dizzy, me.'

'Well, there's three of us in a cupboard with no ventilation and incense burning and we're all type two diabetics. What do you expect?'

'So I'll open the door, shall I?'

'Ooh. Persistent.'

'What's the point. We have to work up a good fug or we can't do the oracle blah-blah.'

'Hang on, I'm getting something...you out there?'

'Yes?' said William.

'Are you a doctor?'

'Yes. Well. Not after today.' Now it sounded like a radio tuning in, not three women's voices.

'Listen, lovey. Every teaching hospital has its own Oracle, a partially-sedated woman seated on a decommissioned mini-step. She's usually stowed in a basement cupboard, asthmatic on cheap incense, and muttering incessantly. Ain't that the truth, girls?'

'Veracity at its purest, m'duck.'

'Today you've got the luxury bundle, three Oracles stuffed in the one cupboard.'

'So, don't I get to see you?'

'Only if you need our pronouncements signed by a BSL interpreter, captioned or translated.'

'Right, no, I don't need any of those.'

'You know how this works, then?'

'No idea, actually. And I'm a sceptic.' said William.

'It still works whatever your arrow points to.'

'I'll be the judge of that,' said William.

'Ooh, get him. Judge and jury. Fudge and fury.'

'Right-oh. Something's coming through.'

'Take the weight off your feet. Sit on a bed.'

The bed bansheed beneath William's buttocks and the

balloons shuffled closer. The door rattled again and the light grew dimmer.

'What bloody man is that?'

'It's the same one we've just been talking to.'

'I fell in a pond on my way to work. It's just scratches.'

'Where the place?'

'On Hampstead Heath,' said William.

'Where were you before that?'

'In my car.'

'In his car. He will go far.'

'How do, William Shakespeare. Husband of Anne, Crime Scene Cleaner, CBE!'

'How do, William Shakespeare, father of Odile, Odette and Odear, billionaire entrepreneur, and knighted for services to industry!'

'How do, William Shakespeare, Global Brand, Destroyer of Death, Cleanser of All The World's Sins. And Pope!'

'Come again? Pope?'

'The earth has bubbles, as the water has. Glug glug pop pop.'

'So, I'm going to be rich through crime scene cleaning?'

'You will disinfect the world. You will wipe away incrimination. You will lose your naval for good. You will inherit a cock.'

'Are you being allegorical?'

'You will nibble on the insane root.'

'What insane root? What does that mean?'

'Time's arrow ends in a suction cup.'

'Toot toot. Ta ta. You've had your lot. Bugger off.'

'And your favourite patient's dead.'

'Who? Mr Kempe? He can't be dead, he's only forty-five and he's just done a sponsored Morris dance.'

'Well, he's just done the Farewell Shuffle and RIP'd his RSS feed. Oh, and ring that number tonight. Ring the number the Butcher gave you.' The Five of Cups (difficulty, loss) bumped William's face as he turned and clattered across the ruined beds, several balloons (the Nine of Swords: fear and nightmare and The Wheel of Fortune: each person has their own path to follow) tangling round both ankles as he commando crawled the length of the tunnel, and a great swathe of them (The Hanged Man, The Lovers, the Six of Cups reversed and The Sun) flew alongside as he fought and scrabbled up the steep corridor until he was back among the familiar departments. He stopped to get his breath back and peel balloons from his wrists and ankles. As he reached the High Dependency Unit a covered mortuary trolley slid through the pegged-back doors.

'Jacques?' said William, recognising the porter pushing it.

'Sorry, Bill. It's one of yours,' said the porter, a sallow, slight young man with corrugated sandy hair, the longest fingers William had ever seen on a human, and an oddly rounded waist as though his upper torso was grafted onto sturdier rootstock or he was pregnant all-the-way-round. 'Nice bloke. Loud but harmless.'

'It's not Mr Kempe?'

'It's not not Mr Kempe. Got it in one.'

'When did he die?'

'Recently, obviously. I don't know what time. Dr Tybalt clocked him off. Sad do. He was singing. Then he wasn't. I thought you'd mended him, but obviously not.'

'Obviously.'

'Better get him to the mortuary. They don't like me procrastinating with this type of cargo. Oh, and speaking of which, Dr Bill, I've bagged up your, ahem, 'friend.' You're not the first to take a shine to their designated 'ahem'. He's wrapped up. I think it's nice you want to give him a decent send-off, despite never knowing who he was, and having chopped him about a bit.'

'Yes. I'd like to do that for him. He's been a good listener.'

'The Dead always are. See yah. Oh, but not here. You're off today.'

'Yes. I'll pick up my...ahem and go.'

'Check your smart car. They've replaced the windscreen wipers with sticks. That'll play havoc with the glass. Okay. All the best, Bill. Nice balloons.'

'Thanks.'

* * *

An hour before his medical career ended for all time, William went and sat at the command station of the High Dependency Unit with the Ward Sister, Lorina. William Kempe's bed was being stripped, with emotionless efficiency, by two charge nurses whose energetic limbs kept punching open the flimsy, floral curtains shielding their efforts from the rest of the patients. Each glimpse exposed the time lapse erosion of William Kempe's last moments. The mussed pillowcase, the dented mattress, the skewed sheets all replaced or flattened-out and smoothed sheer. William Shakespeare saw where William Kempe had vanished. He turned and began to read Mr Kempe's medical notes, the final stats, the last medications, and couldn't track death through any of it. Death hadn't been stalking Mr Kempe, leaving the tell-tale slots behind each observation. William Kempe should still be drawing breath and exhaling it into his repertoire of inappropriate songs.

'Mr Kempe. I'm a bit shocked.'

'Nice lad, wasn't he? Forty five's no age these days, eh? Character. Singing away annoying the grouches one minute, then he made an odd noise, metallic, like a busy road — weird, really — and he was gone. Yes, sounded like he'd sped off on a motorbike, engine gunning. He looked surprised. Post mortem might show what it was. His wife was on her way to see him. In the lift. Would have had a chance to pull his finger, hear a fart, but the lift stalled. When she did arrive she took one look at the deceased and wandered off. People react to death very differently.'

'Tragic thing.'

'Yes. He was a very larky bloke. I bet he thought, when the time came, he'd pop off laughing.' The ward sister, now on her break, took out a magazine, stroked it flat and began flipping through its vivid pages.

Junior Hospital Doctor William Shakespeare was beginning to get very tired of sitting by the Ward Sister. His eyes were wearied by the glowing bank of monitors, and he was weary of having nothing to do — no one approached him since he was anathema, and his tenure was about to expire so, unless it was a problem that could be resolved in that instant, he was of no earthly use. William peered at the magazine the Ward Sister was reading but it was all pictures with very little text. 'What is the use of a magazine,' thought William, 'that is almost entirely composed of pictures, with a sparse number of quotes, and those quotes obviously taken out of context?'

* * *

He dozed fitfully, woke, checked his watch and left the hospital ward for the final time as an employee. As a Junior Doctor.

Outside there were clouds shaped like soft scaffolding. Beneath them, Inspector Benedicke Othello and his copilot, Sergeant Iago McDuff were hovering over the tiny Hampstead Cottage Hospital. Inspector Benedicke Othello felt as though he was the filament in an old fashioned lightbulb, a twist of tungsten as friable and delicate as the first hair on a baby's head, a silken and querulous thing. He felt disembodied. Flying always did this to him, whether it was piloting the police helicopter or as a passenger in a civil aircraft. He felt as though his body was anchored in the ground, like a bee sting plunged into flesh, or guy ropes restraining the spangled hem of a trapeze artist. Or roots. The tap root of a dandelion with the enriched and pregnant parasols commissioned by a breeze. Iago McDuff, all present and purpose and packed in the moment, was scanning the roads leading to the cottage hospital after another reported sighting of Albert Lear.

Yes, yes, there were the senior element on their car crawlers, sliding about quite dextrously. One of them had stopped to chat with a man in the staff carpark. A man with a small bald patch, a tiny fleck of white on the crown of his head from this height. Inspector Benedict Othello tried to imagine their conversation. He liked to invent compliant social interactions. Friendly, impromptu chats. It elevated his opinion of people — that they could rub along in a non-combative manner, disposed in a friendly way to their fellow creatures. Strangers could link amicably and without conflict. Benignity. That was exactly what his new wife was doing every day. Linking amicably with this and that person. Dear Desdemona was a friendly young woman who bonded with all comers. That was how Inspector Benedicke Othello's heart had been ignited. Flames had struck that place where he'd presumed the powder was damp from the misery and tears it was his lot to trawl through. Dear, friend-to-strangers, darling, faithful-unto-death Mrs Othello lifted the skirts of her heart for one and all.

* * *

Down in the carpark, William, his hair wafted by the downdraft of the helicopter's rotating blades, wiped the salt from his car's bonnet. Light from the helicopter and the car park lights made it glimmer in prickles. There was salt under the sticks pushed into the windscreen wiper sockets and he removed this with the squirty water fountains that washed the windscreen, clearing the excess with the car's rag (every car has a rag). William plucked the sticks (the culprits probably called them 'wands') before popping back into the closest examination room (excuse me, it's all right, seen it all before, I'm not really looking and I'm a doctor so if I do see, well, it doesn't count, our sensitivity's been abraded/erased by our training and we call our lack of human responses 'objectivity' — just so you know. Ta ta!' William flicked the Ouija planchette gliding over the patient's bared and gel-slicked abdomen and it coasted off their hips and smacked onto the floor), retrieving his windscreen wipers from a sharps disposal bin which bore the label 'LOST SOMETHING? IT'S IN HERE. MIND YOU DON'T SLICE OFF YOUR FINGERS'). Once they were replaced, William checked tyres and found the car surrounded by a circle of salt. Annoyed, he booted some away and just missed kicking an elderly woman in the face.

'I'm terribly sorry!' William said, exaggeratedly swinging his foot in the opposite direction and hovering it there. 'I never expected someone to slide out from under my car. Oh, god, I could have hurt you!'

A woman cleared the back bumper. She was lying on a car crawler, her right arm in a sling. She cleared the underside of the car and rotated slightly so she could stare into William's eyes.

'Well, you won't have been the first medical practitioner to injure a patient, eh? Now, excuse me, love, you'll have problems if you don't jiggle that out of your pipe. Damage your engine I shouldn't wonder.' The woman pulled the end of a felted wad of human hair that was rammed into the exhaust. 'Prank, was it, or ill-intent?'

'Prank.'

'There's something awry with the NHS. Developing its own sub culture. Secretive. Nocturnal. Fancy putting this in a doctor's exhaust pipe. Part and parcel of patches of NHS going awry and into the shadows of superstition Yes, this hospital's going to the Hounds of the Wild Hunt.'

'I'd noticed. Good people, but....'

'Consultants doing magic spells.'

'Yes. It's wrong.'

'You the one who drew media attention to it? The Whistleblower?'

'Yes.'

'Oooh, hence the unpopularity. Hence the reprisals. Well, look, love, there's a few of us behind you. Back you to the hilt. You know. We don't want hocus pocus. We don't want Charles and his histrionic dilutions.

'Homeopathic.'

'And what's this grit? Human ashes? A year's occupational crack cocaine?'

'Salt, I think,' said William. 'It's a bit of a trademark. Magic uses salt.'

'Corrosive. Damages trees. Roots — messes with the root system. Did you know, lovey, that the gene that causes deafness in humans is present in plants and causes ineffectual roots? I'm a botanist. If I can ever be of assistance, here's my card. That's me. Plantologist, Portia Pease.' William took the card and Portia Pease slid back beneath his car and skimmed away, unseen, into the darkness. William slipped back to the mortuary door and Jacques handed him the large, well sticky-taped box containing the only body William had ever explored with a knife. Then he drove home.

CHAPTER 3

AT HOME WITH THE SHAKESPEARES

Anne Shakespeare always heard William arrive home in the car, whether she was listening out for him or not, because he always scraped the under-edge of the hatchback against the kerb. The kerb shone silver in the daylight, glinted in lamplight and the car's floor was probably taking on a veneer of concrete.

Click clack locked, William paced towards the midpoint of the telephone wires stretched between his house and Mrs Tudor's, lifted his patched-up stethoscope from its box, listened to his own heart —bluhblumbluhblumbluhblum and lobbed the stethoscope over the wire hoping that the rhythm of his heartbeat was still working its way through the metal and rubber molecules. A perfectly pitched shot. The tubing wagged for a moment and the wire shivered. Three metres away, a pair of trainers strung up by their laces clapped their worn sides, twirled and butted toe to toe — Dorothy in her silver slippers. William followed the stethoscope with his blood pressure cuff. His first. A manual thing now replaced by an automated rig. The second attempt secured it close to the trainers. Then all was still. William saluted, retrieved the large box from the boot, and heaved himself into the house, checking his reflection in the hall mirror whilst he shut the door with the sole of his shoe. Did he look any less a doctor? Had that veneer peeled off already? 'You empire-builder, you,' he said after a moment, and that seemed possible, plausible. 'You Holy Father,' he said, wondering how Fate could engineer his ascendency to Pope when he was devoid of any religious belief and also married with a family. 'Baloney.' He dropped his car keys into the vintage biscuit tin, and trod on a doll, flattening it. 'Uh oh, cubism.' Then William stowed the large, resplendently taped box in the cupboard under the stairs, sliding it in on its side and feeling the torso glide and the pared bones thud, patting it affectionately. 'Welcome home, sir!' Then William traipsed into the kitchen to confirm his arrival.

Anne, wearing her usual muscleman apron over jeans and her aquatic ballet teams's teeshirt (Titania and the Titanics) was standing in the tree position and the twins, slotted into highchairs that hardly constrained them, flicked their pappy food at her. Their aim was surprisingly accurate for such tiny fingers. Odette, older by four years, was standing in the living room doorway in her cotton nightdress, imitating her mother, her hair roughly shorn.

'Greetings, lovelies,' William said, and tipped his still sodden, wreaking clothes into the washing machine.

'Poo,' said Anne. 'And why are you got up like a surgeon? Had a change of plan?'

'No. I had an accident. Got out to help another motorist on my way in. Ended up in a neglected garden pond.'

'Could only happen to you, dear,' said Anne. 'You are an Oddity Magnet. Always have been, always will be.'

'Well, I attracted you. Boom boom.'

'Boom boom indeed.'

His brain was still occupied by the prophecies. They seemed somehow too accurate and too concise, despite the sections of piffle and waffle. He'd always believed that these charlatans operated on a kind of second-guessing, with every detail vaguely expressed and open to interpretation. The Oracles certainly hadn't been. Their willingness to be so specific was unnerving. The worst of it was that their suggestions fell on fertile ground — he liked to think he was entrepreneurial. And, if he was going to excel, well, he needed all the advice and expertise he could get. He would ring The Number.

'You also stink of Parma Violet sweets,' said Anne, releasing her raised leg and stamping about on it to knock the pins and needles out. 'Have you bought more?'

'No. I found where you'd dumped my stash and retrieved it.'

'You know what, when I put your underwear in the wash, I do a double take cos I sometimes think I'm about to boil wash a bouquet. Know what else? You could make honey off you if you had a proboscis and the time. I've even begun waggle-dancing.'

'I call that rock and roll, love.'

'And the new bed arrived. Not sure I like second hand. Second hand is second best in my book.'

'It's a good bed...'

'Yeah, yeah made by retired Shaolin Monks with blahblahblah benefits to the back, the front and all quarters in between.'

William imagined the Shaolins. Those bed-making retirees, Shaolins still, but their bodies fragmented by arthritis. Supposedly, the mattress was sprung like floating kicks, the springs matching the rotating elevation of each fighter, and placed in a to-scale reenactment of battles, the point of contact — not impact — supporting your body, aligning your body like a properly strung puppet. 'Excuse me whilst I wash my hands. Okay kiddles?' William kissed the twins' heads and mimed a pair of snipping scissors at Odette, who lifted some of the remaining long, copper-coloured strands and giggled. Then he grabbed the air freshener and slunk back into the hallway. William opened the door to the cupboard under the stairs, stuck his head over the box, inhaled, then sprayed Autumn Berry Spices so heavily the air was fogged with droplets and a dull rainbow arced from the daylight bulb. Anne had installed daylight bulbs throughout the house to elevate her moods and now there was no doubt that she was painfully, permanently upbeat and bouncy as fuck. Now up to the lavatory. Mirror. Washbasin. The towel damp as usual from so much hand traffic. Back in the kitchen again, Anne was wiping her apron clear of the twins' dinner.

'You should stop them doing that, love,' said William, kissing Anne on her left ear whilst tapping Shirley's breast-hovering pinna.

'It's speeding up their hand-to-eye coordination, Bill,' said Anne placing a casserole dish onto a heat mat and shoving a serving spoon under its lid.

'Self-service. And whilst you eat, I want to lay down some house rules about your new business venture.'

'Can I just eat in peace, love?'

'I don't so you're not. Now listen. I don't want you coming home with stuff on your phone. Before and after shots. This job will change you.'

'Everything we do changes us.'

'Don't be facetious. This is cleaning up…stuff.'

'What stuff?' said Odette, climbing back into her chair.

'Daddy's going to be a cleaner now he's not a doctor.'

'Why?'

'Answer that, Daddy.'

'Because …that's what I'm doing. All the people I was looking after, well they're all better now, so…'

'Oh right,' said Odette laying her flattened doll on the table next to him and then crawling under the table where she dug at William's feet with a spoon.

'Funny thing is, Anne,' said William, 'I went to see the hospital Oracle. Actually, there were three of them. Two just, ah, stopping over whilst their cupboards are refurbished. But they said…they said some interesting stuff. They weren't vague. They said specific stuff. Basically, if they're right, well, we're… we're going to do well. I am. I'm going to do really, really well.'

'Yeah, huzzah, like most wives I'll do well by proxy.'

'You'll have the freedom to do your own thing, if the money

comes in like they said it would.'

'Go on, then. Tell me what they said.'

'The business is going to do very well. Top brand. Clean the world so, yeah, global branding. And, now you'll like this. This is good. I'll, ha ha, I'll also be Pope.'

'Go Popollo! Yeah, okay, and will I have to go into hiding seeing as Pope is all about celibacy, cutting women off above the feet and below the neck? Oh those naughty women's things, the twixt and the tween where you, my friend, have been!'

'Okay. Pope's mad but it's what they said.'

'I am warming to these nutters. Go on.'

'That was about it, really. I ought to ring that number. The Oracles knew about it — the number your friend, Helena, gave me.'

'So you ended up out on your ear for nothing. You Whistleblew and there was no need because the magic and stuff actually work.'

'Yes, there was a need. Watching consultants do a tarot spread for their patients, cutting down on x-rays and scans, getting out the Western Medicine Diagnostic Tarot without any nod to their diagnostic training — that had to be stopped.'

'There are more things in heaven and earth than in your belief system, mister.'

'Do you know, just before I left I saw a doctor running an ouija planchette over a patient's gel-slicked abdomen?'

'Hilarious.'

'I'd want to be treated by something that actually works. By people who look at whatever's ailing me and draw their answers and diagnoses from their knowledge and from life, from looking at me and not at a pack of playing cards.'

'The tarot's drawn from life. Just an aid to thought. Casts up possibilities, gives you the clues you're not conscious of clocking.'

'Piffle. I'm surprised at you, a midwife. Instead of seeing what's there in the spread of your patient's legs you'd look at a spread of cards. Oh yes, I see by the King and Swords she's five centimetres dilated.'

'Ha ha. Ha ha ha.'

'I'm not knocking your professionalism.'

'Nor are you praising it.'

'Sorry. I've just been forced out of my professionalism.'

'Here we go, puppy with the liddle hurt paw, aw, be nice to puppy...'

'No, brave husband Whistleblower who's stood up against the current stupid trend which is in fact a ruse to economise and cut spending in certain quarters of the NHS. Oh, Mr Nan, you don't need a scan, have that cup of tea and then I'll read your tea leaves and we'll know how to proceed. The cost of a teabag and some boiling water is sweeter when balancing the books than the cost of a blindingly amazing machine that pries inside the human capsule without having to fillet it, and then shows exactly what's what.'

Anne applauded. Odette copied her mum. Odile and Odear blew raspberries and burped up sick.

'So look, Bill. Ring the number. Let's get Fate out of the pit stop and back onto the circuit, eh? Phone where the children can't here you. And Bill...?'

'Yes, love?'

'Don't make any rash promises.'

* * *

William decided to ring from the bedroom. He smiled as he lifted the phone from its cradle — who was he ringing? What was he about to discover? Being a junior hospital doctor had been gruesome enough. And, had he not just fetched home, illegally, the remains of the cadaver he had gradually, but not completely, dissected during his medical school training? Admittedly, the idea was to give it — him— a proper funeral. A cremation. An urn for the ashes. A place for the ashes in their urn in his home, or a secluded and lovely spot for their scattering. A ritual. A commemoration. A leave-taking. The cadaver hadn't been murdered. The cadaver's current state had been a life choice. Here goes nothing, William thought, and dialled the number. I can always put the phone down if I don't like what they're saying.

'Hello?'

'Hello?' The voice was androgynous. Pleasant.

'The Butcher gave me your number.'

'He did? Oh, he's a one.'

'I'm about to become a...a crime scene cleaner and he said you could help me. With advice. About stain removal. The sorts of stain removal I'll be encountering. They'll be, ah, stubborn stains. Heavy biological stains.'

There was a pause and William was about to repeat what he'd just said when...

'Oh yes. Yes. I should imagine they will be.'

'Can you help me? Please?'

'Come round. The better to talk. Face to face. We are in Montgomery Square. Number 13. If it is at all convenient, call round now.'

'Yes.'

'Dress warmly. The night is cold. Our home is colder. Goodbye until we meet.'

William set the phone back in its cradle. The voice was impossible to place and difficult to recall. Sexless. Ageless, Accent-less. If the scattered stalks of Anonymous were ever gathered into the one collected sheaf, this was it.

William shed the green theatre rig, showered, and then climbed into his own clothes, unsure whether he should suit-up or dress down. He compromised. Jeans and a smart jacket. A tie and loafers. Cotton and worsted and a beanie hat. Earth tones with a button badge of clouds — a magnificent cumulonimbus wandering like speculation itself, like the unfettered mind. Body with a smidgeon of soul levered clear like a hankie showing from the breast pocket.

It took thirty-seven minutes to drive there.

Stepping out of his car, William glimpsed a small procession of elderly people on car crawlers sliding through the space between the parked cars, bagged-up groceries held to their chests. They called-out a genial 'Good evening' which William answered with a wave as he walked along the broad pavement of a tree lined square. The houses faced onto a small, verdant park with an immaculate black and gold iron railing around it. The houses themselves had high copper beech and burly holly hedges and willows with drifting fronds that the wind whipped and spun like streamered carousels. The street lamps were slender and elegant and cast their light above the rooftops as though their purpose was to suggest stars and not illuminate where people wandered. William felt as though he'd walked to somewhere eighty years earlier in a more clearly defined world. Although it was autumn, and close to 10pm, a nightingale sang a miscellany of notes in the key of F major. William stopped by each tall gate and tried to read the brass house number plates. Ten minutes later he was standing on the front step of number 13. A mansion. William could see the flicker of candlelight through the tall front windows. As soon as he'd reached it the door swung open leaving his fist knocking in mid-air. The door hit the hallway wall with sufficient force to crack an antique peer glass. William stepped over the threshold and bent to pick up slivers of mercury amalgam and shards of glass.

'Come in, William,' called the voice he had spoken to on the phone. 'Please ensure the door is locked behind you, there's a dear. And don't worry about the peer glass. We left it there to die. You have been the unwitting executioner.'

William wrapped the debris in his clean pocket tissue and stood for a moment in the dappled ruby and green light falling from the stained glass panel above the door. Then he turned and locked the nine bolts. This is already weird, he thought, before setting off down a long and deep-pile carpeted hallway towards the voice. The plantation style door was opened for him and William was met by nine wispy figures wearing identical grey diaphanous shifts, with their feet in fuchsia slippers. Their colourless hair was abundant, thick, and cut square just above their shoulders. They had aquiline noses, thumb-print eyes, thin blue-tinged lips and teeth so white they seemed fused into the one, undifferentiated and continuous tooth. Nine tall-backed, silvery chairs were arranged around a silver table polished to reflect the darkness between the nine silver candlesticks, and the slender candles blazed with diamond-sized and diamond-bright flames. William shivered. The room was as cold as a winter landscape. Is that ice hanging from the mantelpiece? William thought it might have been plastic or glass until he finger-tapped the edge of one blue-hued icicle and his flesh stuck to it. Dragging his hand clear, the prong snapped and clattered to the floor.

'We are the Nonuplets,' said the person standing closest to him. 'We are,' and the person pointed, 'Roju, Meli, Oet, Teo, Ilm, Ujor, Gunta and Nulet. I am Lumo.'

'Hello.' William smiled at them and was poised to shake hands but no hands were offered. 'Are you related to the Butcher, the one who gave me your phone number?'

'Yes we are,' said Ilm.

'We ate his wife, Gertrude,' said Ujor.

'We hope she will be returned to life,' said Roju as Oet lifted a stainless steel canister from a shelf on a tall bookcase. The canister was plugged into a socket, it hummed, was obviously heavy and began to cloud with condensation from their breath. 'This is Gertrude's head.'

'I'm sorry, did you say you ate her?' said William. 'And that's her head?'

'Yes. We are cryologists so we preserved her so she might be returned to life,' said Meli. 'Life, Death, nothing's permanent.'

'Sweet Gertrude,' said Ujor, giving the canister a gentle shake.

Its contents clinked like ice in a whisky glass. 'She carried one of our cards.' They each flourished a card from unseen pockets and flicked the tip of it. 'It sends out a signal if it registers the sort of impact presaging a car crash. We only eat the bodies of the Dead.'

'The Consensual Roadkill,' said Ilm. 'Genuine volunteers. They preselect the dish they wish to join. Choose their recipe. We spend what would have been lost on wreaths on the ingredients and a new dinner service that we dedicate to their memory and never dine from again.'

'I see,' said William. 'You're... cannibals?' Nine heads nodded. 'So you know how to remove signs of the body from the car...?'

'And from the kitchen.'

'And from the dishwasher.'

'And from our lips, fingers, serviettes and shifts, cutlery, crockery, cook-pots, slippers and bins.'

'Exhaustive,' said William Shakespeare. 'You are the experts.'

'Let us explain our predicament, though, before you agree to use the cleaning fluids we make.'

'Oh, you actually manufacture your own? I see. Please...'

'Our parents died before we were conceived.'

'Unusual.'

'Their parents, guilt and grief stricken, united our father's milt and our mother's ova, and our grandmothers surrogated us in their wombs. Grandmother Alpha contained four of us, Grandmother Omega, five — Friar Laurence having taken the necessary samples from our inert parents. His idea of pastoral care was somewhat intrusive. Anyway, we were brought to full term and raised in great secrecy by our family. We are alchemists. We are hermaphrodites.'

'I see. Oh.'

'And bulimic cannibals.'

'It goes without saying.'

'Our cleaning methods, our potions and fludds have

properties you will not find equivalent in other cleaning products.'

'Right. Yes. I'm sure.'

'We are of such delicate digestive abilities that we can only eat human meat. Even this is a trial to us and we must regurgitate our meals before they pass out of our stomachs and into our colons. However, we cannot vomit until we have the necessary permission from the Authorities because our vomiting is exhumation. Rules are rules.'

'So the Authorities know about you?' They nodded.

'When we were eighteen our grandparents went into hiding. We think they may have assumed other names and new identities. We are therefore on our own in the wide world but we are happy. We are thriving. We have our alchemy. We have our intelligence, which is uncommonly large. We have each other, which is uncommonly comforting.'

William was forced to step back as the nine bulimic cannibals rushed forward to link arms. They formed a circle, clapped the tops of their heads together and began spinning around, their grey robes flailing, their fuchsia slippers flying off. After five minutes of watching them twirl, their heads constantly turning to kiss the cheeks of their linked siblings, as though one kiss passed in a ring. William felt he could intrude on their private ritual with another question. 'Friar Laurence preserved your parents', potential?'

The circle slowed and the nine broke apart and gripped the chair backs till their dizzy spells passed.

'Friar Laurence? It was just something he did. He was following a monk's work. Only that fellow, Gregor Mendel, he worked with plants. Sweet peas. Lovely perfume. The more you cut, the more rise to the scissors' kiss.'

'So Friar Laurence was a eugenicist?'

'He was but his work was rooted in the husbandry of the Holy Bible.'

'We were begat. We were begat down the angel surveilled

aisles of Arcadia. We were begat so that we could blunt the natural edge of Mortality and its sovereign juices.'

'It's what?' said William.

'We will show where and how we make our cleaning fludds, but you must understand the principles by which they work or you will suffer catastrophic consequences, or experience strange events.'

'I'm already experiencing those,' said William quietly, whilst wondering at their mispronunciation of the word 'fluids'.

'But not on a par with what you would be subjected to, if you didn't follow the rules and guidelines.'

'Of course. Yes. I'll follow them and to the letter.'

'It will be in your own best interests.'

'Can I pay you for your advice, as well as for your cleaning products?' William said, having completely failed to remember any of the nine forenames, and now unable to distinguish them one from the other. It seemed to him that they were purposely assuming a single, shared identity. Was it a ruse or were they as interchangeable in private? 'So, what transaction is this? A direct debit. Cash? A cheque? How can I can pay…?'

With one movement nine consent cards — *In the eventuality of my departing this life in a traffic accident, I consent to be eaten* — slid towards William, clutched by nine pairs of immaculately trimmed and angel-delicate hands. 'You will also take two apprentices of our choosing. Nell D'eath and Jacques Mercutio.'

'I'm sorry? What were your wards' names? I think I know one of them.'

'You know one of the already. Jacques Mercutio…'

'The hospital porter who keeps being warned about sumo-lifting quadriplegics by their belts,' said William. 'I know him. I saw him today.'

'And his step sister, Nell D'eath. Both are in need of help career wise. Nell has gone from being a Goth barmaid to performing as a Goth campanologist. Her income is not commensurate with her outgoings.'

'A Goth campanologist?'

'She plays cracked bells retrieved from skips outside the houses of known campanologists.'

'How does she know where any campanologists live?'

'There's an app for it. Let us take you to our laboratory.'

They lifted a rug bearing the portrait of a Medici-looking woman with the moon rising where her bosoms ought to have been and a sloth hanging upside down from her jewelled hair. Beneath the rug was a semi-circular cleft in the fine oak floorboards. Fingers slipped into it and drew back a trapdoor. The Nine extinguished the candles and descended like a thin fog down grey stone steps, leaving William to follow. William did, shoving the nine consensus cards into his breast pocket. The stairwell led into a surprisingly high ceilinged alchemical laboratory — it said 'ALCHEMICAL LABORATORY' on a flaring-sun shaped sign depending from two golden chains. As William joined the Seven Bulimic Cannibals, one of them stripped to the waist, had their hands bound by a sibling, was blindfolded by another, and then they ducked into a squat stone chimney built on a low stone plinth. After a moment, their head appeared above the chimney top and their thick, colourless hair began to billow upwards as though it were smoke. William was guided to an iron walkway above the laboratory floor so he could watch. The room was filled with enormous glass alembics that foamed and burbled and fizzed. He was aware that something fluttered behind him. There was an almost unbreathable scent of violets, and then he fell, his knees striking the iron floor like the twin clappers of a tenor bell.

William woke up in his car hemmed in and pinned down by apothecary bottles and glass flasks filled to their brims, some with black liquid, others white, some had the look of freshly drawn blood. All luminesced. A clock struck. William counted forwards. It was midnight.

* * *

NEXT DAY

William was online. He filled in the form. Entered his card details. Pressed 'pay'. He was informed that his bank was supervising the secure transaction. And voila. William snapped his fingers. 'Yeah!' He had just paid for a medium sized advertisement in the crime scene cleaning industry's trade paper, SPILLAGES AND SPURTS. He read the draft again. Not bad, not bad at all.

Wanted. Two crime scene cleaning technicians. No experience necessary. Full training given. Please apply by email with current C.V. in attached word document. The positions are open to school leavers, college leavers, graduates and people with life experience rather than certificates. The main criterion is aptitude and ability to work in a small team under difficult and sometimes traumatic conditions. A covering note should explain your reason for wishing to pursue crime scene cleaning as a career.

He felt obliged to advertise for trainees, despite the Nine Bulimic Cannibals insisting that he took on their protégés. William felt it was much fairer to flag up the vacancies, otherwise he was hoisting the eagle ensign of nepotism.

William wondered why anybody would choose to work cleaning murder scenes but people, like ants, generated sufficient workers to staff and service all the vagaries and niches that society spawned. Cometh the hour, cometh the (wo)man, cometh the niche worker.

* * *

AN HOUR LATER

An hour later, William was composing a second advertisement. He needed crime scenes to clean. William had to advertise for them, which felt blatantly immoral, whilst reassuring the traumatised clientele that he would clean them well, sensitively and economically. William was intending to place the advertisement in the crime scene cleaners' trade newspaper, SPILLAGES AND SPURTS, but he also needed to advertise elsewhere. He could hardly post fliers through the monied parts of London, could he? He needed the monied sort of murder. How to say that without, well, saying that. Inspiration wasn't exactly dripping in his ear.

'You haven't got any work, yet,' said Anne, hoisting Odile on her hip and pat-a-caking then one-potatoing Odear's clenched and wavering fists.

'I've contacted the people the, ah, cleaning fluid suppliers suggested. The barristers and family lawyers that oversee the families affected by crimes. Who'd have thought that some forms of social climbing involved climbing over corpses. Anyway, I want to specialise in discretion. It'll pay more. Maybe I'm also hoping it won't be so…seedy.'

'That big cardboard box in the hall cupboard, William?'

'Yes.'

'What's in it.'

'Would you mind if I didn't tell you?'

'Is it a secret?'

'Yes, yes it's a secret.'

'Is it something to do with crime scene cleaning?'

'Tangential connection, yes.'

'It smells off.'

'It's quite safe. I'm intending to move it shortly. I'm making arrangements.'

'Aren't we all,' said Anne. 'We're all trying to connect with people who'll do something for us. Ain't that the truth?'

William had no idea how he was going to approach an undertaker about the woefully chopped cadaver without alerting anyone to the fact he'd sneaked it out of the hospital. Perhaps he was going against the Deceased's wishes but William thought of it as retirement. The cadaver had served its purpose and it was time for it to leave behind the peculiar hatcheries of human endeavour. William had learned such a lot from dissecting it and he was beyond grateful. Nobody else could learn as much from it, piecing the desiccated segments back together was beyond the skill and patience of any surgeon. Besides, the trend at medical school was now for anatomical dissection software. It was possible to buy programmes showing a body, dead for thirty minutes or less, that had been factory sliced by lasers into 0.5mm slivers. No embalmed body could teach as much. The embalmed, beloved, tutelary cadaver's time was over.

* * *

William re read his words. Then he crossed them all out.

* * *

'How're you supposed to use this stuff,' said Anne, hoisting an apothecary jar by its neck. You'd have thought they'd label them. Aren't you supposed to list the contents. Sticker it. Say if it's corrosive. What to do if it gets in your eyes? Do you use it neat? No? Yes? Or what's its dilution rate? Ratio? I mean, they pack these round you having obviously carted you back to your car. Then they don't leave a note. If you hadn't passed out would they have shown you how to use it? And why pack them in these cumbersome bottles? That's just … well, they may be eccentric but the job this stuff's got to do is about being in the real frigging world. It's your livelihood. Look, what do other crime scene cleaners use? Google it. Ask around. Take some of what they use with you.'

'Okay. Yeah. I agree with … with some of that, Anne, but I think this might be something special.'

'What if it just eats through the surfaces it's put on and you're liable and get stuffed with compensation claims?'

'I've taken out insurance.'

'Yeah, but your reputation's gonna be stuffed isn't it?'

'I suppose … it wouldn't look good. Especially if we're going for high-end crimes. Murders in expensive homes and venues.'

'You've got to be picky. Cleaning up in a scuzzy place, yeah, you're doing them a good turn but you're not going to do yourself or your family any favours. You've got to aim high. Will this stuff support your ambition? Let's give it a whirl.'

'I didn't buy it from them. It was given.'

'A qualified gift.'

'Yes, but still a gift. They're not a business.'

'Are you sure? How do you know it's not part of their marketing ploy? They make you feel like you're the only person lucky enough to be provided with the complete cleaning kit. Why would they do that? Could be a bespoke brand that goes in for narrative selling. They enclose you in a kind of narrative.'

'Very elaborate for no money. They seemed genuine.'

'You've done nothing but work as a doctor. Okay, you get a few people who toddle along and lie about symptoms, and you get hypochondriacs who think they've got everything, but mostly you're dealing with honesty. Could you spot a bit of skullduggery?'

'I'd like to think I could.'

'Nine bulimic cannibals? That's far-fetched. Some women giggling in a cupboard at the hospital? Yeah, very credible.'

William lifted the jar from Anne's swinging hands. 'Let's try a dab.'

'Okay, but on something that doesn't matter. Something we can afford to lose. Your stinking clothes. Yes, let's try them on the clothes that seem to have been dunked in a Hampstead shit pit.' Anne hauled them out and slapped them onto a polythene sheet. Out in the back garden, eh?' Out they went.

The intruder light snapped on and a cat's ragged silhouette scattered over the wooden fence. 'Miaow said pussy,' said Anne. The smell from the soaked clothes had festered. Water oozed from the heaped trousers and balled shirt, the surface of the socks were scummed, the underpants drooled.

'Let's pretend this is a crime scene, Billy my love. What would you do to get it clean? What is your approach.'

William grabbed a garden cane, sliding it from the green twine loop that held the plant against it. The plant immediately sprawled. 'I'm going to spread everything out so it all gets a dose of whatever this stuff is.'

'Which one first?'

'I'm tempted to try the black …I mean, it looks viscous. I'd like to see what it does, whether we have to clean up after using it. To be honest, I don't mind if I lose these clothes. They carry too many memories.'

'All right. let them be the guinea pig.' Try the red one? The black one? Okay. Actually this stuff's much lighter than I thought. Stopper out. Look at the stopper. It's got something inside it. Can you see what it is? Need a magnifying glass. Maybe it's an imperfection? I bet this glass is mouth blown. I see the signs of the artisan upon it.'

'Okay. Just drizzle a bit on. This might just be coloured water.'

'You sound like Jamie Oliver. Drizzling it on. A chef.

Do we need a cloth to dab it? To rub it in?'

'I've no idea. Okay, that's wet a bit of it. Do you need to dilute it? Should I get a bucket or a basin?

'Let's just see what it does neat. Okay. Something's happening.'

'It's giving off light. Is this stuff flammable? I mean…?'

'There's no heat. Look. My hand's over it. There's no heat.

There's no smoke. Tip a bit more.'

'You sure?'

'Yes, just a bit more. Enough to… that's it. This light's not good. We're working in our own light. And the light coming from it — impossible to see what's happening.'

'Come round this side.'

'All right. Now spread it out. Yes, look, look it's…!'

'You can't tell there was a stain on it.

'How do we know water wouldn't have just rinsed this out? We're not doing a control experiment here. Tut.'

'Okay, let's rinse this. Let's put it in a rinse cycle.'

'Take too long. Let's just bung it in the kitchen sink and ring it out by hand. See what comes off.'

They rushed back into the kitchen carrying the polythene sheet, laden with glowing garments, between them. Anne lifted the washing up bowl out, William dropping the still reeking jeans and shirt and socks into the stainless steel sink, running the cold tap onto them. The whole sink shone, light swirled, mixing with water for a moment, and then it irrupted like a geyser. They both ducked. The light dazzled and fell, disappearing with an exaggerated slurp. Then it showed up gain, shining through the pipes and out of the kitchen unit cupboard. It shone in the wall and William and Anne ran out and it shone through the outlet and then down into the drain and the sewer, and a white light shone through the ground.

'Bloody hell, love! Bloody hell!' said William.

'Is this stuff radioactive? What the fuck have you fetched home? Is this what they kill secret agents with? Bloody hell, Billy!' They ran into the street, the flumes of the sewers and their runnels and shifts shone like translucent veins. The road carried a great almost straight, luminous shuffling line of light.

'What happens when it hits the sea, Billy?'

'Maybe one of the other bottles has something that stops it.'

They ran back inside, breathless, on the cusp of laughing, their hands shaking as though in the throes of invisible cocktail mixing. Grabbing the white liquid — 'well, the light came from the dark liquid, this should stop it,' they poured some down the sink, sliding the trousers out of the way with a breadknife. This liquid made a sound.

'Can you hear that?' said William.

'It's singing,' said Anne. 'Singing. Like fucking singing!' The sound increased and spread. It chanted through the walls. They ran back into the street and the light was dimming but the singing grew louder as though more voices were joining it. They were all following a tune. 'It's a tune. It's an old tune. Serious. Stentorious. Bloody hell, Billy!'

They ran back inside and grabbed the apothecary bottle with red contents. Then they legged it into the street. Williams stethoscope, blood pressure cuffs and the trainers twisted and twirled above them. Were they keeping time with the music?

'Quick, it's getting louder. Is this really cleaning stuff? What have they given you? What in the name of mucker shmuck is this?' Back inside they glugged some red liquid after the white and the trousers writhed, stood up as though filled with invisible legs then lay down. A great sigh went out of them. The shirt filled and flattened and huffed. A great sigh burbled and hummed through the pipes and William and Anne felt something embrace them, felt something in the kitchen, warm, like a draft that contained itself and didn't rush about, like an invisible bag of warm air that rose against them and held them and then vanished. The sink gurgled. They sped back into the road and a kind of heat-mirage bore ran away from them in a soft ripple and the road lay peaceful in the darkness, William's stethoscope and blood pressure cuffs swinging quietly in the night air, the trainers having slid over to Mrs Tudor's where they kicked playfully at her guttering. Overhead the stars appeared as the clouds rolled back.

'Is that sigh shifting the fucking clouds?'

'Circumstantial. Coincidence,' said William.

Okay, the stuff shifted us, but has the stuff shifted the stains.

What do your kecks look like after all that? And the shirt and scummy socks?'

They went back into the kitchen. Anne put on rubber gloves and got the sprung, grippy salad servers and gingerly, nervously, her hands shaking, she lifted the trousers clear and held them to the light.

'For goodness sake don't get any splashed in your eye. You don't want an eye that sheds light beams, sings and then exhales. You'd be dragged off by the security services. Would that be superhuman powers? Well, what would those things let you do? I mean, what could they do against organised crime? Or even a random attack?'

'Spook an assailant,' said William, squinting at his trousers and shifting a bucket under the drips.

'What was that singing? Did that sound religious to you?' said Anne.

'Ritualistic, not necessarily religious. You know, ceremonial.'

'And that sigh, do you think the stuff gave off gas? It gave off something! What gas was it? What have we just inhaled?' said Anne.

'Well, it's not affected our breathing, so…'

'So what about your trousers?'

'Yeah, what about my trousers?

'Oh!'

'Oh!'

'Oh!'

'Oh. Oh. oh.'

'Oh!'

'Oh!'

'Oh!'

'Oh!'

'Was there much of a mark there to begin with? I mean, wasn't it just like scummy water?' said Anne.

'Can't have been heavily soiled.' said William.

'Maybe just a spot. You know, maybe a leaf you could've

picked off when they dried out.'

'Yeah, it seemed worse because of the smell.'

'Ha ha. Yep, the smell was bad. You'd expect really awful stains with that level of smell.'

'Yes, how funny! You know I said I'd fallen in a pond. I think it was probably just wet from the hedge. Fresh rain. Clean in Hampstead, isn't it? Just all darkened with water.'

'What about the smell?'

'Maybe I thought it was more stinky than it was. I do have a tendency to exaggerate. To make a point.'

'There was an animal involved. Did you say a bear?'

'Oh, god, did I? That's typical of me, isn't it?'

'Can't have been a bear, not in Britain. Not in a horse box.'

'That'd be stupid. Nobody'd do that. Yeah. These early mornings and all the stress when I did get to work. I mean, those trousers. They've hardly been worn. They were new, really. There's no stain there because there wasn't to begin with. Yeah. Who'd set an animal on me? Nobody. People aren't vindictive, not really, nobody'd do that to a complete stranger. Bears are asleep this time of year. Hibernating. Nobody's going to wake them up just so they could take a pop at me. What was I thinking? It's okay. Whatever happened. If she did set something on me. Well, let it go. Yes, let it go. That's the best thing. So, these trousers. Drop them in the wash? I think they're my favourites.'

'They don't need it. Just spin to get the water out of them. And they do look great. You look very … you know, in them. We'll have to find something else to try the stuff on. I mean, the trousers, they were nothing. So …'

'How about. Um, the dog blanket with the blood on?'

'We shouldn't have kept that.

'Yeah, but we did. It was tough to throw out. We loved that dog like a son.'

'We did love him like a son. So the dog blanket. That's a big stain. We know that's a big stain and we haven't got rid of it in three boiled washes and a mild bleach soak and the stuff that's supposed to soak stains out.'

'Yeah. That's a tough stain. Which bottle first? Try the red first. Oh, look. Smell. What does that smell like, Anne?'

'Like your bloody Parma Violet sweets.'

'It does.'

'Yeah, that's probably impregnated the blankets. You addict. How many years have you been chewing the fucking things? I'll go and get Grin's blanket.'

William tapped on the red-filled apothecary bottle with his fingernail. Each tap it felt as though his finger was having to extend further to touch the bottle. From upright finger to horizontal digit, yet the bottle remained upright, unmoving, constant in space. Anne returned with the blanket sealed in its airtight polythene bag. She tore it open and shook out the blanket. The blood was in a great, grey-brown stain. Most of the blanket was marked with it, some a deeper more distressing blot.

'Poor old Grin, eh? Poor lad. Poor old lad.'

Anne teared up. William felt the edges of his eyes leaking. Even after eight years the pain of loss, of seeing their beloved dog suffer and die, well, it hadn't lessened. It hadn't lost its edge. The hurt stung William's heart over and over again. It was one of his memories eternal wasps' nest.

'Do we want to get rid of the blood stain?'

'I think it'd be good to. I mean, this will still be Grin's favourite blanket. But without his death all over it.'

'Poor lad just bled and bled.'

'Even you couldn't staunch it. You a doctor.'

William swallowed hard. He thought back to the moment he'd carried Grin in off the road. The van had gone over the poor dog's head. Blood poured. Arterial. A main artery. Oh yes he could have stemmed the flow but why? What would that have done? The dog was mortally wounded, squealing then squealing silently, using the urgent puffs from his lungs to try to expel the pain. Better to have his life blood seep out than to keep his life stoppered in a pitiful body for five minutes' more anguish, a body so damaged that life and death would be a game of pong where the pointless blip would batter back and forth then glide out of the frame. Then came the blame. Why in god's name had they not bought him a new lead. The old extendable one had a broken clicker so the lead would spool out if the dog pulled and there was no lock and no retracting button to reel it in. But they hadn't. It had been like when they'd put cheap garden netting, plastic and nasty a kind of nasturtium-leaf green, floss-thin thing, and they had woken to find a tawny owl dead with its legs snarled up in it. The great wings had flopped out after its last attempt to fly free, its beak skewed with the effort of chewing at what terrified and held it. The carp in the pond seemed altogether smugger. Feathers bobbed on the surface for a week afterwards, the fish rising to swallow them (or seeming to blow them off the surface) until the pond looked as pretty and uneventful as it always had. Sometimes, William believed he saw an owl flying in among the carp, its wing beats slowed by the water, pouncing on reflections. Carrying down a reflected bundle of cloud. Although he knew he hadn't seen it, he also knew he had.

Back out in the garden, Anne having checked on the three sleeping children, William laid the dog blanket on the polythene sheet. The light snapped off so Anne ran into the trigger beam and it blazed anew. Like a starburst. The sudden erection of a starry body in the bleak, blasted firmament. William was starting to feel a little delirious. He thought about light on a personal level. We take with us lengths of light, drag them with us from our mother's wombs, maybe from our ancestors, who knows, he thought. Loose lengths of light snipped from the sun like string from a great wound ball that lessens with each withdrawal, but to such a mass the loss is nigh on invisible. Less than a nail clipping to an elephant. An eyelash loosened and lost. All of us with lengths of light dangling off us like ribbons from the handlebars of kids' bikes. That's us. Blazing through our own days. Then the night comes and the dog dies. Here is the dog blanket he died on. Poor old Grin. Such a wise and loving dog. So lovable. So loved.

William felt the loss was as ripe now as it had been an hour after his death. Up to an hour and you're fighting the loss. It hasn't gained credibility. The soul repels it. There's the tiny iota of belief that there has not been a death. Time will reverse itself. What happened will be dragged back, removed, folded over. Just a small reversal. A moment. The moment when everything drifted out of true, when what should have continued was snagged and forfeit.

'Okay, are you doing the honours, Anne?'

'Watch me fly, matey,' she said.

Anne hefted the red apothecary jar between her first and index finger and twisted the glass stopper loose, dropping it on the grass. 'How much?'

'To go off last time, well, just a small glug.' Out it poured and wind blew off it, a veering wind, one that pushed against Anne's jumper so that it contoured her body then relaxed back, one that came from behind William and pushed his hair forward. The blanket gained bubbles of trapped air beneath it as though the ground was also giving off gas. The blanket lifted and flapped and the air popped out in gusts they could feel against their faces.

'Do you think this stuff is environmentally friendly?'

'I'd kind of think it was. The, ah, makers seemed to be that sort of folks.' said William. Ah, but they were the sort that also ate dead people. Would they care what state the world was in? Maybe? They were cultured, savvy. You'd expect them to be conscientious about how they altered the environment. 'So, yes, probably.'

Poor Grin. Dead these past seven years. Anne was unstoppering the black solution. It came out in gritty slops this time.

'Did we shake it last time?'

Our hands were trembling before so it could be we inadvertently shook the contents, eh? Anyway, it's out now. It's on Grin's blanket.'

'So, is it reacting to the air? Is it okay. Does it smell all right to you?'

Anne sniffed and sniffed again. 'What's that smell like to you?'

William sniffed above the blanket. Cautiously. Trying to keep his nostrils away from it and thinning his mouth into a compressed seal. 'It reminds me of something.'

'Dog?'

'Well, it Grin's blanket. He was a dog. But this is more puppy. When you hold a young puppy. It's not an old dog smell. This is newer. Less established, Faintly milky. But outdoors.'

'Duh. We are outdoors, everything we smell's going to have outdoors tagged onto it.'

'No, this is outdoors hot summer day. When the air's still. The light's kind of fixed, static. A great warmth. A golden tube of light. A cone of light. Like when you see the clouds separate the light into those biblical cones, like the multiple conical cylinders in some vacuum cleaners. That rolling grey-white sky with the light breaks through and falls in pillar-like shafts except they're softer. Like souls are being received into heaven or there's a patch of revelatory business going on and the light confirms it. The light for an epiphany. That's what it smells like. There's ozone. There's something that the wind's let drop like the soft mouth of a retriever placing something living by your hand.'

'Remind me never to take you wine tasting. Fuck's sake, Billy, that was so waxing lyrical they've made crayons out of it.'

'Okay. You try and describe this smell.'

'Never mind that, look at the blanket!' They looked.

The stain had resolved itself into what looked like dog hairs. Dark, freshly shed dog hairs. They smelt of Grin.

'Dog hairs. Been trapped by the blood. Gummed down. into the blanket fibres. Amazing!'

'Yes, he was a moulty old thing. Couldn't go out without using that tacky-sticky lint roller. All pegged to my tights. Not good when you're a midwife to have dog hairs cluttering your dark tights. I mean. Your client's going to take one look and say, 'cross contamination'.'

'You work in your swimwear.'

'I know, but you don't want dog hairs in the denier. Sends out a wrong signal. Suggests 'germy woman'.'

'I doubt it.'

'Anyway, here's Grin's hairs. Thought we'd cleaned up every last one. Nice to see them again.'

Anne stroked the blanket. 'Shit, it even feels like him when you stroke it. It's the grass. You feel dog body. Can you feel dog body under here?'

'We're reminiscing. That's why. We've hit muscle memory.'

'A blanket with muscle memory?'

William and Anne wept, then slept outdoors on the blanket curled beside the memory of the dog they had loved and still loved and wouldn't stop loving. William dreamed of the slaughtered beasts he had seen in this same garden, and as the poor headless things stood with the candles in their bellies their fur had risen out of the ground and fastened itself with Kit, William's step brother and a tailor, sewing them back inside, and their heads had descended from a low cloud and found the necks and restored themselves and Kit had tacked and secured them. Whilst the candles, oh the candles, did what they could to be blood and heartbeat.

* * *

FIVE DAYS LATER

William, unshaven and in lounge pants and a shirt that he'd hiked from the drying rack without bothering to iron it, had his feet shoved inside Anne's fleecy fuchsia mules. He was scrolling through his emails. Thin schists of genuine emails lay between great geological slabs of spam that his server's spam-spotter hadn't spotted. After much routing, William found that there were five applicants for the two posts of trainee crime scene cleaner.

William opened the first.

Dr Doctor Shakespeare,

Let me introduce myself. I am a business graduate and was considering joining the police but this looks more interesting. I'm good at housework and car valeting, have a kind of second-sense where stains are concerned and can mentally tabulate and calculate the ratio and aptness of chemicals needed for stain removal. I have a supplier who allows me to practice on blood stained clothes produced by people with regular nosebleeds. Some of the Nosebleeders have also gamely allowed themselves to flow over a variety of surfaces to allow me the experience firsthand of removing all traces of blood. I am happy working in a team and know quite a few group bonding games with which we could begin the crime scene clean, just to ensure energy's high as is co-operation. I am a driver, non-smoker and easy going, upbeat person. I look forward to hearing from you when you've had a chance to read my (attached) resume.

'Mm,' said William, and pressed the delete button. He wasn't sure what rankled him about this particular applicant but something did. Was it her assuredness, her presumption that game-playing was something appropriate to cleaning a murder site? The next applicant was far more suitable.

Dear Dr Shakespeare,

I have no experience but am willing to learn. I think it must be very satisfying to give people back their homes and places of work, having cleared them of every trace of an exceedingly tragic and unfortunate circumstance. That must be very gratifying. I can't imagine what it must be like having your home or a place you go to every day of the week completely changed by the mess that murders usually leave in their wake. My brother murdered someone in his bedroom but, because he was such a messy boy nobody realised until the flies began arriving. If it wasn't for the flies, if we'd successfully removed all blow flies and their ilk from the planet the murder would have gone unnoticed. As it is, my brother is now serving life and it fell to me to clean his bedroom. It was a tough call but, ultimately, very satisfying. I attach a before and after set of images so you can judge for yourself just how successful my cleaning efforts were. I can't wait to hear from you. It's be a blast being a crime scene cleaner and returning the world to its innocence.

Regards,

Kyle Burgundy.

William paused for several seconds before hitting 'delete' — 'no, even if there are no suitable candidates, that man is not joining my team.' The third email was brief but the attachment was over fifty pages long. The email said,

Hi Shaspeare,

I can do it. I done it before, very reliable.

Bests,

Berowne Boyet

William tapped the dustbin icon. Two left.

Dear Dr Shakespeare,

I am very interested and would like to be considered for the post of trainee crime scene cleaner. I do understand that it will be a tough job, sometimes, simply because murder is murder and it affects you.

Also, my Aunkles mentioned that I ought to apply, and I think their other ward, Nell D'eath, is applying, too. However, don't let that sway you when you're making your decision. You must choose the staff you need.

Yours Sincerely,

Jacques Mercutio

PS Yes you know me. I'm that porter.

PPS We call them our Aunkles at their own request. You see, they're both Aunt and Uncle to us.

'Bingo!' said William. 'Yes, he'll be great. He's a good man.' William had always liked him, he was quiet, genuinely respectful with the patients, seemed quick witted and astute and worked hard. There'd be no problem complying with the wishes of the

Nine Bulimic Cannibals and hiring Jacques Mercutio. Fingers crossed Nell D'eath was as spot on. And they call them their 'Aunkles'. Interesting compound word.

'Yes, welcome on bard,' William typed, smiling. Oops. Typo. He'd written 'bard' and meant 'board'. Ah well. Too late, sent. He opened the final email.

Dear Dr Shakespeare,

This is a career I hadn't considered before but it's oddly appealing. Righting wrong. Working towards normality, removing horrors and reinstating, resetting, the moral compass. I'm hardworking although I have only known artistic pursuits. My relatives, whom I believe you met, wish me to apply. They have been very kind and considerate to me over the years and I know they know me. If they think that this position suits me then I am absolutely sure it will. They have never been wrong in any advice or decision they have ver given or made on my behalf. So, here I am, applying and saying, quite genuinely, I would really like to win this position. I don't think you'd be disappointed if you employed me. Thank you for your consideration.

Sincerely,

Nell D'eath.

'Yes!'
William printed off Jacques and Nell D'eath's emails and took them into the kitchen. Odile, Odette and Odear were all at nursery and Anne was working, bobbing about in the Simulacrum Company's River, holding her breath underwater for up to nine minutes whilst delivering babies. He always thought of her job as a hybrid of Life Guard and Midwife and

Undine.

Did he really need to see the two successful applicants or could he just email them and tell them to turn up for training? Note to self: book a training day for the three of us. These days you needed certificates, bonafides for whatever you undertook — for recreation or career. The University of Life had started issuing credentials. Nobody did anything without expecting, at the very least, a certificate of participation. Surely this was the start of the Enclosure Acts of the human mind?! He ought to rebel. Yes. He'd think about it.

So, no, William decided that he ought to make time to interview both of them. It was protocol. He'd begin right now, drawing up questions on the back of their emails. Question one...? What did he want to know? Were they squeamish? Good point. Was that something he ought to ask at the outset? And he needed to know how they'd work under pressure. Yes, there'd be pressure and each workplace would affect them because of what had happened there. They could expect post-traumatic stress and recurring nightmares. Should he hold off mentioning that? How easily could they expunge what they'd seen from the fridge door of their minds.

The mind had the biggest fridge door and with the greatest number of magnets available to peg things directly in your line of sight whenever you went to collect something from the sophisticated fridge freezer of memory. Yes, William had always imagined memory as a magnificent fridge freezer with everything in the immediate memory pinned to the door with fridge magnets. Then short term memory, that was the fridge part, well lit and with any emotional impact cooling down. Now, when you were sorting through the freezer drawers of long term memory, everything had become solid and permanent and heavy with its own importance. It had also assumed a new shape and was losing definition as it collected ice. Oh, William liked his metaphors. Would they add magic to his instruction?

Would he be an inspirational team leader? William rather thought he would.

Look at the power endowed by his mnemonic system for prescription medication! He had designated characters, places, powers to the entire contents of the British Pharmacopoeia — prescribing medication meant that, in his mind at least, his patients embarked on the pharmaceutical equivalent of the Hero's Journey (or cosplay if the prescription was short-term and meant to treat an acute illness and not a chronic), travelling a route along which certain aspects reared up as archetypes. One woman, Mrs Mendicotte, had (allegorically) travelled into the Hall of the Mountain Troll, grown a troll tail, danced in front of the throne made from horse bones and car horns. William had begun to notice a wildness in her previously neat-as-a-paper-napkin hair, and in her age-pale eyes there grew a fire that bloodied her cheeks and flicked her limbs, limbs so indisposed by arthritis, that she cavorted with agility but at a disadvantageous tilt. He remembered thinking that each new prescription drug would give her a new mentor and a new quest. It was like sending her, and the rest of the people he treated, out to live their own lives inside the shell of a fairytale, like grubs living inside peaches. They fed and they transformed. Meanwhile, his peers were dabbling with scrying on toilet mirrors for diagnoses, and divining appropriate treatments by considering broken teabags, biscuit crumbs, lost gloves leaking wet onto pavements, the wear on their patients' car or mobility scooters' tyres, traffic reports and the weather forecast.

Days of glory. Days of jubilation and contentment. Gone.

So he had two people working for him. Jacques, whom he was sure would be an excellent crime scene cleaner having worked in a hospital and seen what he had seen. And Nell D'Eath was intriguing. He'd already reversed her name. She was Death Nell, a name suggesting a woman of great individuality and resourcefulness, someone left unintimidated by anything chance could bowl at her feet, even if that something was a pod of burning skulls. This woman would cope. There was nothing bleak about her. Yes, she was truly death-defying.

Anne was due home from her shift in the Simulacrum River, and she'd fetch the girls from nursery, so William limbered-up, trimmed his beard, experimented with his hair using Anne's waterproof hair products, and drafted several emails to people who might be able to recommend his services. Here was his business and it was stepping into the real world. Lalala, William's heart sang, and William sang descant with it. William thought he'd tidy round. Spruce up. Impress Anne. He opened the cupboard under the stairs, to air it, certainly, but also so he could chat with his partially dissected companion. He liked to feel that the house was't empty, his friend was there. The dear, dead man still had his ears and could listen, oh this long-standing and physically diminished friend, cohort of many secrets, the constant supporter during William's tribulations as he fought the onslaught of superstition — why, that cadaver was like the dried riverbed ready to draw-off William's tears of anger and frustration. Oh, here he is!

'Hello, Shreds,' William said, patting the box as though it contained a hibernating dormouse. Yes, that's how William chose to see his beloved dissection buddy. He was hibernating. His body shredded into bedding for the rest of it to curl into.

'I think I've got my personnel,' William called to the man-in-the-box — 'one I know, the other sounds interesting and she's connected to the Mysterious Cannibalistic Nine. Do you think she'll be a cannibal as well? Oh, a cannibal working on cleaning a murder crime scene, that would be very different for her, wouldn't it? Be like scraping the scraps off plates after dinner.' William dragged out the upright vacuum cleaner with its clear plastic torso, his head turned away whilst he addressed the box, his hands remembering the coordinates for the socket and flicking the switch. 'Yes, I know, I need to be given a crime scene to clean, but my guess is that the Cannibals are onto it. I suppose they must have contacts. You can't eat people, even willing ones, and not have your antennae quivering across other forms of human demise, eh? The questionable and illegal ones, eh?' That's when William became aware of two significant anomalies. Two shocks were aimed at normality, normality, that softly decanted bit of the brain that flows like a public water fountain — a psychic public water fountain alongside all the other primed little public water fountains of his Cultural Mates, connected to the plumbing of What's Expected. The pressure fell. Normality dribbled into the porcelain pan and vanished. Why? Well, smoke was corralling him, a pall had covered the hallway carpet and was rising up his calves, hiding the vacuum cleaner's base (the base always looked hunched — its shape made him think it was a chunk snapped off his sleeping wife, that domed hunch of a sleeping policeman, his wife snoring over the floor and inhaling her own dead, shed flakes of skin). That's when he clocked the contents of the vacuum cleaner's cylinder. There was a baby inside it, inverted, its limbs folded as they would be in the womb. Its fingers flexed as he accidentally caught the 'on' button and the vacuum cleaner inhaled and roared. At the same moment William saw the reflections of flame cast against his hall wallpaper, dancing on the inside of the vintage biscuit tin. Fire! A house fire! A baby inside the vacuum cleaner! William fell backwards, tripped on the invisible flex beneath the rising smoke, dragged the plug from the socket, hiked the vacuum cleaner into the air as high as he could and staggered with it down the hallway towards the flames inside the cupboard under the stairs. It was a white hot fire, like a dough made of industrial lasers kneading the box in which his friend, the precious, dissected cadaver, lay. The baby cried softly within its plastic womb, audible above the loud insufflation of the fire. 'Ring the fire brigade. An ambulance. For fuck's sake, get the baby away from the fire, the cylinder will melt around it! Get the phone, get the phone!' he yelled.

Cradling the heavy vacuum cleaner against his chest, William hurtled into the kitchen, grabbed the phone and began beating 999 into it. Then the light changed. The smoke was sucked back. The baby opened its fluff-bunny eyes and its body flowed into its head and the head disappeared with a pop.

'Hello. Emergency services. Which service do you require?' said an operator.

'It's gone,' said William. 'It's all right. It's gone,' ending the call with a heavy jab of his finger as though to make sure he could feel it, he wasn't tripping, sleeping or having his mind torn into tiny shreds by humdrumness, the everyday shredder, slivering anything that didn't add to the humdrumness. He dropped the vacuum cleaner and went back to the cupboard under the stairs. A tiny wire of smoke, a thin capillary, twisted above a heap of cinders and ash. The fire hadn't touched anything else, nothing was blackened or scorched or damaged other than the cadaver's remains and the box in which it had been packed. The ash dribbled away and revealed teeth. Two rows of teeth like an unstrung abacus, and one boney hand. The bones and teeth were a crisp white as though bleached or painted. William dipped his fingers alongside them. Cold. He tapped the teeth and finger bones. 'A perfect partner for Shirley,' William said. 'Two ears and a nipple meet two rows of teeth and a skeletal hand. I'd call that a marriage made in heaven.' As he watched, the teeth and hand sank into the ash. 'You never know the day,' said William and plugged the vacuum cleaner back into the socket and began to remove the drifts of sticky soot thrown off by the spontaneous combustion. He arranged the teeth and the hand bones on an empty shelf, wiped the grey film from the cupboard lightbulb, sprayed the hallway with Winter Berry air freshener, had another think and tipped the ash, teeth and bones into the vintage biscuit tin (removing the keys), sliding a layer of clingfilm over everything to stop it wisping away like his mother's ashes in their fluffy dice, and firmed on the biscuit tin lid. Then William put a chipped enamel pudding basin in the biscuit tin's place. Somewhere for the keys. He pulled on a pair of marigolds and gave the vacuum cleaner an internal. No sign of any baby. Was he suffering from stress? Even if he was, the fact of the spontaneous combustion remained. If that was real and true and factual, so was the baby in the hoover. There was only one source of this kind of intrusion, this mashing of normality: Fairies.

William made a brew. Stuffed two teabags into the mug. Soya milk to the brim. Sat in the chair back that was like the banister of a spiral staircase. Sat and thought. Sat and remembered this.

Portia Avalon, first time mother and barrister newly called to the bar, was expecting her first baby. William had gone into the ultrasound suite on his brief stint on obstetrics (a taster offered to him because of his wife's fame as a water specialist midwife — senior management had thought he may have the aptitude). Watching the midwife place the pestle-resembling ultrasound generating hub over the gelled stomach, William had gasped, inhaling his own spit so he choked momentarily, in shock as he saw what looked like the Cottingly fairies assembled round the developing foetus, poised, attentive, a pert fantastic tableau. Their wings twitching up and down as though in strobe lighting. He bent closer to the monitor. His breath screened it. The midwife tutted, whipped a tissue from the slow explosion of the open box and wiped it clear. 'What's this?' William said. pointing at the fairy throng. 'What's this?' The midwife just tutted and muttered, 'you know what it is.' Portia Avalon, fingers to the side of her belly asked them if anything was wrong. William nodded. The midwife shook her head. 'He's out of his depth, my love,' said the midwife. 'He's not used to reading the monitor. He's not used to this.'

William left the room and went to the WRVS cafe to drink tea among the unsuspecting patients and their relatives. The

Cottingly Fairies installed inside a human womb. Unthinkable.

William's father had drawn up a fairy eye chart in one of his many pamphlets about The Weird. There was an untouched copy up in the attic.

William collected the biscuit tin with his dissection buddy's ashes in it, and went up into the loft. He'd stow the ashes there until they could be scattered or tipped into an urn and buried or retained by some authorised facility that would keep them inside the equivalent of a post mortem safety box. In a reredos. In a bee bole.

William opened the skylight to let in the unseasonably mild air and the crystalline sunlight. Over in a nook stood a fragile handmade book case (Anne's fragile mother's handiwork). Its thin shelves were slumped under its modest load. William hunkered down in front of it and trawled through his father's works. *From Knock to Nation, Poltergeists Equal War, Fairy Diet, Divination by Canal Narrowboat, Ectoplasm Fashion Patterns, Fairy Senses and Vital Stats.* William slid *Fairy Senses and Vital Stats* free, its glossed cover adhering slightly to the other pamphlets. William riffled the pages and then opened them out onto the contents page. Fairy's were evidently prone to acne and hormone imbalances. And here it was. A fairy eye chart. The page was blank. Haha, it would be, he wasn't a fairy. A fairy would see something. A fairy with perfect eyesight would see a page filled with recognisable symbols. Evidently, William learned as he flicked through the information, the Fairy alphabet was very different from any form of human writing. It was not so much runes as wrinkles. Their fairy books looked like bits cut from badly crumpled linen pillowcases or handkerchiefs. There was a page describing what they saw…. Bless him, his dad, John Shakespeare, had been a very thorough man.

WHAT A FAIRY SEES

Whatever their size — the fairy from the seelie or unseelie courts, their eyesight is shaped by different abilities. Things are visible to them that we would have trouble believing existed. But that's what senses define. They are the parameters and guardians of our beliefs. What we cannot see by any means (and humans are ingenious at extending the natural range of human oprics) the fairies have no such apparatus or instruments. Creating anything that extends their natural senses is anathema to them. They have a far more rigid belief system than humans. They are by comparison inflexible. This is both a strength, since it unites them, providing them with a base and basis to agree on since nothing is open to speculation nor interpretation. On the back foot though it means that they are liable to ignore information gleaned from observing humans and non-enchanted and non-fairy animals and ignore sources of danger. Fairies are stubbornly confined to their own realm which can neither extend or suffer retraction/contraction. They see the spaces between stars but not the stars themselves, readers of what we humans would call 'negative spaces'.

William shivered. It was returning. The Noise was sneaking back. There'd been a buzzing, dismissible as a fly negotiating the rebuttal of freedom, restrained by the invisible boundary of a window... the Noise coming forwards at walking pace. William ran to the skylight, lifted the catch and pushed his head through the gap, the better to stare down into the garden. He listened. There was that horrible hubbub but it was like hearing a sound seven layers deep inside an onion skin. Bang! The front door shut. 'Anne!' William shut the skylight, hid the biscuit tin under some old duvet covers and hoped he'd cleaned up the spontaneous combustion sufficiently well to avoid questions. How had that happened, though? He'd never believed in spontaneous combustion. Alcohol was at its base. Perhaps the cadaver's preservatives had been at the root of the conflagration — vulnerable to ignition away from the far more controlled environment of a hospital.

'WILLIAM!' Anne shouted from the hallway. 'Where's my biscuit tin?'

William tucked his father's pamphlet into his back pocket and shinned down the extension ladder, closing the attic door with the pole. 'I'm here, love. I was in the loft.'

Down in the hallway, the children scattered around her like dropped shopping bags, Anne was holding the chipped enamel pudding bowl, flicking it with her index finger, her eyes searching the rest of the hall table for the missing biscuit tin, despite the fact that it obviously wasn't there.

'I borrowed it. I'll put it back in a few days.'

'What for? What did you borrow it for?'

'Scraps. Scraps and receipts and stuff for the new business. I'll get a proper box. I'll visit the stationers. Then I'll put it back. Promise.'

'There's just something comforting about it. Sometimes, when I come in, the light in here, maybe the keys already in it, the tin looks like its refilled itself with vintage biscuits. The sort of biscuit they don't make now. Bigger. More chunky. Different shapes. Lovely old-fashioned biscuits of our youth. Can you have biscuit nostalgia? I'm not nostalgic about anything else.'

'Don't see why not.' William scooped Odile and Odear from the floor and dropped them into their highchairs in the kitchen. Odette demonstrated her new ability to do forward rolls. They took a while for her to organise her limbs and push herself over but they were pretty neat for a three year old. William realised he was doing that parent thing, talent scouting, spotting the promises his children were bound to have, flushes of inheritance from all their forbears, talents and skills that may have lain dormant, skills he and Anne had that were repeated or magnified. It was something he was slightly ashamed of doing. But there it was. He had an empty trophy case in his head and phantom awards and cups floated in to fill the shelves, changing with the shifting abilities his children were demonstrating. It was exciting.

Anne's hair was still wet from work. William stroked it tenderly. They smiled at each other, the same smiles they'd given each other from the first time they met — where had they met? At a competition. Like air guitar but air artillery. Miming to audio recordings of modern battles. Miming the correct artillery to previously unheard remastered tapes. It was geeky but the camaraderie was strong. They all looked down on air guitar. Also, the practitioners of Air Armament, the enthusiasts, were, without exception, vegetarian. It was a hobby that attracted life-style pacifists.

'I have two perfect applicants for my crime scene cleaning business.'

'Oh, said Anne, stepping over Odette and filling the kettle.

'One of them's the hospital porter I know. He's a good man and recommended by the Nine YouKnowWhats. I think he's wanting to broaden his horizons.'

'By sliding a mop and bucket over a murder scene. Much more panoramic, that.'

'And the other one also seems to be related in some way to the, ah, people who provided the cleaning fludds.

'You said 'fludds'.'

'I did. That's how they pronounce it. Fludds.'

Anne, kicked off her shoes and slid on the fuchsia mules. 'Oh, is that wise? I don't mean pronouncing the word the same way, I mean taking on people related to a family of cannibals.'

'It seems to be what the 'suppliers' want. They both sound okay.'

'But are they both cannibals?'

'I don't think Jacques, the porter, is. And the woman doesn't

70

sound like one, either. Not from her email and resume.'

'But you don't know. She's hardly like to write, 'must dash, the postman's buttocks need basting'. Unnerving thinking a cannibal might clean the scene of a murder. I mean, for them it's like scraping the dinner plates and washing up after a meal.'

'That's what I thought. But I don't think I'm about to employ cannibals. '

'Although you're going to employ a product used by cannibals after they've cannibalised. Can I smell smoke? Have you been smoking?'

'I don't smoke. Haven't in an age.' William rolled up his sleeve and displayed the transdermal patches on his arm. The nicotine and the contraceptive. Side by side.'

* * *

Under the whistle of the kettle, someone could be heard knocking on the door.

'I'll go,' said William. You sit down. Then I'll make tea. Odette, stay with your mum...'

William opened the door to a uniformed courier holding a cardboard box with air holes punched into it and the words 'Fragile. Bird.' drawn above the address label in black felt tip.

'I didn't order this,' said William.

'No,' said the courier. 'You William Shakespeare, though?'

'Yes, I'm William Shakespeare.'

'Then the box is yours. Maybe you weren't expecting it. Because somebody's sent you a surprise.'

'Well, it's a surprise.'

'Sign here.'

William signed and the courier disappeared around a corner. Holding the box in one hand, William saluted his stethoscope which looked, from this angle, as if it was examining the left trainer, its disc pressed against the trainer's heel. Then William carried the box into the kitchen, 'What's that, daddy?' said Odette.

'My sentiments entirely,' said Anne. 'What's that, daddy?'

'I have no idea.'

'Who's it from. There'll be a sender name and address.'

'Oh, St Largesse hospital.'

'Maybe they've sent stuff you left behind.'

'It's a live creature inside. A bird of some sort. I didn't leave a bird behind.'

'Haha, funny if it's a cockerel. Didn't you say your consultant gave you a totem animal? That's one of the reasons…'

'I blew the whistle.'

'Fucking hilarious if that's what it is.'

'Funny in a threatening sort of way, certainly. '

'Well, open the box — and I noticed you'd got rid of that big stinky box — good man.'

* * *

Two hours later the children were in bed and Anne and William were watching television with a small bantam cockerel asleep on a cushion in the corner of the room. 'I'll send it back tomorrow.'

'You can't stick it in the post. That was a courier. Pricey to return it.'

'Well I don't fancy turning up in the car with it and dropping it off at main reception.'

'I'd like to see their faces if you did.'

And I've thought of a name for my start up business. Got it when this chap arrived.'

'Oh right. What is it? Shitter and Shouter?'

'Not quite. It's Crow. He crows a lot. I thought I'd have a cockerel in silhouette and try and find appropriate words so that CROW is an abbreviation.'

'Or an acrostic.'

'An abbreviation. Yeah. Crow.'

'You don't want people thinking of carrion crow because, given the nature of your work, that would be ghoulish.'

'Or we're gone by cockcrow so the cleaning's done before the sunrise. We have to have a unique selling point. Maybe that's it. We clean at night. We might turn up at dusk or late afternoon to set up but the cleaning happens secretly, quietly, discreetly in the hours of darkness and we're gone by dawn and the room or whatever has been returned from the nocturnal nightmare of murder to its previous diurnal innocence.'

'I wouldn't look at any room in the same way if someone was murdered in it.'

'No, I wouldn't either, but people can take quite a lot. Psychologically robust. Plus they'll have spent a fortune on its decor.'

✺ CHAPTER 4 ✺

THE INTERVIEWS

William bought three coffees. Jacques and Death Nell had commandeered one of three window tables and were busy hiking an extra chair over to it from an unoccupied corner. William carried the tray over, noticing how the low, grey skies slid their undifferentiated cloud mass across the city. An image came to mind: cloud-cutter ants, a species that carried slivers of condensed water vapour and used it, mixed with their faeces, to grow a crop of weather on which the colony fed.

Most of the interview was spent with William speculating what might happen. Explaining they were going to specialise in murders among the rich and wealthy.

'Why's that then, Billy?' said Death Nell, tipping sugar into her latte so the foam was crushed beneath it, rising back like correction fluid.

'I just thought it might make it more bearable. These murder victims had something before their lives were lost. Better than when someone's had nothing. The world's been abysmal for them then they get murdered.'

'Money is no indicator of a life well lived,' said Jacques chewing on a wood-stirrer's payload of coffee foam.

'I don't know. It seemed the better option. And we wouldn't have to clean so many because they'd be better paid, so, ah, kinder to us.'

'I can see your reasoning,' said Jacques. 'Maybe, say several times a year, we could clean up after a poor person's murder as an act of charity.'

'That's a good thought,' said Death Nell. 'Yeah, we could help them cope. I mean, till you showed us what happens after a violent death, I always imagined the police went in and did a spot of tidying. But they don't, do they? Even when they've flung fingerprint dust everywhere and yanked up floorboards. People have to mostly clean the place themselves. Pretty tough deal, that.'

'And the fingerprint dust is carcinogenic. So that's another problem. That's why we'll be doing training. It's not just the shock to our systems, it's the physical health risks, too.'

'Right-o. So what's the salary?' said Death Nell.

'Good,' said William. 'What are you getting now?'

Jacques and Death Nell scribbled down their salaries on the till receipt. William considered the numbers, nodded and smiled.

'This will pay better,' said William. 'Sometimes there will be a lot of work. There are the Murder Months when it's statistically more likely that people are killed unlawfully. It varies from culture to culture, country to country. Here it's mid-winter and mid-summer. Of course, there are years when these stats are overturned. And sometimes national events — war, pandemics, elections, something compelling on the telly, well, these can be the trigger for homicidal tendencies.'

'Have you got any work yet?'

'No, because we need to train first and then advertise our availability. I've booked us on a one day course run by the trade journal. Once we have the certification and backing of the trade experts, then we'll be able to flag up our expertise.'

'It's a bit exciting,' said Death Nell. 'Except for the fact that it's all to do with murder.'

'Yeah,' said Jacques. 'Except we're part of the, er, healing process. The recovery.'

'I think Christianity missed a trick,' said Death Nell.

'Like what?' said Jacques. I'd say it had all bases pretty much covered.' William smiled encouragingly. To him, the Bible was a campsite that languages passed through on their way to obsolescence. A trading post for lingusitics.

'Well, if I was writing up the Bible, the New Testament bit, then I'd have made Lazarus a murder victim. Then along comes Jesus and brings the murderee back to life. Imagine how much more powerful that would have been, eh? Much more hope for the Hopeless.'

'That's one for the Bible fanfic sites, Nell,' said Jacques

☙ CHAPTER 5 ❧

THE NOISE
RETURNS IN DRIBS
AND DRABS

On the way home, William had a text from his step brother, Kit Marlow. Sewing Kit, the Savile Row Stitcheroo.

Got u a .mnt at ur old hosp. come whn u get this.Kitx

Kit was waiting for him.

'That Noise thing. If Anne's not heard it then it's something going on in your ears. I got you in — pulled a few threads.'

'Thanks, Kit.'

'Try getting a referral from your GP and this hospital will have its staff go sky-clad and back-combed to get the mumbo-jumbo in place to block you. They'd postpone indefinitely, there'd be dates leapfrogging off every line of latitude, a mirror facing a mirror. You'd never have been seen.'

'True. Thanks, Kit.'

The clinic doctor was an old, if secret, associate. There'd been four of them — supposedly anonymous — undertaking clandestine experiments with blood. The Doctor was called Lafew Aumerle, and he was a decent man with a fetish for bowler hats worn over Tibetan earflap bonnets.

Doctor Aumerle examined William Shakespeare's ears as

thoroughly as though they were an expensive wedding present. Then William and Kit waited whilst the data was collated and studied.

'Come back in, Bill, Kit,' said Doctor Aumerle. 'Sit down.'

'Thanks, Lafew.'

'It's tinnitus of sorts,' said Dr Aumerle. 'Basically, you have a whole road system in your head.'

'What?'

'Are you saying 'what' because you can't hear me or because you're finding it tough going to believe me?'

'The latter,' said William.

'I want you to come and look at these scans.'

William went over to the wall-length light box.

'See. It's a great road system. Overpasses, underpasses, motorways, autobahns but all in microcosm.'

William could not gainsay him. 'Go on.'

'It's the Fairies.'

'Those Eustachian Tube botherers, right,' said Kit.

'I believe that they have transferred their entire transport system into human ears so that their environment isn't marred by track and road building, nor by the emissions from their dainty fuel. From this sequence of images you get a time lapse glimpse of Fairy rush hour. All the little headlights and brake lights. The magic comes in when they arrive at their destination. They step from the vehicles into their own Fairylands. You'll be relieved to know that once Fairy commuters step from their vehicles they put their feet down in their own world, the one they share with us.

'Hahaha! You're telling me some sort of a story.'

'No. You have tinnitus. That's the noise. That's the great noise in your head and why no one can see it. The thing is, it's the entire Fairyland Transport System miniatured and hidden in your ears that you're hearing.'

'And what I saw? Did Kit tell you about the poor, abbatoired animals? '

'I did.'

'He did. All I can suggest is that you check your garden when you get home. Check your garden for clues. Fairies build on what's already present. They also play on fears. You're vegan.'

'I am.'

Kit studied the scan. 'Can cochleas grow? Can the inner ear change shape? Obviously I am no expert but there seems to be an awful lot of doodahs in such a small space. This bit here — it goes back, back, back and there's probably even more just behind this bit. Is there another scan from the front top or behind?'

Pale lipped Doctor Aumerle handed Kit another set of images which Kit pinned to the light box wall. 'Oh! Good lord. Bill, my dearest step brother, your skull is a frantic and frenetic place. Look, William, you know me. I'm part of the old gang, the blood experiment — you knew it was me back then...?'

'Of course I did.'

'I wore the Tibetan bonnet and bowler.'

'And I wore the... you're telling me some sort of story.'

'No. You have tinnitus. That's the noise. That's the great noise in your head and why no one can see it.'

'And what I saw?'

'Check your garden when you get home. Check your garden for clues.'

'And in the meantime?'

'Have you had tinnitus recently?'

'To a lesser and lesser extent, yes.'

'I think they've added baffles. To mute it. I think they've tried to make it better for you.'

'Better for me? I'd have been better with my ears left as my own green belt property.'

'True, Anyway, it's good to see you, Bill. Look after yourself. I'm glad you did what you did. The madness has to stop.'

☜ CHAPTER 6 ☞

TRAINING DAY

One Week Later

William was driving to the Crime Scene Cleaning Trade Journal headquarters in Battersea. It was 9am and the roads were quieter than he had anticipated. There were a lot of bicycles.

'Thanks for the lift, Bill. Much obliged,' said Death Nell.

'S'okay. I was coming this way,' William grinned.

'What, oh? Hahahaha!' Death Nell rummaged in her bag. 'How's Jacques getting here?'

'He's staying with a friend who lives nearby.'

'Oh, which friend is that? Did he say?'

'Vignette.'

'Oh. She's an idiot. I stayed with her once. Never again.'

'How so?'

'She works at a planetarium.'

'Oh, she must be an idiot then,' said William.

'No, obviously she's not an idiot for working in a planetarium. She's just an idiot who works in a planetarium. She wears white Goth makeup, like me, but she manages to look like the moon. Fatter face. She bigs up her acne scars — I've got more than she has. She builds extra bits up using the sticky tape method.'

'Go on.'

'Sticky tape your skin. Where you want the effect. Rub the back with a cloth soaked in warm water. It peels the top shiny bit off and you're left with this malleable tacky slick. Shape it. Add your white panstick. Et voila, ladies and gents, a woman with a moon face! Not'

'I might try that home.'

'Anyway, she's in the Shrewds. That woman-and-girl gang, they moisten linen handkerchiefs with synthetic spit and come and scrub your face with it. Lab-made spit. Saliva. The sort pumped into the chronically driy mouthed.'

'And they scrub your face with it?'

'Disarray your makeup. Muss your grooming. Not exactly actual bodily harm. Can't really report it as a crime.'

'What do they do it for?'

'Feminism.'

'Oh.'

'One of its many facets.'

'Have they got a sense of humour?'

'Yeah, but its braided into their sense of destiny.'

'Is it a big gang? I've seen them in action. Once. And not very long ago.'

'International. They do exchanges. Gang exchanges. Scholarships.'

'They're that organised?'

'They got money, money organises. It's when you've got nothing it goes ad hoc. Unpredictable. Money makes 'em more predictable. It also makes them less arrestable.'

'As I said, I've come across them. Seen them in action.'

'They got their own cocktails, their own mixers. Own currency.'

'They're sounding less and less like a gang.'

'They're expanding the boundaries. The parameters. They dance the cotillion.'

'And here we are.'

'Yeah.'

William parked up. A man was pushing a mobile hanger on castors along the street towards a row of market stalls. The hanger was loaded with uninflated inflatable grandfather and grandmother clocks.

'They're the choice for trendies who don't want inflatable dolls. You can have sex with time or just cuddle it. They're marketed as 'ME TIME'. Objects that are unmistakably objects. I mean, okay, inflatable dolls are objects but they're designed with more accommodating human proportions. This is honest. You can Fuck with Time. Popular with CEOs.'

'Sex with inflatable time pieces?'

'Yeah, the faces have a digital implant and the time changes. Some people feel that's an improvement. They're getting a response. Something's being measured, eh?'

* * *

William and Nell were escorted through the Spillages and Spurts headquarters. It was unusual. Everywhere was lit with flickering daylight, daylight broken by the flight of birds and the calumny of clouds channelled through periscopes, expressed by bioluminescent plants, and phosphorescent sea life in wall-length aquariums. 'Look carefully, Dr Shakespeare, Ms D'eath, and you'll spot the recreation of a sea-bed crime scene — and, yes, specialist crime scene cleaning divers were fetched in to mop up.'

'Wouldn't the, ah, scene clean itself?' said William.

'Not when steps had been taken by the murderer to restrain the bodies and it's on the lea of a very large reef.'

'Don't fish eat that sort of thing?' said Death Nell.

'That's a bit of a myth.'

'They wouldn't know it was a murder scene,' said William. 'Would they?'

'Dolphins tend to prevent the scene being disturbed and the remains desecrated.'

'Trained dolphins? Or, um, general fin traffic?' said Death Nell.

'Some marine biologists train the already respectful bottle-nose dolphins to police the ocean floor. They will sometimes carry clues and loosened biological material back to the marine biologists's fleet.'

'They have a fleet of boats?'

'Marine biologists are quite a sea power. Oh yes, everyone raves about the space station but few ever toss a gladsome hiccup in the direction of the permanent Marine Base out in the Atlantic Ocean. It's difficult to get into space. It's just as hard to make your way across the terrible Atlantic and it's a known fact that all academics are seasick. It goes with the territory.'

William and Nell tried not to smile as they were ushered deeper into the building.

'We have a black museum, and our training rooms use A.R. and V.R. All our crime scenes are based on actual sites and genuine crimes, reconstructed from eye witness accounts, filmed footage, artist's renderings, photographs and police and witness descriptions. Some are famous, most are not. Using haptic gloves and aromas and odours you will gain experience of what it is like to confront an area where tragedy and evil have had a mash-up. Your constant companions will be the repellant stench and obduracy of old blood and human detritus, the sort that isn't scraped up and collected for dignified ritual disposal. There will be insects. Moulds. Vile slops. You will vomit and faint. Your responses are genetically programmed. You must learn to cope as best you can. Remember, the area you are cleaning you are also cleansing of memory. You are making homes habitable again. Returning workplaces to the economy, restoring areas to their natural ecology. Their unremarkable contingency. It is a vital job. You are professionals. You will make a difference. Here we will let you loose on a variety — a whole cross-section — of crime scenes and you will be guided though the processes. With their banishing you are allowing Time to heal and memory to forget. Both are important factors. A place must not remain out-of-bounds because it played host to violent death. Now, put on the suits provided and the headsets and you will be taken in your teams (or as individuals) into the crime scenes and guided by a computer-generated mentor. Marks will be awarded for successful completion of tasks. At the end of your training day certificates will be presented. Be aware that, should the standard not reach a professional bench mark, then certificates will be withheld, available only if another training day is booked and the standard then passes muster. Any questions?'

Nell and William shook their heads.

'Please help yourselves to coffee and the Information Pack.'

* * *

'Where's Jacques? He's not normally late,' said Death Nell.

William lifted first one buttock then the other. The chairs had a veneer of padding, a scraping of blue plush like an untanned skinned toy. One or two people — anglers, William thought, had gathered themselves to the rim of the chair and were sat in a fishing position, the propped-up by watchfulness, the speculation. Others had the demeanour of people in free-fall through their thoughts, thoughts airlifted like pollen. The woman giving the introduction — 101 in Violence-Induced Debris and Staining — had poised the power point display and rocked back with great difficulty on shoes that resembled praying hands forced open by her feet.

'I'll begin,' she said, and the chatter subsided.

'Murder leaves thirteen types of blot, requiring five methods of deletion. Violence creates two types of ghost the murder snappy, the murder durational, the murder accurate, the murder incommensurate, the murder solitary, the murder communal and complicit, the murder scheduled, the murder ad hoc, the murder elementary, the murder urban, the murder irresolute, the murder intended, the murder for murder's sake, the murder revengeful...the murder hierarchical, the murder canonical, the murder of equals, the murder of disadvantage, the murder devotional, the murder pathetical, the murder commodious, the murder involuntary, the murder scatological...' she handed a young man sitting on the front row a sheaf of printouts. 'Pass them round, please.' He dropped them and they fell with a wallop and slithered into disarray. 'Hah ha sorry,' the man muttered, scooping and dropping the weight onto his laptop to settle and order them. Then they were off round the room like a ballad sheet through the seventeenth century.

'I could email you this diagram but I prefer to hand it out during the seminar.' William lifted his into the powerpoint beams. It showed a body with something of a butcher's chart to it but a lot more disturbing. Lines led from the outline of a body, sexually neutral, and led to rash of elliptical windows in which photographs showed what was spilled from wounds to that area. Then there was a timeline of leakages, how they corroded or remained inert above the surface of whatever hosted them; how microbes varied their activities according to temperature, time of year, location, humidity and cleanliness or otherwise of the host surface. It showed regional variations. It showed the type and processes of the insects drawn to inhabit and tenant it. It indicated the level of microbial contamination and the level of bio hazard. It also indicated the type of cleaning materials that would efficiently deal with it. Then there were the stains from police procedures. The toxic and carcinogenic dustings — everything had its danger, its significance and its stubbornness. Every surface had its quirks. Chemical bonding was a problem with both natural and synthetic materials. Animals would sometimes get in and add their own wet intransigents to the stains. Some stains had to be allowed to stay and these were the ones around which superstition blossomed.

William looked round the full room. It was hot and the last

few images from the power point presentation shone on the speaker, a tall women with fine, brown hair, giving her the blunt, blurred look of a missing person's poster. Jacques hurried in, his eyes hidden by dark glasses and there was a strip of surgical microporous tape over his left ear.

'Why're you late? What's happened?' said Death Nell.

'A bloke sleep-drove a forked lift truck straight through my friend's front room window. The forks were raised. It knocked over the settee we were on and my ear hit a glass. Had to have the lobe reattached.'

'Someone sleep-drove a fork lift truck?' repeated William.

'Yeah. There's a factory nearby. The driver was on nightshift and he must've dropped off and kept driving.'

'Is he okay? And is your friend okay?'

'He drove off afterwards and we're not sure which fork lift driver it was. There's about a dozen of them. They ganged together. Like a line up. "Okay, pick out who you claim did it". All burly men. All got that grey-black whip-around haircut. All launched their paunches like a fleet of threats...'

Aftermath

William scrutinised his two employees. His trainees who knew just as much as he did. Death Nell sleek and wound-in as a liquorice cartwheel, Jacques with his lower abdomen bulked into Tweedledee-ness by ten metres of sumo loin cloth. William caught his own reflection in the giant aquarium. It rippled, bubbles spun through it like a school of silver buttons, sparkler-ing his soft, dark suit. And look at that collar length hair! It stuck to his skull like chased metal on a sceptre. They were all outsiders. Non conformists, reared by fortune to shuffle and leap in the campus of uncertainty, circumnavigating the main events like the supportive underlings in a pantomime. Tra la la, cleaning the mess caused by fellow outsiders, the isthmus, the cursed-sort, here he was with the acuity of a kaleidoscope, tangents sparking off his thoughts like sparks from a grind wheel, from an welding arc, from hooves clattering across stones.

'All right Mr Shakespeare, Mr Mercutio and Ms D'eath, we think this locus is the most appropriate to get you started. It's like the nursery slope. The crime is vintage — historical, actually, and the stains limited to flesh fragments consistent with multiple stab wounds by multiple assailants. There was some attempt to limit the damage, to create a dead body that retained its dignity and wasn't sawn out of true by unmeasured knife strokes, the sort tendered in anger and brutality. Political assassination with some finesse. Haha, I know, unusual! A coup d'etat. A game changer. Multiple assassins so they were all equally guilty — like an Agatha Christie novel where no one knows who delivers the killing blow. The blame shared. A politically correct assault. Now, each blow of the knife was delivered cleanly. No tugging or redirection once the blade was inserted. Yes, kind of commendable, clean, disciplined knife thrusts. The assassins struck two blows each. Conterminously. Synchronised. The later wounds had less depth and show less certainty. The final wounds are superficial. You have multidirectional blood spatter. I'll just switch on the computer and bring up the Virtual Reality and the Augmented Reality. That's it. And three pairs of haptic gloves. The Odouriser's switched on so the scene will smell like the authentic thing. There are sick bags behind the door if you should come over queasy. Well, I'll leav you to it. Your attempts at cleaning will be monitored. Good luck. Oh, and pop on the paper overalls and face masks. Get used to them.'

They dressed in the designated outfits and waited. After a few moments several screens lit up. A video game style man's face appeared. Golden ale coloured. Friendly.

'Hullo, I am Richard mark 3, your crime scene cleaning virtual wizard. I will guide you through the crime scene and explain the types of stains you will encounter. Your employer might be reluctant to tell you the exact nature or specific details of the incident whose aftermath you are repealing. You are the normalisers.'

'Yes, that's us,' said William, donning the virtual reality headgear and the haptic gloves. 'Let's wipe Evil from the face of the earth!'

'I'm in,' said Death Nell. 'Wish I'd had a vape, though. This smell's started to haggle with my cornflakes.'

'Cometh the hour, cometh the mop,' said Jacques. 'Ugh. Nausea's definitely trending.'

'Can you knock off the switch to the Odouriser, Billy?'

William snapped the switch back up. 'Probably lose points but there you are.'

'I can smell violets now,' said Death Nell.

'That's me,' said William taking an unopened packet from his pocket and offering them round.

'Well, I suppose it's apt. In a way. Violets symbolise Death and Resurrection.'

'Fancy that,' said William and cracked the sweet between his jaws.

☙ CHAPTER 7 ❧

THE CLEANSING OF WYUEN PINE*

WILLIAM SHAKESPEARE'S NEW START-UP BUSINESS, *CROW*

Two weeks later

'The pornography industry isn't affiliated to fertility treatment is it?'

'Nah.'

'Even so, maybe they should talk. Enter into communication.'

'That'd be weird. So, Billy, what's our first crime scene cleaning destination called?'

'The mansion's called Wyuen Pine.'

'Hawaiian Pine?'

'Wine and Dine?'

'Wyuen Pine.'

'Is it like a spruce?'

'No idea.'

'Can't believe I'll be mopping up the clarty that's come out of a body being killed,' said Death Nell. 'I mean, I knew that's what I'd signed up to do but it's different when it leaps from

---

* literally 'women's punishment' from Langland's Piers Plowman.

hypothetical to in-your-face-ical. Now we're nearly there and I'm feeling a bit wobbly.'

'I'm not,' said Jacques. 'Think I got it out of my system by having a nightmare this afternoon.'

'Afternoon mare,' said Death Nell.

'Well, they don't know it's night,' said Jacques. 'The nightmares don't abide by the day-night division. When they arrive they bring night with them.'

* * *

So, on the 21st of December, at an unearthly hour, William was driving his father's vintage hatchback through quiet London streets. CROW's logo had been printed across the door panels, and and mesh-printed across the back and side windows so as not to obscure the visibility. In silhouette, William's pet cockerel, Mr Ruby, rocked in mid crow. Yes, here was his new business start up, CROW (Crime-scene Rebuttal is Our World, with the silhouette of a crowing Mr Ruby, his pet cockerel, as the logo) en route for its inaugural crime scene clean-up. Jacques and Death Nell were semi foetal in the back seat, hips lower than knees, the angle of a tilted dustpan. A pair of pink fluffy dice dithered from the rear-view mirror, fat with William's mother's ashes.

'Those fluffy dice really packed full of your mum's cinders?'

'Ashes,' said Jacques. 'Cinders is one step closer to reconstitution.'

'You are so finicky.'

'No I'm not.'

'Are they really your mum's earthly remains?' said Death Nell.

'Yes,' said William. 'They are. It was in her will.'

'Bloody hell, had she slipped a bit when she made it?'

'That's not a nice thing to insinuate, is it, Nell?' said Jacques.

'Well it's unusual. If I was making out a will it's not something that would have sprung to my mind. Oh yeah, stuff me in some fluffy dice.'

'The fact they're fluffy dice, it's a metaphysical statement,' said Jacques.

'Get out of here,' said Death Nell. 'They're just fake fur novelties.'

'Jacques is right,' said William. 'Dice — God doesn't play dice.'

'Two of you at it now. Why can't something just be as it is. Let it alone. Was that what your old mum thought?'

'She wasn't old. She was younger than me when she died.'

'Did they have fluffy dice back then?'

'Obviously.'

'This is my dad's old car. She wanted to stay with him.'

'Bits are coming out. Dust. She'll gradually empty herself out all over the floor. Every valeting will carry a bit of her away.'

'I think that's the idea. Not being scattered or contained at one place.'

'Spooky, though.'

'A vintage ride. Ten more years on and you'll be able to hire it out to wedding parties. Transport for the bride.'

'Brides. Are you a bride from the moment you get your engagement going or only on the wedding day? Is it time sensitive?'

'You can't be a bride after you're married.'

'Unless you're remarrying.'

'William glanced up at the fluffy dice, a strange whim of his mother's will. They luminesced faintly, as though boxed in a halo. Occasionally the road threw up a lump or scutched a little hollow and the car juddered and dust clapped from the dice. In the boot, thirteen apothecary jars, brimful of alchemical cleaning fluid and encased in styrofoam cells, swirl and slosh. Is it the bumpy road the trio traverse or is it the darkness rocking them, rocking them? Vlooooosh go the apothecary jars. Slish slosh slish.

Is the darkness uneven where it meets the earth, does it ripple at its base like an upended sea, William wondered? *Why do we always imagine the night, the darkness, as something smooth and settled? Perhaps it's not.*

Splish sploosh dlop shheeesh shuff. The resurrected hatchback sounds like an urban water feature packed with flailing Morris Men. William could see them outlined on the road ahead, and he grimaced. Morris men, he knew where this was going…. They wouldn't be dancing, though. Not dancing. Oh no, not these Morris Men, this is a re-run of William Kempe's inflammatory final sponsored miles. They're pounding each other's jaws, these Morris Men, because they're under attack from a girl and woman gang whose territory they've trespassed on. Some Morris Men have thumped the girls and the girl/women-thumpers are being attacked by the small contingent of Morris Men who think hitting girls/women, even when being struck by girls/women, is indefensible. The name of the gang? William wracks his brain — Death Nell mentioned it. Their moon-imitating friend was in it. The Shrewds! The Shrewds. William had witnessed them in action. The debacle happened at a water feature, the kind with channels too narrow for anyone to drown in, the hydrant-fat jets sparking up, then subsiding, whether triggered by movement or placed on an automatic sequence, it was impossible to tell. The water always regrouped, was recouped and then recycled. When it shot up again, heads were shoved in it. A girl of about fifteen, overdressed, grew saturated and was felled by the weight of her sodden clothes, she lay face down in the flow, drowning, unable to roll away, turning her head but the water always contained it.

Shploosh floosh shlop. They're at it with fists, sticks, ankle-bells turned knuckle-dusters and their iron paling rapper swords. There's even the billowing crack of a hobby horse having its oaken ribs kicked in. William sees it all, all over again, promoted by the featureless, urban road, the starless, moonless sky, the sweep of his headlights showing nothing more than the indifferent weather and wheel torn tarmac and taxis. But look at those faces the colour of used flyswatters! Look at their cambered guts! These aren't William Kempe's companion jiggers, this is a substitute crew drawn from the hopping, bell-rigged ranks of the recent Dead. Testosteromeos, so much male hormone they're shoving their knotted handkies down each other's moonlit throats (that's where the moon is — elsewhere, apportioned among ghosts). William sees nakedness beneath the Morris costumes, he knows their morbid cargoes. These Morris Men are all his former patients, all the ones whose lives ended abruptly and unexpectedly in his care. Death set up his ironing board by their cardiograms and flat-ironed the ruby ribbons twitching from the weak gymnastics of their hearts. Crinkled, flapping red ribbons. William had watched Death flat-ironing every inch of fight, pressing and scalding their foreshortened lives into oblivion. Now they returned as ghostly Morris Men too vigorous for dance, too angry not to vent their rage, and kicking off in a pond composed entirely of the sound of cleaning fluids capable of expunging every trace of death. Capable of wiping away any trace of death at all, as though Death had never been. William felt the intersecting ripples spreading from the jars, the wash latticing him. The car. His passengers. His mother's ash sprackling the air in geometric lines.

1)Morris Men. 2)Death flat-ironing cardiograms. 3)Hearts wafting their ribbons. William had always thought that Doctors were natural metaphor-mixers. Prescribing umpteen drugs for one patient was literally mixing metaphors. Some were more cogent and workable than others.

Cshash flooooossss gruggle shlock plock.

Sploosh sloosh shlosh

'It sounds like we're riding the flume at Blackpool Pleasure Beach,' said Death Nell, rousing Jacques from his torpor. 'So much sloshing. Least we're not getting soaked.'

Jacques huddled his crotch, 'I feel a squall blowing up, Billy. I'll have to get out.'

'Jacques views his member as a cloud formation,' said Death Nell. 'Always has. Nothing to do with his sumo fixation.'

One day, when William knew Jacques better, he would ask him about the sumo thing. 'Okay, I'll pull over by the petrol station. Go and use the facilities.' He watched as Jacques hauled out, disappearing to precipitate at the back of a forlorn, neon blistered forecourt. The sloshing was subsiding.

Jacques returned holding his jeans draped between his forearms like a child rescued from danger.

'You came running out onto the street dressed like that?' said William.

'Yeah. What's with the snow white panties, Jacques?' said Death Nell.

'I am an amateur rikishi in my mawashi. I'm wearing the mawashi, my sumo loin cloth.'

'But why?' said Death Nell.

'I want to approach my first crime scene cleaning with the mind and attitude I bring to sumo.'

'Might not be appropriate,' said Death Nell.

'You'll see.' Jacques and wiped his window with the cuff of a trouser leg, as though that would make something more wonderful appear out of the darkness. Nothing did. 'Are we nearly there yet, Billy?'

'Yes. You'll see it any time now,' said William. Not that anything like a mansion was visible ahead but William had been told that Wuyaen Pine was an hour's drive across London and they'd been travelling for forty seven minutes.

SHLOP SHLOP SHLOP

The road turned to potholes again as they passed a great girth of roadworks. The car pitching in umpteen directions at once and William felt as though giant hands were gripping either end of the car and trying to wring it out like a sopped rag. In the rear-view mirror he watched Death Nell and Jacques pitch and bounce off each other, a perfect two-ball Newton's cradle.

SHLOP

'Do you believe in ghosts?' said Jacques.

'Oh, honestly! Not now,' said Death Nell.

'I do. Spirits, anyway. They're like great big, wafting amoebas that only speak in soliloquies.'

'Never heard of them described like that,' Death Nell laughed. 'Where'd you get that from?'

'Here we go,' said William.

'When you die it stands to reason you take all your thoughts with you. The stuff you've heard in your head all your life. The spirit grabs them when it leaves. Then all the thoughts you ever thought percolate through your spirit. Thoughts are soliloquies, aren't they? Nobody else hears what you say to yourself. You come across a ghost and that's what's going on. Soliloquies.'

'But what about the amoeba bit?' said Death Nell. William wondered about that, too. Amoebas?

'I've seen amoebas through a microscope and the stuff inside them looks like trapped speech bubbles. Like, er, verbal wind.'

'Okay,' said Death Nell. 'If you say so. Anyway, Billy,' she stared at William through the rear view mirror, 'why are we going to start cleaning the crime scene before daybreak?'

'Before cockcrow,' says Jacques. 'Billy's fetched his cock with him.'

'What a surprise.'

'Couldn't book him into the hen-minders. She was full up.'

'You've got a wife. You've got Anne. Why didn't she volunteer to look after the wee beastie?'

'You wanted him along to crow, to see-off any lurking malevolence isn't it?' said Jacques.

'Maybe.'

'Are we always going to start before cockcrow?' said Death Nell.

'I felt it was important — at least for the first one.'

'And Mr Ruby, he's your totem animal from when you were a junior doctor?' said Death Nell.

'Yes, given to me by my supervising consultant.'

'And what was he, what was your supervising consultant?' says Death Nell.

'A labradoodle.'

'Bonkers.'

'The NHS is weirder than you could imagine,' said Jacques. 'You don't know the half of it.' William had begun to wonder how aware Jacques and Death Nell were of their 'guardians'' predilections and oddness.

Then the moon popped out of the cloud and brightened the universe around it — revealing their destination directly ahead.

'That's Wyuen Pine, then? I can't see any trees,' said Death Nell.

'It's horrible,' said Jacques, returning his legs to his jeans and undoing several metres of mawashi which he draped across his chest...

'Like a sari,' says Death Nell.

'Like a toga,' said Jacques.

'Same difference,' said Death Nell.

'A-ah. Status,' said Jacques. 'Togas trump saris'.

'Women trump men,' said Death Nell.

William drew up and Death Nell reassembled the aluminium trolley and they unloaded everything onto it. Jacques then lit the way with his 5000 lumen torch. '

'A sparkler, ain't she?' said Death Nell. 'Bet they see you from deep space.'

The trolley clanked, the liquids gurgled, and they walked forward with small steps. Something onerous assembled in the torch beam and they gasped in unison.

'It's a marble scarecrow! A marble scarecrow!' said Death Nell. 'Touch it. Fucking hell!' And around it the ground is gouged in the likeness of animals.

'Like the White Horse on that hillside. Only these are animals of the discreeter sort, rodents mostly, and drawn to size,' said William. They thread like a ghostly eco-system between the flowers and shrubs.

'The family paid to have a two metre depth of chalk laid beneath the topsoil... so they could draw on it,' William told them.

'More money than sense,' muttered Death Nell.

'Actually, the family had a bank balance that matched their collective ego.'

'The place looks like it's built for slaughter,' said Jacques, sweeping the torch across its front, making the windows glitter and waking the darkness inside. 'Yes, Wyeun Pine looks like a bunker that's been dragged out of the earth, a rotting tooth drawn from the Jaws of Hell.'

'I'm looking forward to it, thanks very much,' said Death Nell.

It's a wriggling sort of darkness that makes you want to scratch your skin, thought William.

They went in. Darkness was darker indoors.

'Find the light switch, Jacques, you're nearest the wall,' said William. Death Nell pushed the trolley into something solid and the bottles crashed together and several mops clattered to the floor.

'Quick before I smash everything up,' said Death Nell.

'Here it is.' It's over bright. The hallway's thick with elegant marble pillars —

'Doric columns.'

'Eh?' said Death Nell.

'Doric columns are designed to suggest the vigorous male form,' said Jacques.

'Skirts up, ladees,' said Death Nell.

The pillars acted like body guards or bouncers, shepherding with a grotesque civility, a nuanced enforcement. William noticed that if they stepped beyond a prescribed area they nudged their elbows.

Every movement casts an echo.

'So, where's the crime scene, then?' said Death Nell.

'It's described as extensive,' William replied, turning over the stapled notes sent by the family's barrister. 'Kitchen. Banqueting Hall. Service corridors.'

They shuffled forward again, the trolley rattling like ten coats of agitated armour, Jacques snapping on every light switch until their progress was stopped by what looked like a snarled, goal-mouth net. Crime-scene tape stretched across a broad doorway. It was woven. Latticed. Artisanal. Neat until someone had come by and flung themselves into it.

'Okay, Death Nell, Jacques, this is where it gets, you know...'

'Messy?'

'Where you begin clicking and saving the slide show for your post traumatic flashbacks.'

'Thanks.'

'What's that smell?' said Jacques. 'Smells like the Odourisers followed us here.'

'Okay. This is where we'll set up the decontamination area. On with the protective gear. Yes, this is where you start collecting the the slide show for your post traumatic trauma.'

'Thanks for that,' said Jacques, zippering up his disposable overalls.

'Yeah, thanks Billy. This place os shockingly cold. Next time I'll wear thicker socks.'

'Well, it's a learning experience,' said William.

They slid on face-masks and flimsy plastic aprons, ankle-high, white wellingtons and light-blue latex gloves. William checked the trolley, the buckets and containers and mops, the plastic bio waste bags, the decontaminants and disinfectants, the scrapers and the stacked absorbent wads. And the fludds from the Nine Bulimic Cannibals — William was still unsure whether he would use them. Death Nell gathered the police tape into a loose ball and kicked it back towards the hallway where it bounced and disappeared behind the pillars.

'Ready Jacques? Ready Death Nell? Ready…?'

Into hell we go. Into hell. Into such a hell, thought William. Sartre was right. Hell is (what has been violently gouged and hammered out of) other people.

Jacques threw the light switch. It ground like a stone rolled from a tomb.

'Bloody hell, they've enjoyed mucking about with the psychoacoustics haven't they?' he muttered. The lights fizzled on, eco-bulbs with their drowsy wattage shod in carpet slippers shuffling up opaque glass spirals to assemble like a moon viewed through shut eyelids. They lent the floor the look of a flung trifle. There was ruby jelly. Fruit clumps. Custard dollops. Cream hardened into little leather caps. Except, the smell didn't match. It stink like gangrened sugar.

'Ugh!'

'Ew! Somebody's had their just desserts.'

'Ah…' said William.

And in the air above them something floundered, casting oddly hollow shadows.

'Has a bird got in?" said Death Nell.

'Are we imagining it?' said Jacques, pointing.

'It's real' said Death Nell. 'The slipstream's rocking the black meringue of my hair.'

Something was nipping, airborne, between the architrave and the umpteen arrases between the crowding columns, slapping about in the draperies. The thing was clumsy the way birds are when their sky is reduced to human ceilings — but it looked more like a pink PVC mitten or a rubber lolly than anything avian. Yes, there it went, agile in a twangy sort of way.

'Bloody weird-looking object,' said Death Nell, trying not to slip on the reeking mess.

Then William caught enough of a glance to know what the thing was. He'd cut one out of a human body, eased its root from his beloved designated cadaver. Shock seared Williams chest.

'What's up, Billy?' said Jacques.

'That's a tongue,' said William. 'A human tongue.'

'Don't be daft.'

'Is.'

'No way.

'Gross!'

'Can't argue with that,' replied William. 'I have no idea how it's flying about or why.'

They leant on their long handled scrapers and mops, and watched. It wasn't just a tongue.

'It's got bird legs,' said Death Nell. 'Why's it got bird legs?'

'Because it's a Tonguebird,' said Jacques. And he was right. There was no other word for it. It was a Tonguebird with bird legs sprouting from its underside. And it was flapping in great spit-spattering, muscular waves. Tonguebird.

'Is this...normal?'

'No,' said William. 'It is not. How can you think this might be normal?'

'Sumo,' said Jacques. 'We take it in our stride and so we make it comfortably unexceptionable.'

'Bonkers,' said Death Nell.

'Okay. So what do we do about it?' said Jacques.

'Nothing. Not our problem. It belongs to the house,' said William. 'As long as it doesn't attempt to injure or impede us, we leave it alone.'

'Have you got a sweet or something to lure it away? I think I'd find it a bit distracting,' said Death Nell.' It'll take a bit of getting used to.'

The Tonguebird was now beating itself against the wall, flipping and somersaulting and gliding against surfaces then waggling, pushing off from the brink like a swimmer from the edge of the baths. Sounds came from it. Death Nell cupped her ear.

'It's saying something.'

They all listened, stepping over the terrible slops to hear it better…

'Bastards!'

'Did it just say 'bastards'?'

'Yes,' said William. Now it was frip-frapping round the light fittings.

'It's shitting shadows,' said Death Nell.

'Hello?' said William calling up to it.

Hello,' replied the Tonguebird.

'Where do you come from?'

'Mouth,' said the Tonguebird. 'Mouth mouth mouth — where do you frigging think I came from, stupid?' It's lippy without lips, mouthy without mouth, gobby without… 'Avenge me,' it said.

'Yeah, okay. Give us the details,' replied Jacques.

'You're going to avenge me, then?' said the Tonguebird, slapping the back of Jacques' head to form the words.

'Yeah, if I'm not too concussed,' said Jacques. And Jacques put out his arm and the Tonguebird perched on it, sliding up to his shoulder where it slapped against his ears.

'Whoa, that tickles like a lover,' said Jacques.

That's when they all screamed and the Tonguebird took flight — a woman had shuffled into their midst. She was wearing a grey-green tulle veil which ended mid-way down her ribcage in a wide, hula hoop roughly sewn into the tulle to weight it. She wore red gloves very conspicuously, holding her hands so that they were always noticeable. If you took a photograph, they would be the only things in focus. She held them up, sometimes like a surgeon, and then out in front of her like a sleep walker using them like a cat used whiskers, to test for the sides and ends of things — if there was breadth enough to enter, or obstacles that needed circumventing.

Her feet were hidden beneath the frayed hem of a long, dismal skirt which dragged along the floor like one of Life's intransigent burdens. She coughed continuously, a small, low cough attached to the beginnings and ends of each breath, the middle billowing audibly between them. And she was very cluttered with belongings. Her pockets bulged, she wore an army surplus knapsack so full and heavy she lurched, arched and recovered as she walked. Her hat atop the veil was sewn with numerous little pockets from which a clutter of vaguely familiar items dangled.

'It isn't safe in here,' said William to her. 'Germs are everywhere,' and he waved his hands so that the vast bacterial armies amassed on every surface and in the air were included in his gesture.

The woman said nothing, but bent her knees and executed a series of little jumps that took her over the unpleasant parts of the floor. She jumped without looking, as though she knew very well where the nasty blotches were. She was light on her feet but her hands swung heavily by her sides like the pendulums in a clock. Like Irish dancing infusing the everyday. The net stirred around her, twisting her hair into tags and knots. She looked as though she were being mixed like a stiff drink with an unrelenting core of bitters.

Obviously, the fairies have been mucking about here, enchanting anything that took their fancy.

She stared up at the frantic Tonguebird, moaned dismally, and slid back towards the door.

'Who she?' asks Death Nell.

'Who indeed,' said William.

William ushered the woman back through the door. As he turned she kicked him in the pants with an unseen foot so that he staggered, his arms plummeting up to the shoulders in the soiled water of the mop bucket.

'Uh, bad luck, Billy,' said Death Nell as she and Jacques lifted him out. 'Least it's not gone further than your rubber gloves. Nice woman, though.'

They scrubbed and scraped and wiped. They sluiced, slopped, mopped, dried, polished, damped a fresh cloth and worked away, scouring in circles. William took the ultra violet wand out of the bag and its journey across the floor and wall was followed by a trace of magical spatters.

'Blood gets everywhere,' said William, scrubbing the blood's track.

'So they've caught the people who did this?' said Death Nell.

'That's the thing, it's a self-contained crime. The perpetrators ended up dying, too. It's like a loop. Now, that's unusual for crimes. That's why I thought it was worth being aware. Who knows, there might be some sort of highly elusive criminal at the back of this. Let's see what other crime scenes we end up working on. But this, yes, something feels skewed. Everything's too wound up and tidy. I believe there's a murderer hiding behind all this neatness and responsible for every death her.'

'That's a bold statement, Bill,' said Jacques. 'Got any clues?'

'No, no clues, but from what I've been told by the family's barrister, well, it just seems far too neat. When you work as a hospital doctor you begin to understand how ragged everyday things are. Nothing in real life is this neat, is this simply concluded. That's all I'm saying.'

'We're listening, Billy.'

* * *

When they had finished and changed back into their normal clothes, they sat side by side on the top step of the entrance, still an hour before dawn, the welcome mat tugged under them to keep off the cold.

'Cold rises through marble,' said William. 'You can get post mortem haemorrhoids. Caused by the chill of the tomb. The bodies in family mausoleums suffer from them when they're exhumed.'

'Oh, get on with you. That's not possible,' said Death Nell, searching her pocket for her E-Cigarette.

'I've seen it myself. It's true,' said William.

'That's on the verge of being funny,' said Jacques.

'It also means that whilst the rest of the body decomposes, the back, which is in contact with the cool marble through the coffin, well, that's preserved. Skeletons at the front, a skin covering at the back, from the back they look normal, if a little foxed and dangly.'

'Don't,' said Death Nell spluttering her first lung full of nicotine vapour.

William looked up at the moon. Such a clear and lovely light. The moon, a full moon, drawing tides and lunatics and werewolves out into its beams. Like tweezers locking onto hairs and raising them free of their roots. That was the moonlight working on the mad and the werewolves and the top layer of sea that closed over the sand. Would werewolves go for a swim in the high tide under the moonlight? Dogs swam.

They shared a flask of coffee and sat hunched and silent, their thoughts as varied as the global breeds of dogs. Death Nell vaped, sucking through the black and silver pipe held such a different angle than cigarettes. More introverted. More like you'd play a private tune on a private whistle. Could you play tunes for your dog on a dog whistle? No it's just a summoning whistle. It must sound authoritative otherwise the dogs would just hear it and think, ah, okay. Jacques wafted the the vapour away with his palm.

'Well, gang,' said William,' we've completed our first crime scene clean. We did a good job.'

'That Tonguebird bothers me,' said Death Nell. 'That was a phenomenon. Was it something psychic?'

'I don't think so,' said Jacques. 'It's as psychic as something out of Alice in Wonderland. Most of what your modern mediums do would not look out of place as regular occurrence in children's books. It's all about where stuff happens that makes them spooky.'

William noticed something odd. He blinked. Stood, walked

around and viewed it from this angle and from that, did a small circular tour of it, but the strange thing remained strange wherever William fetched up, no viewpoint made it normal and it was still there wherever he viewed it from. William coughed to clear his thoughts and assemble his words. This was going to be a difficult sentence to say out loud. *But here goes*, he thought. *Here goes.*

'You're exhaling ectoplasm, Nell.'

'I'm what?' said Nell, puffing out a particularly clear spectral leg that rolled as though it had once been part of the Isle of Man gig but had left to pursue a solo career in kicking and hopping.

'You've breathed out ectoplasm. It's taking shape. It's ghosts.'

'Thought I felt odd. Is it —are they— still coming out?'

'Yes. If you're okay to keep vaping whilst we see who turns up.'

'Apropos this crime scene?'

'I'm hoping,' said William. 'I'd be surprised if they were random entities.'

'If I pass out, if they ask, I'm allergic to penicillin,' said Death Nell. 'The emergency services always ask.'

'Righto,' said Jacques. 'What about egg albumin?'

'Yeah, that too. Phew. I'm getting a bit stalked on the nicotine but, hell, if I'm actually vaping the Dead, great, rah rah me! It's a mall initial outlay for great returns-from-the-dead.'

After half an hour the sky began to lighten. Death Nell looked like death warmed up.

'Come on, let's get home,' said William. 'Jacques and I have filmed what emerged and I'll write it all up whilst I remember it. But, Death Nell, I think it might be an experiment worth repeating on our next crime scene clean. We may gain access to information only the actual murderer knows.'

'It'd be thrilling if I wasn't so atrophied on nicotine,' said Death Nell.

William packed everything back into the boot of the car and they left.

* * *

A week later, William went to visit the ash and bones in his attic. He tapped the tin affectionately, and took out WAR EQUALS POLTERGEISTS, a pamphlet authored by his father, John.

'So tell me about poltergeists,' said William, and sat down cross-legged on the floor beneath the skylight, and read...

He could hear his father's voice.

War is a species of poltergeist. John Shakespeare knew that. The problem was that people who didn't believe in poltergeists believed themselves responsible for all the carnage and destruction. These deluded souls, let's call them Commanders, Admirals, Colonels, War Cabinets, Fuhrers and Kaisers, presumed that cities, objects and people were thrown about and blown away because they, or their enemy counterparts, were doing it.

'Thanks for that, Dad. I'm sure it'll come in handy.'

* * *

Work had begun to come in. William was excited but always made sure his excitement was dampened and abraded by remembering why he was actually getting the work. A person, or people, had died horrifically through acts of violence.

Anne got on with her aquatic ballet practice, worked in the Simulacrum River, brought numerous babies safely into the world, and bought more expensive underwear. The three girls grew a little and none wore hand-me-downs. Some things were improving.

✍ CHAPTER 8 ✍

THE SECOND CRIME SCENE CLEAN

They had arrived at midnight. The cleaning was going well. They were in a large and expensively kitted kitchen. William switched on the ultra violet wand and checked the floor and wall for any remaining traces of blood spatter. Clear. But there was something. He coasted the cold blood-seeking blue light over the floor and along the skirting board, then gave a wide sweep up again. Death Nell and Jacques leant forward.

'Go from right to left, Billy. Whatever it was seemed to start over on the right.'

'Yeah, there's something,' said Jacques. 'Is it me or did it look like it was moving?'

'Moving,' said William. He'd jumped, both feet leaving the floor, as the shape coasted towards his hands. He was almost certain he had heard it slide. There was a faint 'swooshing' noise that had raised the hairs on his nape.

'Light it up again, Billy.' He did. A ghostly shape was outlined against the wall. In fact, it was just an outline. Like a chalk mark round a body — or if someone had scattered flour, rather than crushing a stick of chalk into the surface. There was something loose and scattered about its edges.

'Like an aura print,' said Jacques.

'Bit like a Hiroshima shadow,' said Death Nell. 'That terrible sooted gloom left by the Vaporised.'

'Says the woman who 'vapes',' said Jacques.

'I never connected the two things. Go on, you've put me off my ecigs, Jacques. It's back to fag-land with me. It'll be your fault I bugger my lungs.'

The thing on the wall was moving. It was following William's hand.

'All we need now is that Tongue thing and the gang's all here!' said Death Nell.

'Shush. I think it's speaking.'

It was opening and closing like a jelly fish but nothing came of it.

'I hate to ask, Nell, not after the recent conversation, but I'm wondering whether your vaping might help. We've got something here...' Nell got out her E-Cigaratte and started up. A voice began to find a path out of the vapour. The shape spoke.

'The passing — you feel it like a kind of white-out expansion, not exactly an explosion, but some terrific force that billows against you. A car airbag inflating that doesn't come to an end. And here I am. a ghostly outline. A ghost gliding across walls.

'Could somebody paint over you? Or would you rise through the paint?' said Jacques.

'Your guess is as good as mine. However, there seems to be a vent, whether mouth, anus or bellybutton I wouldn't know, and it's where you can insert your breath — or even a bicycle or balloon pump. I have been led to believe that if I am filled with air or breath, I can part from the wall and wander. Yes, I'll peel off. I shall have volition although I'm not sure I'll be able to control where I go. You may need to guide me.'

'Who are you?'

'I'm not sure. The word 'Recipe' keeps coming to mind. Could I be a ghost of a recipe?'

'Not heard of that before,' said Death Nell.

'Perhaps you were part of a recipe. Like an ingredient,'

William said, thinking about the Bulimic Cannibals.

'I recall pouring a libation,' said the Shape.

'A libation? What's that?' said Jacques, but the Shape didn't answer, it simply disintegrated and tumbled to the floor in a million little dots.

'I do that on our grandmother's grave. Pour libations. Jacques and I share a grandmother.'

'What do you pour on it?' said Jacques.

'It varies.'

'You never said.'

'You never come with me'

'Can't see the point.'

'Memory's the point. Connection's the point.'

'I can remember and connect without going where their mortal remains lie under the earth.'

'Yes, well, I like to think they have a geographical location.'

'I see.'

'I've invented a city round her. Not a necropolis. No, a city with her as the only inhabitant. There's a take-away. A planetarium. A library. A natural history museum and a live music venue. And a town hall. Town council. The things she loved.'

'Why?'

'Because I like doing it.'

'Does that milkman still do his rounds in the cemetery?'

'Yes, he follows a mandala. One of Jung's mandalas actually.'

'Does the dairy mind?'

'He works for himself. He pours milk into the graves. Exhumations show the bodies encased in their own distinctive cheeses.'

'No they don't'

'Ha ha.'

'There's a marble snowman out there.'

'That trumps the marble scarecrow.'

William lifted the apothecary jars. The red, black and white.

'Not seen anything like that for cleaning before,' said Jacques.

'No, you wouldn't. These are specially made. Not commercially available, made by the Nine people you both know.'

'Are they hazardous? I know they have a laboratory. They're always there, they've even installed their beds among the equipment.'

'I presume it's all safe — they seem to know what they're doing. I've used this stuff at home and nobody's died, ha ha.' William gave them the kind of reassuring smile he'd given to patients but since he was wearing a face mask he had to hope that the expression in his eyes was sufficiently convincing.'

'Your eyes are a bit glassy, Billy.'

'Well, we're all a bit tired. Sleep deprivation,' said William wondering if the smile only worked when he held the authority of being a doctor. 'Anyway, I'm going for the black.'

'Does it need diluting?'

'No, it's funny stuff. It spreads out. Covers the stains exactly, no excess.'

'Sounds very hi-tech. Did they charge you for it?'

'No. Well, maybe there are hidden costs.'

'He speaketh in crypticisms,' said Death Nell.

'Well, a lot of what we're doing is still a new science. I mean. okay, abattoirs clean stuff up but it's fresh blood.'

'Uh, don't talk about that.'

'Well, murder scenes are a bit abattoirish.'

'Noirish.'

'Come on, show us what happens, then,' said Jacques. "the quicker we clean the sooner we get home and kip.'

'Look out, Bill, it's that woman from our first clean. She's following us!'

The woman, still tulle-draped and hula hooped, traipsed in as though her legs were working in opposition to each other. William wondered if the woman was being ghoulish. As a doctor, sometimes, he'd come across a species of love and grief and fear that seemed tinged with ghoulishness.

'This is a bio-hazard. Can you leave whilst we clean, please?' said William.

The woman turned but her legs carried her in a small circle and she was back facing them again. Death Nell started to giggle.

'Sorry everyone.'

'Please leave so we can work,' said William. 'I'll let you know when we're done.' The woman took a step backwards and raised her arms.

'Is she about to take off?' said Death Nell. The woman began to wave her arms about. 'I get it. She's spelling out words using the Village People font.' And that's what she seemed to be doing.

'You're closest to the door, Jacques. Is there a lock?' William said.

Jacques nodded. 'Several, actually. Clear plastic. You wouldn't know they were there.'

'Unless you knew they were there,' said Death Nell. Jacques pointed to three newly installed bolts fashioned out of clear plastic polymer. They looked very recent additions.

'Older plastic acquires a patina, a soft opacity because it scuffs,' said Jacques.

'Well, I'll guide the woman out and then you can shoot those bolts so we have some privacy.' William took the woman's arm and gently guided her out of the door. Her arms were as heavy as lead weights.

'Mind she doesn't kick you in the trousers again,' said Death Nell.

William shot back into the kitchen and Jacques threw the bolts. The woman could be heard bouncing off the other side of the door.

'You would think, if you turn up in the wee small hours to clean, that a pitch invasion would be unlikely.'

'Mmm, no, the odd 'uns go on patrol at night, don't they? Sleep deprivation. Insomniacs. People who are dragged about by the moon.'

'What?'

'The mind waving wicked images at you from behind its bone balustrade.'

'Behind it's what…?'

'Just …'

William imagined the murderer arriving home with a bag from some hardware store, then fastening the transparent bolts with clear plastic screws, quietly, secretively. Maybe even the screw driver was see-through so it looked as though the perpetrator was waggling his fingers mysteriously in front of the door. On the wall above the cooker there were brackets showing where a CCTV had been mounted, the sort that could turn and scrutinise the room, one with an active watcher connected to its controls. Who would watch? Was there a monitor room here or was the feed sent to some centralised security firm. Imagine the murderer gesticulating. The way fingers sometimes twitch when they hover over objects. The brain is working. The fingers flap as though the brain has shaken a string to which they're tied. All the better to butcher a human body. Prepare a human head for the pot. William had an intrusive image of the person placing the head upright on its dish, combing its hair. A good and careful cook inadvertently copying the head's expression. Would you want the head to have a mellow, resigned twist to the lips? A look of contentment? A scowl of disapproval or an inscrutable stare? Or plain old indifference? Would the expression affect how you baked it? How many onions you scattered around it, the sort of stock and oils you'd coat it with? Would you match expression with seasoning? Or had that milestone been breached at the moment of decapitation. Had you thought a plain pan roasting, chicken-style, an unfussy slick with the basting brush? Filleted the cheeks, the double chin, the tongue. Liquidise the brains for stock. The folds and billows, wet marshmallow strips you could lattice? Would the reptilian part of the brain, the brainstem, would its consistency be different? Like, say, the parson's nose of the brain. Really. Were there ancient recipes. The Sawney Bean Cook Book? William was surprised how many readily available tangents had been planted in his own brain. Imagine his own brain cooking. Very celtic. Very... very much the absorption of power, ability. Life force. It was a marriage a la mode.

'You've stopped mopping, Billy,' said Death Nell, nudging him gently in the middle of his back. 'Bad place to brood or be struck by a random thought, eh? Moping not mopping.'

Jacques was humming.

'Not the Death March, Jacques!' said Death Nell and puffed out her face mask in exasperation. 'Honestly. I mean, you've got to be a bit upbeat. Respectful, yes. But we've got to be able to walk away from here without too much psychic damage.'

'Nobody takes the Death March seriously,' said Jacques. It's just one way of responding. You know. But not a tears and travail way. Just a trope.'

'Trope?'

'Yeah, one of the signifiers of a genre. A little flag waved to catch your bearings. It's awful that people have died here. Been eaten here. Raped...'

'Shut the fuck up,' said Death Nell.

'That was elsewhere,' William said. 'Absolutely terrible business. Of course, it's all sub judice so I shouldn't be telling you.'

'Oh... there are some vicious sorts around...'

'... yeah, but she came back here. Then she was murdered. By her own dad.'

'That's the thing with some dads. You men in general. Too few responses to choose from. They don't have the range. Send her away, mate, if you feel that devastated. Think how she must feel. Give her a chance. Let her recover. New life and that. Support. Ever hear of 'support' mate?'

'Not everyone can handle stuff. It's the honour thing'

'Fuck honour. Whose honour? What's honour? They've got honour, they can't help being attacked can they? Honour's a really wobbly thing, isn't it? It's one of those stupid things where someone who's not been the victim can sort of make out that they're damaged. Not with grief, but harmed more than the victim. Makes me sick.'

'Yeah, I know. But…well, they should at least think before doing something so sadly drastic.'

'Well, if it's any consolation, he was murdered too.'

'In here? IN the kitchen?'

'In the dining room. Next after this.'

'What a family, eh?'

William thought about his family. He allowed his ruminations to loiter among his second cousins. To consider them. Had a little tour taking in what he knew about their activities. How they behaved on the few weddings he'd met them at. Really, any of them could commit savageries. Impossible to swear none of them would do something so terrible. Could I, he wondered? What would make me think someone's life should be cut short? Because something had happened to them? Something more psychological than physical? Something they grieved over? No. He didn't try and slide his family into the roles established by the murder. That's too game-y. That's wrong, Cosplay of real-life murders. This was a locked room crime — not that it had been committed under impossible circumstances, but that the killers had killed themselves. Everything wound up. Neat. Unequivocal guilt although the reasons behind the slaughter, cannibalism and the rest had yet to be determined. Coroners' court stuff.

Two hours of cleaning, silently, the light without shadow, bin bags filling with the aftermath. Mop and bucket, mop and bucket. Steamer. Sprakle, fogger.

'Not wishing you were still a hospital porter then, Jacques?'

'Nah I'd had enough. I was about to be cautioned for using a sumo lift on a paraplegic patient. The sling they usually used to transfer him from his wheelchair to his bed, it'd broken. There was only me. To be honest, I was miles away. I was visualising the forthcoming contest. My opponent. I was there. So I lifted the poor bloke by his pyjama belt. I was starting to drift. The superstition stuff was getting on my nerves. I was kind of glad you'd spoken out about it. Weird stuff going on. They shouldn't have tipped piss in your locker, though. Bang out of order if you ask me.'

'Thanks, Jacques. Right, this looks about done — great job both of you. Let's move to the next room.'

'Nope that woman isn't loitering again. Who do you think she is?'

'To be honest, I'm not interested. I just don't want this second job compromised. I mean, she could complain that we let her in to watch. That's not following the basic rules of hygiene. Or of morality, eh?'

* * *

The next room, a palatial space messed about by columns —'They don't even hold up the ceiling, they're just fancy. What do they have these for?' said Death Nell.

'Well, they're too big to be a tripping hazard but I bet they take a lot of energy to warm up,' said Jacques. 'After the first gig I left my mawashi at home and got out the thermals.'

William noticed, despite the persistent lack of shadow, tiny lettering, ancient script with the 's's like 'f's and the names that no one had been called by for the last several hundred years. Very old columns. If inscriptions had the equivalent of whispers, this script, never chiselled deeply, whispered. The whispers, away from the rains and frosts and sunlight remained as audible to the soul as they'd been on the first day they'd been cut.

'How old is this mansion?'

'Dates back to the nineteen twenties, I think. But the family seat was elsewhere and was very old. Greece, possibly? I'm not sure, why?'

'These columns. They bear inscriptions. People are buried

inside them. They're crypts of sorts. For ashes, and upright inhumations probably. The ancestors are buried here among the living. How've they wangled that over Environmental Health? Back handers? Maybe the tombs are empty? Niches. Perhaps for ashes or a tradition of hearts inside skulls. That was a tradition.'

'Maybe,' said Jacques. 'Bit freaky, though.'

'Jacques, can you just check that the veiled woman's not loitering in the hall?'

Jacques peered round the door. 'No. Not a living soul.'

'Funny how that sounds so spooky saying it here. I mean. That's like admitting there's a spot of haunting going on, something unaccountable,' said Death Nell.

'Okay, people, I must away to the bathroom.'

'Well, I hope that woman doesn't follow you there. Better lock yourself in,' said Jacques.

William set off along the preternaturally silent corridors. He had to remove all his contamination kit, his suit and boots. Inside what he called the 'trap zone' — the decontamination buffer zone. Then he padded in his socks along the carpets and coves, guessing second-guessing the route of the plumbing. After fetching up in several terrifyingly ornate rooms the size of olympic swimming pools, the size of a city night club, and one entirely filled with a bonsai forest, William found the lavatory. He noticed a strange mark in the marble cornice. Like a door. Black marble, a dark door with a glimmer outlining it — an expansive light source behind the door. William flushed the lavatory. Is this a solid gold pan, he wondered? He knuckle tapped its base. The metal chimed, muted by its s-tube's wriggle of lodged water. He touched the black marble shape and it swung open, growing as it did until William was standing in a tall gateway and staring into a moonlit courtyard. 'Oh,' he said. 'Fancy that.' The ground was bare, compacted, the kind of dry that a relentless summer sun imposes, creating a pattern of dry micro-chasmed lozenges. In the moonlight stood three men, their heads lolling, two of them with their cheeks and temple resting on the shoulder of the other. Each held an implement. A rake, a spade and a fork. The men were dressed in ornate costumes that caught the light and responded with twinkles and glimmers. Wide boots, damask breeches, satin frock coats with wide trimmed cuffs. On their heads they each had a broad-brimmed hat topped by fern fronds. Moonlight silvered them and made the surroundings into grim streaks, suggestions of things, the tops dusted with light as though the earth had been torn asunder and the depths lifted up but light still couldn't pervade them. A strange feeling of having sunk into the earth. William was about to turn round and go back into the bathroom (which he sincerely hoped was still there) when the three men snapped awake and stared at him, their stares drifting around the moonlight night until they'd all found him. Then they began to dig. Or, rather, the man with the spade started digging, the man with the fork loosening the soil ahead of the spade and the man with the rake dragging what had been dug up away from the hole that was forming. A darker darkness. William turned to go but there was nothing at his back. Quite literally nothing. He leant back a little way and felt something solid. He couldn't see a wall but it felt as though he was leaning against a painted background although his hands just felt air, air solid as stone or brick or a tree trunk. When he turned back the hole was as deep as the man with the spade's thighs. He stepped out. The rake worked the soil a little bit and the spade man climbed out and struck the edges of the hole with the back of his spade. The hole rocked. William blinked. The hole was still rocking slightly. Then the man with the rake walked over to where a stack of something lay on the ground, rolled and lifted and sorted amongst them, coming back with a STOP CHILDREN road sign on its metal pole. He stuck that in the centre of the hole and again the hole swayed and rocked. The man with the rake, now slung over his left shoulder, walked up to William, bowed and held out his hand towards the hole.

William wondered if they'd dug his grave. If they were now going to kill him. He also wondered why this was happening when he'd simply wanted to go to the toilet. '

'I don't know who you are. I don't know where I am,' said William. 'I'm cleaning a crime scene.'

The men gestured at the hole. One drew him towards it, his grip stronger than anyone William had ever known. Yes, that was a grip two notches off being painful. It was a grip that intended to be irresistible. William felt three pairs of hands each placed one pair above another from his waist upwards and he was propelled into the hole. The hole swung and dipped as he entered it. It felt like it was floating in water. Like a sunken island. Floating in water. He put his hand to the soil around him and it was solid. The three men walked in unison, their footfalls matching each other, and stood behind the sign and blew. Their leaning forward, one foot ahead of the other, leaning with the right hand on the left leg, they breathed in again and blew and the road sign chimed like buoy out at sea and the hole began to move forward, jolting William so he fell down into it.

'What's this about?' William called. 'Where am I going!' The men had drawn closer together and by the loll of their heads resting on each other's shoulders as their feet shuffled them into a circle so they faced each other, the men were asleep. William tried to jump out but when he managed to get out onto the ground outside the whole, the hole slid under him and he was back in it again. Off he floated. He found a small piece of paper stuck round the stem of the road sign. This is an Ark, it said. It is taking you where you need to go. It will fetch you back to where you want to be.

'Well, that's all right then,' said William. And he found himself feeling a little bit thrilled that he was on some kind of adventure, something that he hadn't expected. Then he thought to himself that perhaps most of his life was currently so fluid and unpredictable it could dissolve calendars. He didn't have a working mobile phone so couldn't see if wherever he was had a signal. He doubted it. On he bobbed. He sat down, his head just at the right height to peer out at everything. The night was turning darker. He passed a great forest then realised that they were tall grey statues like a forest of caryatids and telemons, some bent to watch him pass, others patted his head with their great hands. As the forest thinned out he passed several who had formed a small copse and were talking.

'So we steal the M25 London Oribital Motorway and we fold it up and stow it for safe keeping on top of Centrepoint. No one'll notice. Even from the air. Careful bit of folding, maybe loop it across to other buildings. Add a touch of glamour to hide it.'

William watched as several telemons and caryatids trotted by with a library, giggling about how they were going to hide it, then leave it in West Bromwich Goal to be found. The Ark continued and stopped outside a tower. William thinking, well, in for a penny, in for a pound, climbed out of the Ark, hoping it would stay put so he might be able to get back to the crime scene and home, pushed open the large wooden and iron nail studded door. It smelled of forest. He climbed a stone, spiral staircase and realised that either side of him were trees, not just tall trees but trees growing on top of trees, the tree above's roots in the canopy of the tree beneath all surrounding the stone stairwell. At the top there was a trapdoor that William heaved open with his shoulders. The hatch flew back and William emerged into a room with a fire and many carved figures. As he stood up and his eyes grew accustomed to the firelight, he realised that although the bodies of the figures were carved from wood, and their costumes differed historically, some seemed to be dressed in very ancient fashions, others were Edwardian, there were even two clearly wearing clothes from very recently. The most surprising thing was that each beautifully, life-sized carving — each in a different wood — had a concave neck on which was balanced a skull. Each skull faced into the room. On a table by the trapdoor lay a platter filled with pinnate, evergreen leaves. Oval and glossy and smooth. The skulls turned towards William. He felt his skin crawl as he heard their jaw bones scrape against the wood on which they were balanced. The fire became brighter as a large log rolled itself in from a trug by the hearth. The mantelpiece was ornate, carved, letters interwoven in such a confusion it was impossible to say whether there were words to be read in it or it was entirely decorative. William walked over and touched them letters rose from the stone and butted his fingers. The skulls now resolutely stared at the platter and leaves. William walked over and lifted a leaf, sniffed it and jaws set a chattering.

'Should I give you one of these? Is that what they're for?' William counted the skulls and counted the leaves and their number matched. Thirteen. He walked to the closest and slipped a leaf into it. The jaws began chomping and the breath hissed through the teeth and slowly a voice rose with it.

'Please give each a leaf. They allow us to speak. Briefly speak. We may speak as long as the leaf remains whole then we are silent again until the next.'

'The next what?' said William.

The skull turned and angled its eye sockets at him.

'Yes, I'll give everyone a leaf.' He walked clockwise round the circle sliding a leaf into each jaw, sometimes the jaw was slightly open, other times he had to force the leaf in through the teeth, trying not to damage the leaf in case this meant the skull would be denied an opportunity to speak. William was half-panicked that what they would say to him would be something he really didn't wish to hear. Once the platter was empty, William placed himself over the trapdoor and waited. The hissing increased. Every jaw was working. In some skulls the leaves blew around in the eye sockets and seemed to be in danger of being exhaled onto the floor. If that happened, would it mean they didn't wish to speak? So he waited. He waited. He was on the point of going back when he realised that the skulls were singing. He didn't understand the language of their song. But their song was beautiful. He waited. The song continued. 'That was my purpose. 'I've run an errand,' he said to himself.

'I've run some kind of errand. An errand boy. But if it means that a silenced choir of skulls can resume singing then it was no bad errand to embark on.' William was at the bottom of the stairs and the song was as clear and audible as it had been in the room. No fainter, no stronger. He opened the door, jumped into the hole, the ark, which rocked with his momentum and then slid back through the forest of caryatids and telemons. The moon shone down. The song stayed with him, the words still a mystery. Then he was back in the lavatory bathroom of the Wyuen Pine. Zipping his fly, washing his hands, the song inside his head like an annoying memory. He hurried through the halls and service corridors, climbed back into his cleaning kit and rushed into the kitchen.

'Gosh, you've been quick,' said Death Nell. 'You've only just gone out of that door.'

'I thought I'd dawdled,' said William, completely confounded, the song still slithering through his brain. Carrying a kind of white tracer light with it. He could see where it led to in the room. How it travelled. It was exploring the crime scene. A song that drifted through time and space and gathered information like a living thing. Absorbing and memorising what it came across. Death Nell and Jacques couldn't see it. He had pocketed one leaf. He wondered what plant it came from and thought a trip to the library's botanical section might edify and educate him.

Of course, when he trawled through every reference book, no leaf resembled the one he'd fetched back with him. William began to wonder if it was, in fact, a leaf at all.

☙ CHAPTER 9 ❧

RELIGION

One evening William had a phone call from a barrister with a voice like a broken exhaust. The barrister's plosives popped emerged in violent pops and bangs. William thought that there would have been enough spit to form the barely serrated drip from a tap with a spent washer. Yes, thought William, that voice probably worked very well in court. It was tuned to intimidation and only voice exercises had allowed it a little leakage into the brusque edge of the conversational, the uninterruptible.

'Two violent deaths in a family crypt,' the barrister said. 'A double suicide. Teenagers. Can you do a sensitive clean-up? There are two notable families concerned. No publicity. There's also a priory involved,' said the voice. 'The friars are of a very particular and secretive order. They are specialists and had some involvement in the deaths — a double suicide — but are not facing prosecution. The families have fully exonerated them.'

William had never met a friar before. Friar Laurence's forearms were enormous and one of his eyes was partially closed as though he had tried to conceal it by papering it over with a cigarette skin.

'Welcome, Doctor Shakespeare. Please follow me.' The friar walked with a gait that suggested a buoyancy aid on a choppy sea although he was in fact shod in new Birkenstock sandals.

His rope belt matched his teeth, they had the same neat, strong pattern as though his teeth were a thin rope twisted at the back to form a loop like a Mobius strip. William imagined Friar Laurence's crucifix dangled against Friar Laurence's tonsils. Everything was made holy going in, every was made holy coming out.

'Sit down,' Friar Laurence said, indicating an overstuffed hassock as big as a large beanbag, the embroidery on it showing a disputed goal in a Premiership match but the shooter being the devil. 'Allegory, eh?' said William pointing. 'No,' said Friar Laurence. 'Fact.'

'Monasteries and friaries depend on creating product. Cheese, beer, retreats. We're a bit different. We are scientific pioneers. Just as Gregor Mandel studied genetics through his experiments with sweet peas, we breed anaesthetics.'

'Can you 'breed' anaesthetics? They're not alive, are they?'

'We treat them as living entities. They have a life cycle. We mate them. We have an anaesthetic stud farm. One superlative stallion and mare anaesthetic can create a multitude of horses for courses. Each patient mounted on a steed created specifically for them in the, ah, steeplechase of unconsciousness.'

And that's your monasteries.

'We are guardians of the crypt. I had induced a coma in Juliet. Which worked very well. Keeping her pulse undetectable until her new husband could reach her and then the two of them could go away, live free from the constricting feud. Possibly end the feud forever — that was my hope. Ah, but the text we sent didn't reach him. Or, as we now believe, was seen by a third party and deleted. These two were proficient on social media but both had their phones confiscated by their parents. And the home WIFI's switched off. Home Office surveillance is suspected. It's mostly blood that's causing the problem. Old stone. Absorbent. There's quite a lot of it. We heard you were proficient.'

* * *

William fed the extension cable trough the iron grate and into the family mausoleum. Low stone archways with their delicate embellishments, the coves and ledges containing aged but beautiful coffins recently swept of dust and cobwebs, their nameplates polished, a marble angel poised thoughtfully between the generations. William noticed that someone had drawn a borstal teardrop on its face in biro, and the words 'love' and 'like' on the delicately balled fingers. An obviously new golden statue, two faces kissing fused into one, three times life size, the lover's hair clipped and spiked like the medieval sun fresh from a visit to the medieval barber's. The statue had been shoved against the wall, scrape marks showing its original position. William took out his UVA wand and waved it over the floor, the granite plinths and the immediate coffins. The spray was so extensive and finely placed it was as though someone had trodden on a crystalline night sky and walked it into the crypt. William looked up as Death Nell entered.

'You should see what's next door,' said Death Nell rustling in wearing her paper overalls. 'Come and have a look! Jacques is taking photos of it. Bling does gruesome.'

William followed, pondering why he felt that this apparent double suicide had something suspiciously murdersome/murdery about it. Teenagers lived (and, apparently, died) in the land of hyperbole. They could outdistance superlatives and often did.

Walking into the adjacent crypt its floor seemed full of too many shadows as though there was a shadow sump in the chapel above that drew them here where they could rise to the ceiling before draining away to wherever shadows went after what they'd represented in a patch of pulled darkness had vanished. Shadows as representatives. Could something be reconstituted out of its shadow? Jacques was kneeling on a stone partition his back to a modest ossuary that reminded William of a bee bole, and he was taking picture after picture, the flash sounding like a freshly laundered sheet of lightning being shaken and folded for the drawer.

'Look at her!' said Jacques. 'They never said she was here, did they?'

'That's, um, resplendent!' said William. 'Is it a saint?' William was staring at a skeleton with the vestiges of its original face locked beneath a film of wax. Gold hair stood out from the skull as though God had given it a century long tousle. Each eye socket was packed with a sapphire (the left eye's slightly larger than the right) and the lips were a thread of pink seed pearls.

'I like the togs,' said Death Nell. 'Gorgeous.'

Jacques nodded. 'Anything looks swell on a size zero model, Nell.'

'But this is like death by glitter. The cloth and embroidery and lace — everything's jewelled. I mean, they've shuffled the cloth around her, if it was heaped on top it'd probably crush her to graded grains.'

'Enough here for a million million millionaire's tarmac driveways. And some left over for a sun-lounger sized patio. Wow.'

'It's a bit low cut at the front,' said Jacques. If she wore that when she had a proper body, well, people wouldn't have stared so much at her goodness as at her two hills standing so, like twin Glastonbury tors.'

William lowered Jacques's camera. 'Work time,' he said. 'And the costume is low because this saint had a true heart. Look at the jewels on her ribs and clavicle. Rubies. Like the pictures of Jesus with his sacred heart.'

'Sounds like that fairy tale with the three crones — that's sexist, isn't it — anyway, the three crones with only one eye between them that they pass around. One heart threading throughout heaven.'

They went back next door and began cleaning.

'Bet you think this was murder, too, Billy?'

'There's something not quite right with it.'

'So you'll be wanting me to vape when we've finished?'

'Yes. If you don't mind.'

'Got to thinking this is part of the process,' said Death Nell.

'It is. Take the cost of equipment out of petty cash. It's work related.'

'Do you think it's happening to anyone else?' said Death Nell. That was something William had wondered about but, having tried it himself and asked his wife to vape whilst he watched (bit kinky, William or what is it you want to see, shall I pout? Are you going to tell me what it's about? Then he'd asked Anne to watch whilst he vaped. What am I looking for exactly? Shapes in the vapour, said William. It's an experiment. Something to do with the crime scene cleaning? Yes. A clue. Actually, yes. Does it stay then, vaping. Can you see the signs with your chemicals? Almost. Just a new technique. Death Nell's very good at it. Jacques and I can't quite match her technique.)

'So the two dead kids, is this them here?' Jacques knocked on the two newest white coffins, each painted with summer scenes.

'Yes.'

'Yes. They all fell silent and stopped mopping. 'I'd have liked to brought roses. Or something. White roses.'

'Did you know they'd be here, Bill?' said Jacques.

'I did, but I hadn't realised we'd be working right next to them. It's an old family so their crypt is a bit full.'

'It's not horrible in here, though, is it? It's peaceful. Except for the blood. The blood gives it an atmosphere. When the blood's gone it will be peaceful.'

'Empty. I'd call it empty,' said Jacques. 'Not peaceful. Like a candle that's gone out.

'Oh, oh that's very sad. And this is where they died?'

'Yes. Oh, That's a first for us. The bodies here whilst we clean what spilt out of them.'

'It's very affecting,' said Jacques. 'I'm affected. Blood. Vomit.'

'Sad that it was suicide, terrible if it was murder.'

'And that's them kissing in that gold statue?' said Death Nell.

'It's supposed to be a good likeness.'

'It'll end up in somebody's garden.'

'What?'

'It has something of the artisanal garden ornament about it. Like Henry Moore's statues. Early Barbara Epstein.'

'Is it real gold?'

'Supposedly.'

'It'll get nicked.'

'Not if they have the choice between her next door and this. She's stayed burglar proof for centuries.'

'True.'

They stayed silent and worked. Gently coaxing the blood from the stone.

'Like getting blood form a stone,' thought William. This is exactly what they were doing.

Three hours later, everything bagged up and sealed, the effluvia disposed into a sealed container, William back in his own clothes went up the staircases through the chapel, skirting the walls since the monks were at prayer, moonlight falling through the stained glass windows not flowers but the small branches of trees in leaf, greens, with leaves and blossom on the hawthorn crown on the figure of Jesus on his cross. It was peaceful. As though everyone had settled into who they were and what the day and night expected of them/what they did/ there was a drowsiness (anaesthetising incense). Out through the porch where a friar sat with several hospital canisters of gas on a gurney and the transparent tubes up to his nose. In his hand a metronome. William nodded. The friar nodded and pointed to the metronome. 'I'm collecting all my experiences at moderato. I have a natural tendency to largo. It's my thyroid. I'm on anaesthetic. Dreaming whilst awake. To get spiritual messages. Visions.'

'Do you get any?'

'Aren't you one?' said the friar.

'Sorry,' said William. 'I'm here to clean the crypt after the tragedy.'

'Ah,' said the friar. 'What about the fellow standing behind you with the hank of human hair?'

'Yes, you're all right with him,' said William turning round to make sure there was no one behind him fondling a shank of human hair. 'He's definitely a vision.'

'Pity it's that way round. You are by far the most vociferous and friendly.' Then the friar turned to stare at the vision, upping the metronome's tempo to presto.

Wiping his feet on the huge bristly welcome mat, William walked along the polished granite flagged corridor to Friar Laurence's office. Before he had a chance to knock, Friar Laurence called out, 'Come in, Dr Shakespeare.'

The office looked very different now the sun had left it. The bare glass showed a remorselessly black sky.

'We've finished,' said William. Friar Laurence gestured to the hassock. William sat.

'We are a scientific order. We use anaesthesia as a form of meditation and prayer. Our retreats are all about reversing into ourselves. We never usually look behind us, at what we've turned our backs on or what has slipped unseen and unbidden to a place we won't bother to look.

Our order has been experimenting using what you might consider 'occult forces' and inexplicable and destructive energies. We have turned poltergeists into bombs and other forms of munitions.'

'Did you just say you've turned poltergeists into...?'

'Bombs and other forms of munition. Yes. Our main problem — and I'm talking to you in utter confidence — is how we clean up the area once order has been restored. The problem with traditional methods of warfare is that explosives often create contamination. Poltergeists don't, not on a physical level. And we've managed to use anaesthetics on poltergeists for a more controlled effect.'

'Why are you telling me this, Friar Laurence?'

'Because I wondered if you would undertake a little experiment for me. On behalf of the order. It's safe. But we are unable, by dint of our vows, to wreak havoc directly into the world. We are also unable to experiment as much as we'd like to, again, our vows prevent us.'

'What vows?'

'Our order is unique. Yes, we have poverty, chastity and obedience but our founding father and saint had other requisites of his followers. We must explore and map the hinterland between Life and Death. That is our calling. A side effect of our use of anaesthetics is that of floating or levitating. We can, those of us who have racked up twenty or more years use of general anaesthetics to assist prayer and meditation, we can hover. Volition is easy but with one major caveat. To propel ourselves in the direction we want to go we are back to swinging like apes using our hands as a means of propulsion and as anchors.'

William imagined it. The image forced him to control a fit of giggles.

'Birth is a terrible spectacle akin to war. I am told by those whose job it has been to monitor and measure the procedure, the pain is equivalent to being critically injured, yet few women suffer post-traumatic stress. We want to our armed forces to have some of that. To forget. To feel that the pain fetched something good into the world, a good that they can bond with and love. Your wife, Anne, is a midwife specialising …' he checked his notes, 'in water births. She works for the Simulacrum river company.'

'Imagine this,' William's wife had said, late one night, a few millimetres away from the sinkhole of sleep, the room crumbling around him. 'Imagine this, William,' said Anne. 'The Simulacrum River Company have built this one river with many tributaries in which women can give birth. Free birthing. One river kept so pure and warmed by solar energy, one river in which the women of the United Kingdom give birth. And here's me, one of the free-diving aquatic midwives. There are those pedicure fish eating the loose meats of labour. The women are brought into the river in bathing machines when their waters break and we, who remain in the river during work hours, swim to their aid. We who can remain submerged for nine minutes. That is the future of the world.'

'Your wife, Anne, is also a poet?'

'She is. And she also choreographs Titania and The Titanics, an aquatic ballet group composed of her fellow free diving midwives.'

'Interesting. You've maybe seen the relic of our Saint.'

'I was surprised the saint was female. I thought your founders would be male.'

'That is where our friary differs from most. We believe that everyone is male when they're dead. It's like the default setting. Female is simply a paradigm shift. An accommodation. Women and men are equal because we are all men. We have no problem with any form of sexuality because we are all men.'

'Except against women.'

'No, because we are all men. A woman is a quibble.'

I can see that upsetting a lot of women.'

'No need to. They are all men when they're dead so it's a fight not worth rolling their sleeves up for.'

William shut up. Friar or not, the man was an idiot

'Somebody said you have a special method of cleaning. I'd like a small sample of the liquid. To analyse. We analyse things here. It might have a formula we can adjust to further our work on anaesthetics. Anaesthetics allow us to hover between life and death and to be either fecund in dreams or barren.

We also believe that we are judged not on our actions but on our dreams. Because we cannot remember our dreams then none of us knows the outcome of God's judgement. Therefore, living a good life is a choice with no agenda attached to it.'

The moon had crawled part way up the window. Clouds

mobbed it. 'Would you allow me to take even just one millilitre of the cleaning fluid you are reputed to have received from some rather curious people.'

'My cleaning methods are not matters I would discuss or details I would disclose. Why don't you contact these curious people yourself if you believe they have something that will further your research?

'Because we are inimical enemies. Not because of their habits but because of who they are. We friars dangle by quite another set of strings to quite another set of manipulators. We are unable to communicate at all. The rules of our order forbid it.'

'What about asking me to mediate?'

'No, no, we don't want to seek permission from them. We want to be given, gratis, a very small amount of what they're creating.'

'Like industrial espionage is it?'

'Yes.'

'The answer's 'no' then.'

'How about spiritual espionage. Would that make it sweeter?'

'No, sorry Friar Laurence. It would not.'

Friar Laurence shook his head, his tonsure flying out in a perfect white horseshoe. Then he took William by the shoulder and turned him towards the door. 'Go out, I'll follow you.'

They walked along a corridor and down an iron spiral staircase. There were friars' cells, all occupants lay inert on their beds connected to heart monitors. 'This should be a familiar sight, Doctor Shakespeare. We keep everyone monitored because the drift between life and death must be horizontal. We are interested in this liminal state. And now I must show you something I know you will never forget. Come.'

They walked for some time and the corridor grew narrower and darker. They went down an ancient flight of stone steps and emerged into what looked like a silo.

William expected to see poltergeist armaments guarded by

an ossuary. Dispensed in human skulls — the fiery skulls of Baba Yaga.

Instead William saw beautifully illustrated vellum cylinders with paper cone tops, and all stacked and secured with red ribbon and red sealing wax. The silo was stacked with warheads, each loaded with a high impact poltergeist. Each canister was fed by a line bearing anaesthetic, each tended by a friar.

'These are the weapon grade anaesthetics. These are warfare anaesthetists. They keep the armaments, the poltergeists, stable. The poltergeist has its origin in emotions not in the human soul so it is comparatively safe to handle. One has to know what one is doing, though. The canisters are vellum paper tubes sealed with wax with hand-illumination. Vellum paper cones. The poltergeists remain inert until the anaesthesia is withdrawn.'

'You're still not having any of the cleaning fludd,' said William, and found his own way back to the priory car park where Death Nell and Jacques were packing up.

'Home,' William said. 'Let's just get home.'

* * *

In the car priory park, Jacques was performing a hybrid form of Tai Chi. It was crossed with British and American sign language. Jacques could feel the energy of the letters, and words, softly solid between his palms and against his fingers, firmer than blowing out the candles on a birthday cake. Jacques was controlling a great balled roster of vocabulary, a dictionary, bound by his body but extending beyond. Death Nell was leaning against the hatchback, checking her phone, tapping the keypad with the stem of her e-cigarette. As he approached, William thought that the e-cigarette looked stupid, like a half-arsed ball point pen, one of those tall as a ring finger efforts dropped into wood-laminate stalls at betting shops and catalogue stores, an under nourished ball point pen balanced on a spark plug, with that spark plug defaced by the stringed pith of an aged tangerine. Yes, William's exhaustion had reached the point where he was banjaxing his similes at the same time he was setting them up.

'Okay, we can get off home straight away if you like,' said William. 'I think that'd be best. We're all exhausted.'

'You don't think something's being covered up here, then, this doesn't fit your hunch about a hidden perpetrator?' said Jacques.

'Something odd is going on. In fact, a lot of odd is happening here. And, yes, it's the same thing as the previous crime scenes. The heirs of influential and powerful families die. Who will inherit the amassed fortunes and the power bases? It's always the same question, isn't it? Who stands to benefit? Who's getting most out of these murders?'

'Well, you are,' said Jacques. 'You know, it's keeping you in work and getting you publicity.'

'That's true,' said William smiling. 'I know I'm benefitting, and so are you by association…'

'By employment.'

'But there's someone I can't, for the moment, see.'

'I'll vape, I'm the Volunteer Vaper,' said Death Nell, 'although there's some reports about these e-ciggies being a bit detrimental.'

'You don't need to vape, Nell. Really.'

'Matter of honour and pride, Billy. If clues come through my vaping then I must vape. I'm young. My body is resilient.'

'It's all vape and mirrors,' said Jacques. 'Except we don't use mirrors.'

'Let's go somewhere a bit less visible,' said William.

'Most of the friars are anaesthetised,' said Jacques

'Most. Not all of them. We need to be close enough to the family mausoleum to get the connection. I don't think the vaping will fetch much if we're out of range.'

'You think there's like a transmission range, then, Bill?' said Jacques. 'The ghost bandwidth. Do you think WIFI will have extended it? Or are psychic phenomena rooted in the analogue age?'

'Paranormal activity's always kept up with technological innovation. The returning Dead used to be as solidly built as they'd been in life until the church intervened and did a kind of reverse transubstantiation on them and turned them into ghosts. Ghosts can be passed off as figments. Now, if we had two dead but animated teenagers galumphing about in the priory herb garden...'

'I'd put it down to the absolute rule of teenage hormones. Like electricity to the severed frog leg, I could believe a hormonally-charged body would jump start itself, however much Death had mucked it about,' said Jacques.

'Hah, yeah, Frankenstein could have just found a youth, given him a slight shake to distribute the testosterone and stood back. Job done,' said Death Nell.

'Watch the firework light its own blue touch-paper!'

They walked over to the suite of mausoleums standing apart from the priory the way the Bates' family house kept its watchful distance from the Bates' motel. Death Nell took off her jacket and sat on it. 'Bum comfort.' Then she began vaping. Straight away there was a great deal of vapour, like somebody had sliced clouds the way they sliced bread. It was a great slab and it slowly pulled itself apart to create a balcony. Standing under the balcony, dressed identically in skeleton suits and caps, each with an arm around the other's neck, were two teenagers and William knew which was which in a moment, because one of them had 'ROM' embroidered on their collar, and the other 'JUL'. 'I suppose they've each got 'lovers' round at the back of the collar,' William said to himself.

The pair stood so still that William quite forgot they were vaped, and he was just going round to see if the word 'LOVERS' *was* written at the back of each collar when he was startled by a voice coming from the one marked 'Rom'.

'If you think we're wax-works,' he said, 'you ought to pay,

you know. Wax-works weren't made to be looked at for nothing. No how!'

'Contrariwise,' added the one marked Jul. 'If you think we're here to entertain you, well, you ought to speak.'

'I'm sure I'm very sorry,' said William.

'We must sing a song,' Rom and Jul said in unison. At first, when they opened the mouths wide enough to sing they simply broke up like the small clouds they were. After a lot of attempts and a good deal of sifting through the air for any stray steam, they recomposed themselves and began to sing.

'The sun was shining on the sea
shining with all his might
he did his very best to make
the billows smooth and bright
and this was very odd because
Juliet was the light

The moon was shining sulkily
because she thought the sun
had risen early in the east
when all was said and done
that light on yonder balcony
suggests we'll have some fun!

The stars, the stars were head-lit cars
beside themselves with glee
they'd hit and squished a girl and boy
and one of them was me
yes, one of them was me was me

yes one of them was me!'

'You were run over?' said William.

'No, we were overrun,' said Jul.

'We overran,' said Rom.

'Over there,' said Jul.

'Or somewhere like it. We'd recognise the wind if it blew us again. If we felt that same wind we'd know we were in the same place.'

'Whenever the East wind blows you're standing where you stand when the East wind blows.'

'It stands to reason.'

'Ditto the other winds. You're always standing where the North wind blows when the North wind blows.'

'That's how we get our bearings.'

'That's how we get our bears. In rings.'

'What bears?' said William, recalling the bear that had chased him into the Hampstead garden pond.

'Bears thinking about, don't it?' said Jul.

'Bears comparison,' said Rom.

'Better than that, it bears witness uck uck uck...'

Nell was coughing and wafting the vapour away from her face where it had congregated.

'Sorry, Billy. I'll have to stop. It's gone like that film, The Fog. It's like I'm trying to inhale grey galoshes, not air.'

'Yes, stop — always stop before you feel you have to. Are you okay?'

'Yes, I'm fine. I think there's too much nicotine on an empty stomach.'

'That was pretty impressive, though, Nell,' said Jacques, helping her to her feet, shaking out her jacket and holding it up for her arms to find the sleeves.

'Got anything you could use?' said Death Nell, stowing the e-cigarette in her back pocket.

'Yes, I rather think I have. Thank you. Well done. Now let's get home.'

CHAPTER 10

ANNE SHAKESPEARE & JUST WILLIAM

Anne Shakespeare was a free-diving, water-birth specialising midwife. She worked for the Simulacrum River Company. The Simulacrum River was a wonderful watercourse. Entirely artificial, it wasn't a canal but a properly functioning river with tributaries feeding into it, and an outlet that allowed the flow to trickle down into an estuary and away into the sea. The Simulacrum River's tributaries were numerous. Anne could name them all, she had been taught them by her employer. She recited them at company functions. It was imperative to know the names of the individual waters whose confluence created her workplace. Say them again, she said to herself. Say them aloud because they are lovely to speak. Whilst Anne said them she thought about all the babies' heads rising above the communal surface, taking their first breaths from the green, golden, sparkling air held by the water's surface like a great silver platter laden with soft leaves.

'The Froissart, the Painter, the Holished rill, the Boccaccio, Elyot, Anonymous brook, the Brooke brook. Gascoigne, Hall, Fabyan, Grafton, Hardying, Foxe, Hall, Baldwin, Spenser, Kyd. The Ovid. The Seneca, More, Livius, Chaucer, Plautus, Warner, Plutarch, Huoun, Petrarca, Bourchier, Fiorentino,Pecarone, Romanorum, Lyly, Daniel, Ariosto Harington, Bandello,

Belleforest, Whetstone,Castiglione, Appian, Lodge, Riche, Bandellio, Roydon, , Homer, Chapman, Caxton, Lydgate, Cinthio, Giraldi, Africanus, Marlowe (like my step brother in law), Lucian, Campaspe,, Buchanan, Gower, Twine, Livius, Camden, Averell, Greene, Strachey, Jourdain, Beaumont... The inlets and the outlet of my lovely place of work, a high rise built horizontally, each tributary adding to its stories.' Anne wept like a source.

* * *

William was sitting in the kitchen at the old 1950s upcycled dining table with its diner's dining history mapped across it like the blotting paper imprint of an inked time line. Like a heat shrunk plastic facsimile of the time line. As if a period of lush, green time, as big as a field mouse, had been eviscerated and spread two millimetres thick across a rectangle large enough for two adults and three young children to dine from together without touching elbows. William was doing his paperwork and preparing everything for their next crime scene cleaning job. Reconnoitring with the bereaved family's 'people', the paid collective who assumed the tasks that poorer families themselves had to undertake, or ignore.

William also thought about the transport system in his ears. The fairies did seem to be aware of the inconvenience and anguish they'd caused and had installed baffles. The baffles effectively lowered his hearing range but William wasn't too concerned. Not being able to hear his children's harmonica-like outbursts was a plus.

Whilst his brain was still craning backwards at the past, William spotted two memories that connected with his immediate situation. They were bookmarked. Both were from the year before. The first happened just before he realised he'd have to leave his profession. Then second, just after he'd left it for good. Both involved visits to his GP's surgery.

He was having his left ear syringed. The nurse, a fretful brunette cobbed by moles the size of map-pins, cupped a kidney dish above his shoulder. She released her inner chatterbox once she could reasonably expect to be heard.

'There's some big nuggins coming out. Bet you've been thinking your stethoscope was bust, eh Doctor.'

'Haha. Actually it was. It was broken.'

'Oh. Right. Um, how? There's not much to break.'

'The tube split.'

'Ah...'

'I mended it with a bicycle puncture repair kit.'

'That worked did it?'

'Not quite. It make it sound as if my patients' innards are whispering conspiratorially.'

'Did it? Is this water too cold?'

'S'okay.'

Nurse was now at William's right ear, power cleaning the other royal driveway to his brain. Slosh squish gurgle. A nub of wax bounced out of the kidney dish and onto his lap.

'Whoa we have a leaper!' said the nurse.

'Got it,' William replied, turning the blob between his thumb and forefinger exactly as his six year self would have done. William remembered the joy of discovering earwax with its strange, harsh and stumpy taste. William stared affectionately at the yellow pellet as though this piece had remained lodged for the last twenty years, waiting for the moment it could emerge and broker the distance between now and then. William smiled at it, then he flung his hand as far away from his body as it would go. The kidney dish slopped, pooling earthy water onto his shoulder. ' Sorry! Hiccups,' said William. But it wasn't hiccups, no, there was a fairy embedded in his earwax like a fly in amber. Malleable amber. William pinched the wax and the fairy flailed, buckled and stuck. William held it as close to his eyes as he could focus. Squeeze, squeeze, this way that way. Is it alive? William pocketed it whilst the nurse did whatever nurses did with the flocculant. Drank it, sold it on to data harvesting agencies, used it to water the exceedingly waxy rubber plant on the window ledge.

Out on the street William rinsed the fairy's head with bottled water. Back home he severed a toothbrush bristle with his nail scissors and poked it up each tiny nostril, drilled into the little mouth to clear its passages. Oops, a mini nosebleed. Ooo! Projectile fairy vomit, bright and reflexive as a sun flare. The eyes, however, remained gummed in golden spectacles. William was not going to open the eyes because that was the fairies' locus of oppugnancy, that was how they enthralled you. He was going to keep this tit immobilised in its tacky orange papoose.

I'm not unkind, he thought. Then he checked his father's reference pamphlet on Fairy Diet — the thinnest of the pamphlets lined on the drooping bookcase in the attic — fairies were obviously picky eaters. Newly wise to their needs, William hurtled back downstairs and fed the fairy on a Barbadian dew drop (well, condensation from the kettle), crystals that had formed in an ancient jar of honey, a sliver of dandelion (there was one under the rose bush) made pappy with his scalpel. The fairy's hair was still slicked with earwax so William used the toothbrush bristle to fold it into a kiss curl, but it looked more like an antennae. When the fairy seemed to have eaten its fill, William hid it under the lowest leaf of a pink flowered, window-ledge geranium.

Next day William 'borrowed' an endoscope from hospital and fixed it onto the plant pot with gaffer tape. Even now, William remembered watching the live feed whenever he get bored with the telly. Anne hadn't noticed, but then she was tired, she was still breast feeding Odile and Odear, and sometimes giving Odette a little soothing tot.

Close-up the fairy's face was as unformed as a green plastic toy soldier's. It moved its lips and all the leaves fell off the geranium.

'That was mean to the plant,' said William. 'You needn't have done that. Now I'm going to think you're peevish.'

William remembered the curved feeling of excitement, it was almost like licking his first Parma Violet sweet of the day.

This fairy was much too special to keep secret so William rang his step brother, Kit, and Kit came over. Kit was less overcome with proof of the existence of fairies than he was perturbed by William's treatment of it.

'That's just cruel.'

'What's cruel?'

'Captivity. Keeping it in earwax.'

'It put itself there.'

'Let it go.'

'No. I want to find out what it was up to.'

'Ask it.'

'Helping diagnose patients. Guiding you.' Said the fairy.

'You know you don't speak to them. It gives them power. It's like ghosts. They don't have souls.'

'They don't need them. They're immortal. We're more like space rockets that shuck off the boosters when we reach sufficient velocity clear of the earth. They circulate galaxies just as they are.'

A week went by and something untoward had happened to William's navel. Kit came back. William slid his tee shirt up to show him.

'Fairy's worked a malison on you, mate,' Kit said. William thought that that was a fair assessment of the situation. His belly button had grown enormous. A number of previous conversations were still swirling around in it. And the volume was turned up on his body's churnings and drummings.

'What happens if you end up all navel?'

'I'll look like a giant inverted fingerprint, won't I?'

They both stared. William's giant belly button was neat, circular, the skin around it like a thin nest of interlaced, pink-tinged twigs that dipped into a soft magnolia cone, and it was acting like a bass speaker on Glasto's main stage.

So William went to his GP's surgery. He was poised outside Doctor Nostler's consulting room. William knocked. Then he thought, who taught me to knock? Who devised knocking? All those stone age hand prints on cave walls, were they markers in the evolution of the knock — were they the precursors before they got the hang of rapping with their knuckles? You knock and the knock is never solo. It's musically phrased. Percussive. It's the crossing of territories, isn't it? The knock is the first defining moment of territory and diplomacy, the principals on which the idea of country is founded. All that, of course, was what William's father's pamphlet propounded. William smiled as he remembered the pamphlet's title: From Knock To Nation. Spot on.

'It's all right. You can go in. Doctor Nostler's expecting you,' the receptionist called, baffled by Williams door stall. William knocked and felt the depth of history in his fist.

'Come in.' In he went. 'What seems to be the trouble, Doctor?' Why hadn't he doctored himself? Because he wanted proof that he, and his step brother, Kit, weren't imagining things.

'It's my navel.'

'Is it crusty? Fungal? Is there a seepage of urine into it?'

'No...'

'What's that noise?'

'My navel.'

'What? Better lift your shirt up so I can have a look.

'WHAT THE!?'

Five minutes later and Doctor Nostler went over to the sink to wash her hands. William followed her to the sink and washed his hands as well, and Doctor Nostler obligingly pumped a squirt of pungent antibacterial gel from the dispenser into William's cupped palms, for which he thanked her. They washed in unison. They washed identically, text book illustration perfectly. William and Doctor Nostler dried themselves on disposable paper sheets and dropped the litter into the immaculate peddle bin. Then they returned to their respective chairs either side of the desk, the twofold status re-established.

'Congratulations, Doctor Shakespeare. You have made medical history. Your navel is so large you're the first person to be diagnosed as acoustic'.

Back home, carrying a stapled pharmacy bag containing a tube of cortisone cream, William went into the kitchen and found the window ledge in disarray. His cockerel, Mr Ruby, had escaped from his pen and ransacked the plant pots. The endoscope had rolled under the table but, thankfully, still seemed to be working, but there was no sign of the fairy embedded in earwax. The soil where it had lain was scratched and pecked. Mr Ruby looked up at William. The cockerel's expression was quizzical.

'Have you eaten the fairy?' William asked him. William knew he had. The poor bird was walking normally enough, it was just that its feet didn't reach the ground. Mr Ruby was walking on an invisible surface an inch above the floor. That was the reason William had left him behind at the hospital when his tenure ended. When he'd served his notice. He'd left Mr Ruby in the staff totem animal kennels. Anne never knew about the cockerel coming home with him from time to time, nor about the episode with the fairy and the endoscope. As far as Anne was concerned, Mr Ruby was an impromptu and totally unexpected leaving present from St Largesse. Ann now seemed fond of the bird and had written a poem about him.

ANNE SHAKESPEARE'S ODE TO WILLIAM'S COCK

from Anne Shakespeare's first volume of poetry:

ANGELS HELP ME WITH MY WASHING

*My husband's cock is an Old English Game bantam. He is
Mr Ruby.
His body is spherical, a cannon ball latticed with muscle.
His beak is ochre flint. His comb is the red silhouette of
an army amassed before the sun. His voice is moonlight in
formaldehyde.*

*His turds are stinks drawn from the earth's core. His food is
Tradition on its death bed. His eyes are the last frap of sand
to disappear into the bottom of twin hour glasses.*

*But he's just a chicken with his knees on back-to-front. He's
but a fowl with wire feet and a comb like a smashed nose.
There is, however, an otherness about him. Mr Ruby.*

Along with the other junior doctors, William had accompanied
their supervising consultant on the ward rounds at St Largesse
Cottage Hospital, and the supervising consultant had allocated
each of them a totem animal. William's was a cock. Others
received budgerigars, goldfish, rabbits, guinea pigs, cats, dogs,
hedgehogs, snakes and an amoeba. They were supposed to
adopt the gait of the animal totem when they accompany the
consultant (a labrapoodle).

'How the hell do I move like an amoeba?' asked a perplexed
junior doctor.

'Glide? Surround your patients and absorb them?' That was
the day William decided to be a whistleblower. Enough was
enough.

* * *

Kit was working late in the sewing room of his tailor's shop. Kit was sitting cross-legged in the middle of an enormous circular oak table. Hundreds of silver needles of different sizes, some of them curved, all with particular credentials, were arranged around him in a perfect circle. It had taken him hours to arrange them, it was a bit of a habit but these were the signifiers of his trade, these were the small, sharp things that fetched together pieces of cloth and threatened them and made them work together to one agreed end. They were the dangerous-in-the-wrong-hands tools of peace and of patching-up, of decorating the body with shapes that amplified the body's purpose, rearranged the body's shortcomings and gave grace to the beast. People were beasts and beasts of some beauty and potency and clothes gave them back their glorious pelts. Kit wanted the pins to seem as though they had been exuded like sap from the lumber they lay across, leaked like amber from the tree's thousand rings.

Kit Marlowe loved his step brother and his step brother's wife and his three step nieces. Kit was proud of William's whistleblowing. When certain people came to have suits made they spoke to Kit Marlowe, Savile Row stitcheroo, about William Shakespeare, crime scene cleaner. William had been Medical Kit, Kit was Sewing Kit. Now William was Cleaning Outfit.

Reels of cotton hung from the chandeliers in place of candles or light bulbs and yet the room was always bright enough to see and sew in. Kit stuck out his arm and carefully selected a dangled strand, licked the cotton and threaded it with one precise jab. Then he set about the worn plectrums of tailors' chalk into a kind of pommel made by stitching together a very old linen tape measure he'd discovered dangling from a tree overhanging Hyde Park's railings. Yes, a pommel for a tailor's sword, it would be the biggest kind of sewing needle there was, the pommel having an eye through which thread could be threaded.

Kit's sewing room was reached by numerous winding stone steps hollowed by hundreds of years of feet. A thick rope handrail helped visitors haul themselves up and down them. In one corner of the room stood a locked glass showcase with a large old book in it, open on a page depicting hand loom weavers, each seated in a cloud, each weaving a star onto their looms, one larger weaver weaving a large, sulky-faced golden sun. The book was very old and had been bound in the skin of a convicted, hanged murderer. the book had been bound in the skin of a convicted murderer. Kit hadn't heard anyone mounting the stairs and jumped when a man stepped into the room.

'Interesting table you've got there,' said the man whom Kit noticed had a most sensuous, polar white moustache, waxed into a cupid's bow. Pearl grey curls drifted out of a black swim cap. And he was tall, dressed in white silk with what looked like a row of birds emerging in a line down the loose cloth flowing like a milk riptide across his torso. 'Yes, a most interesting table.'

'I dare say it is. How may I help you, sir?'

'My trousers are too short.'

'Perhaps sir ought to buy longer trousers.'

'They were fine when I bought them. I, ah, I'm growing taller, something I did not expect to do.'

'Expect the unexpected is what I always say.'

'Which is wise advice for your step brother, William Shakespeare, too.'

They had then fallen into conversation.

* * *

It was late. The children were asleep. Anne had gone up to bed. William went to sit on the family sofa. He checked his phone. There were five missed calls from his step brother Kit. Sewing Kit. The Savile Row tailor, the stitcheroo, a whole performance when you met him, pretending to swallow needles and twine and then disgorging fifty perfectly threaded needles moist with saliva and dangling above his tongue like a swag of miniature icicles dragged from a cold, cold heart. Kit Marlowe lived with a milliner called Richard Spivey the Third, an American who had applied for British citizenship. They called Kit's partner Richard the Third. If you were talking to him and he needed to go to the bathroom he would leave his phone on 'record' until he got back so that everything continued in his absence. Richard the Third hated any form of hiatus. He regarded hats as a means of capturing space and ensuring it was filled, at least for part of the day. Richard had an army of hat blocks on which every one of the hats still under his guardianship practised what they had been created to do.

William hugged a cushion. It was sometimes good to hug the nonliving. It made a kind of sense of death. He was holding one of the numerous cushions in the shape of dogs that Kit had made as a present for Anne's and William's wedding anniversary. Unzip each cushion and you got a handful of crossbred pups, wonderful things, dog cushions filled with exquisitely sewn puppies, and you could track across from cushion to cushion to work out their parentage. Even the male dogs were puppy filled, it was a physically egalitarian sort of canine world Kit had created. All jumbled now, of course. Puppies with no shared attributes to the containing dog. All had names. Each night Odette kennelled them in new combinations. William often thought Kit could be unloaded like the cushions. Kip consisted of numerous litters of self, all participating in isolation wherever they were played.

William leant back into the sofa, pushing himself with his heels until he was as far into the sofa he leant against hard dowling. It felt like there was a doorframe inside the sofa. Was that somebody knocking on it? No, of course not. Somebody was knocking but they were outside the door for which William had inviolable empirical proof. He got up and opened it. Kit was standing on the doorstep.

'Thought I'd better come round.'

'Why?'

'When gossip reaches the tailor's it's been stitched into the lining of belief.'

'Oh, has it? And what's the gossip?

'About what you came across when you did your first crime scene clean.'

'Seeing as only Nell and Jacques were with me no gossip should be given credence.'

'People might not have been there in person but you were being watched.'

'I saw the brackets where the CCTV cameras had been but the police had removed them all.'

'The family reinstalled them. But the covert sort. Cameras secreted in innocuous objects. The kettle was a complete camera, picking up three D footage.'

'What if we'd switched it on?'

You're a professional outfit. You're not going to use a kettle at a crime scene to knock out a brew. You'll be an honourable flask man.'

'True.'

'Somebody was watching and somebody close to the somebodies watching have set off several rumours about what happened there. The family installed cameras just to ensure nothing was taken. They also wanted to see the crime scene first had. You showed them where all the detritus was. But rumour has it there was some sort of occult manifestation. And a female visitor.'

'Care to give me the details?' said William, wondering if the Tonguebird's antics were a perplexing blur because of the speed of its antics.

'Some kind of creature. Flying. But flew badly. Misshapen thing. You said it was a tongue.'

'That's a bit ridiculous,' said William. 'A tongue moving of its own volition at a crime scene?'

'A tongue that ricocheted around the room before it landed on Jacques. Rumour says it spoke.'

'They're right.'

'You're joking!'

'No. It happened. The tongue had bird legs.'

'Flipping flying fffffs.'

'All of you saw it?'

'Yes, we did.'

'And your assistant. Apprentice. Nell D'eath... she's a bit of a medium?'

'I hadn't thought of it like that but, yes, I suppose she is. When she vapes. The vapour comes out in ectoplasm. I don't think she can do it without vaping. Must be the chemical combinations in the E-Cigarette — and she says it doesn't happen away from crime scenes. She's a regular vaper everywhere else.'

'Maybe it's the voltage rather than the liquid nicotine? Aren't ghosts greedy guzzlers of electricity — they drain batteries and make houselights flicker.'

'Your guess is as good as mine. What I do know is that Jacques and I have tried but we can't do it. Nell's definitely got some sort of a gift.'

'You're going to have to be careful. I'm not saying Nell's in danger. But, also, I am saying she's in danger.'

'Somebody's had a very long and fantastic conversation. What were you fitting them for?'

'Don't get shirty with me, William,' Kit grinned. 'That's a cheap and nasty shirt you've got on. Just thought I'd say.'

'Thanks, Kit. So who told you about all the crime scene stuff — do they know our connection?'

'We're not a secret, your step mum's my mum... easy enough for someone to discover if they had a mind to.'

'What was the context of the conversation?'

'They came to warn you. Through me. I asked them for proof. He took me over to a cubbyhole.

'Oh, right, maybe this is the bit you don't mention?'

'Forced me to stick my head in the cubbyhole with them.'

'Okay, you're mentioning it...'

'Their breath, I swear, glowed a bit.'

'You mean it smelled?'

'No, it was like it was condensing on invisible things in the cupboard. And it was my cubbyhole so I knew what was in there and it wasn't what I was seeing.'

'And it was a man'?'

'As far as I could tell. I didn't take their inside leg measurement so I couldn't be certain.'

'And he'd heard of you how?'

'A recommendation. He knows one of my customers. Or several.'

'Who?'

'Albert Lear. That peer who gave up the peerage and distributed his bank accounts among his family. Funny bloke, influential, started this senior citizen cavalry thing —'

'The car crawlers gliding under roadside parked cars?'

'Yes. The same.'

'Captain of industry — once, anyway, old royalty. Once the money goes their families break up like a kicked jigsaw. There's an addendum to that rumour, that you've been given something very powerful by a group of eccentrics.'

'Don't know who or what that could be,' said William, immediately thinking of the nine bulimic cannibals. 'Did they hint at that that might be?'

'He winked, pretended to gnaw my arm and then mimed being sick. Very vulgar I thought. Mean anything to you?'

'No. So what can I do to protect Nell?'

'Give her paid leave.'

'I need three people. We'd be a third understaffed.'

'Better than being a third deceased.'

'What, is it a death threat?'

'Of a kind. A threat by death is probably the right sentence structure there.'

'Are you mixed up in something, Kit?'

'Tailors always are. Time is a paper pattern and a pair of sharpened shears.'

'What?'

'The tonguebird thing. Did it speak?'

'Jacques charmed it. Got it perching on his arm. It spoke to him.'

'Did it say anything cogent?'

'It said 'bastards'…'

'Pretty on the ball there, so?'

'Then it said it wanted revenge. Jacques promised to help it.'

'Careful what you make promises too. There's danger in committing to some small percentage of a person. You don't know what the rest of them is like.'

'Are you staying? Do you want something to drink? Eat?'

'No, no thanks, William. Then there's the pre-existing matter between us. The fairy that came out of your ear. Where is it?'

'I think it got eaten.'

'What!?'

'Mr Ruby. I think he ate it.'

'You know what 'ruby' stands for in folk lore, and folk beliefs, don't you? 'Ruby' has connotations. It signifies communication with spirit guides. Lucid dreams. Hallucinations.'

'Great.'

'Sounds about right?'

'Yes.'

'So where is Mr Ruby?'

'He's hovering and he's laid an egg. He's hovering over it.'

'He's a hen?'

'Nope. He's a rooster and he laid an egg. He's protecting it. Growls if he suspects you're after it.'

'Roosters don't growl.'

'This one does.'

'Let me have a look.'

'He's there. In the corner. Don't disturb him, though. He can kick up a racket. Wake Anne. Wake the kids.'

Kit went over to the corner. 'Knock the light on will you, William?'

'No. Use the flashlight on your phone.' Kit did.

'You're effing right. There's a space between him and his egg and the both of them and the floor. Have you got something I can slide between them? A ruler or, I don't know, a knife?'

'No, it's not a magic trick.'

'I can see it's not a magic trick. It's just me — I measure everything.

'You want substantiated proof. You want Mr Ruby's inside leg.'

'There's that, yeah. When did it start?'

'After he ate that fairy. I'm seeing causality here, Kit'

'This is a wild conversation for two grown men, isn't it? Did I see the fairy?'

'You told me off for keeping it trapped in my earwax.'

'I saw something that might have been one of those Guantanamo worry dolls. A little wire and cloth thing.'

'Guatemalan worry doll. You saw it through the endoscope.'

'I thought I'd seen something. I'm not used to viewing things through medical optometry.'

'He's eaten a fairy and now he's laying an egg. I'd be an idiot if I didn't think the two events aren't linked.'

They watched the cockerel slowly circle over the egg and the egg spin and rotate beneath him.

'And you don't believe in magic?'

'It's not that I claim there's nothing beyond what we call 'normal' just that the NHS shouldn't be shaking shamanic rattles over seriously ill people.'

* * *

Anne shuffled down stairs in oversized fuchsia mules and a floor-length knitted cardigan coat, buttoned out of sequence, over her nightdress. The colour and texture gave her the look of a tree trunk over which her newly dyed green hair shot like new growth after pollarding.

'Oh. Hello Kit. Bit late for a social.'

Kit distractedly hugged Anne and scurried back to the cardboard box with the Mr Ruby in it. 'Anne. Enchanted. But this has ninety per cent of my attention at the moment.'

'You novelty seeker, you.'

'Hello love, have we kept you awake?' said William, hugging his wife who returned a brief embrace then pushed him abruptly away.

'I was awake. Reading. I kept thinking the voices were on the radio — they usually are. Then I recognised your laugh, Kit.'

'Did I laugh?'

'I heard you laugh.'

'Then I must have laughed. This bird of yours. I don't know what to say.'

'It's weird, yes, but it's not threatening weird so it's been shunted to the bottom of the list, hasn't it William?'

'Yes. Bottom of the pile. Birds fly so maybe the next step in their evolution is levitating. Hovering. We take away their nesting areas, their habitats, and they go 'fuck you humans, we'll just float, drift to where the ozone still filters cosmic rays.'

'So evolution in process?'

'Got to happen somewhere so it happens in a front room in London...'

'Look, better go, Richard'll wonder where I am. He's taken a consignment of hat blocks. It's like a police procedural, he has to process them as though they're being inducted into a custody suite not his workroom.'

'How is he?'

'Visa problems. British citizenship got turned down. Nothing a civil partnership won't solve. We'll just shunt the date forward.'

'You never said — oh, congratulations.'

'It was a secret. It was only a secret because we hadn't anything else to be secretive about. It's all shared commons and open access with us.'

'Goodnight.'

'Night, Anne, William. Let me know what happens with egg of Chucky. Maybe even capture it on your phone and, ha ha, wing it across?'

'Maybe. Love to Richard.'

Anne went into the kitchen and returned with a long handled spaghetti spoon.

'Going fishing, dearest,' she said, sitting on her knees, sliding the spoon under Mr Ruby, and gently tapping the spinning egg till it floated out of the box.

'Mind you don't crack it.'

'Mr Ruby, you're some guardian. See, he's let me snaffle it out from under him.'

'No he hasn't.' There was a mad chase in which the tiny cockerel shot after the egg and tried to wrest if from the spoon and Anne attempted to put the living room door between her and the furious, roaring rooster. William grinned as he watched the strangest egg and spoon race in the history of the sport. A noise was coming from the egg. A horrible noise. Anne stopped running and gasped. William's yolk ran cold. The egg slid into the wall...

'It's going to break!' said William. It didn't, it ricocheted gathering velocity as it went. Bang whang ching. Duck! They covered their faces with cushions. The egg pounded them. Winded them both almost simultaneously, striking their bellies, kidneys lungs, hearts, angling beneath the cushions to pound their throats. They hugged each other but felt the egg slide between them and pound them again despite there being no room for it to take a swing back. It was like a bomb that could explode at will, targeting them with pressure waves, shock waves travelling in from the flesh to muscle and bone.

'Anne, this egg could kill — could stop the heart. Run! Come on!'

Hand in hand they out of the room with the egg pounding the back of their heads knocking them senseless. They both came-to outside the door. Grey daylight showed in the arc of glass above the front door. Something was scuffling behind the shut front room door, a dark shape — a nose? a muzzle? a beak? sniffing under the door at them. Then the owner of the snout padded away over the carpet.

'That wasn't Mr Ruby.'

'Oh, dear lord, I hope Mr Ruby's all right!'

'What are we going to do? If the egg was violent, what about the creature inside it?'

'Ring an animal welfare society — tell them a wild animal's got in the front room. Let them deal with it.'

'That'd hardly be fair.'

'This is all because of your crime scene cleaning!'

'No, actually it's a legacy from working at the hospital.'

* * *

A woman turned up. She arrived in a brown paper coloured, unmarked Humvee. They let her in. The girls were still asleep.

'We do exist. And we don't exist. We will do all in our power to help, but you won't see us doing it. These creatures exist but what creatures we are referring to, well, we're not going to tell you,' she said wiping her feet enthusiastically on the welcome mat. 'How big is it?'

'We don't know.'

'And you don't know what it looks like?'

'No.'

'But you're sure it's in the house?'

'Positive. Listen.'

They listened. Something was trotting about and, quite possibly, shaking the rug.

'It hatched out of an egg.

'Oh? That's normal. Hatching.'

'Egg laid by a cockerel hovering three inches above the ground. Is that normal?'

'In some circumstances. Boffins have been hatching eggs in wind tunnels and with some success. Now Nature is suddenly able to do something similar — levitation minus the wind machine. Good old Nature. Rupert Sheldrake calls it 'morphic resonance'. Any other animal in there with it?'

'A cockerel. Bantam. It's mother. Father. We couldn't grab him. He's got a bed in there. On a fleece. Little thing.'

'And you don't think whatever else is in there is a threat to him?'

'Well, it's his chick. Of sorts. I… we had to get out so fast, but there's been no squawks. No screams. It's quiet except for that sniffling and snuffling. But we were attacked. We were beaten unconscious.'

'It knocked you out but you didn't see it?'

'The egg attacked us.'

'You're not the first and you won't be the last.'

'What'll you do with it if you catch it?'

'Kill it.'

'Oh. Oh that doesn't seem right.'

'What do you suggest, then?'

'You've no sanctuary then, for these kind of things?'

'Are you mad? It's not like keeping owls and cats separate. Cryptozoology might have a 'zoo' in the middle of its name but you try keeping aberrations and violent anomalies apart. Behind bars. In cages. Containers. In silos. Too dangerous. Now stand, back, please, let the woman see the whatever it is.'

The woman went in, her green veterinarian overalls giving her a military mien, her patch badges made her look like pack leader of the Brownies. Anne and William peered in after her.

The cockerel was floating but seemed unflustered. Shadows frisked across the wall around it. An eggshell was rocking near the door. The woman bent to pick it up and was seized by the back of the neck by a blur and flown-slammed into the wall opposite. Her head spun round, mouth agog, the thing, still blurred by its speed, bit deep into her neck and blood washed over the furniture. William slammed the door shut.

'Get the girls! Get out!

'Where shall I go?'

'Okay, no, shut yourselves upstairs. Ring the police! Ring Kit!' There was a great crash and William shot back into the room with the upturned enamel basin on the end of his fist like a metal boxing glove. The window was smashed — there was a jagged creature-shaped hole through the panes of glass — the creature had gone. Flown. William went over to the woman. She lay crumpled on the sofa, and he took her pulse, despite the fact that there were quite a lot of her essential parts missing. Anne came back down the stairs.

'Has it gone?'

'Flown. The woman's dead. It's killed her. But it's gone.'

'You sure it's gone? You certain the woman's dead?'

'Yes on both counts.'

'Oh dear lord. I haven't rung the police yet. I thought it might sort itself out. I'll ring the police.'

'And tell them what?'

'What happened. Except about the egg hatching. The rooster levitating. Poor Mr Ruby. And he's still floating.'

'Let's put his food and water dishes on my stack of Spillages and Spurts so he can reach them. Now let's get the cleaning stuff.'

'This poor woman's lost her life... we can't just pretend it's something we can clean up.'

'The paramedics won't be able to do anything for her but I think we can. Let's get the cleaning fludd.'

'You said 'fludd"

'It's what its manufacturers call it. Fludd. Look, you can ring the police. Ring an ambulance. But let's just try some of that cleaning stuff first. You saw what it did with the dog blanket. You felt the dog alive under your hands. We began to doubt he'd died. We began to think he wasn't dead or that his death was different to the one we remembered. And now we can't remember his death at all.'

Anne sped out of the room and came back with the apothecary jars on a tray. She unstoppered the black on and tentatively allowed several drops to splash onto the woman, and into the blood seeping from her. A door opened through the blood stained sofa...

'Was that the door I felt?' said William.

'What?' said Anne. And the Ark builders stepped through it, dug a hole in the floor —

'Tell me that's not going to be a problem, they'll dig through the dap course of they keep going.'

When the hole was big enough, and vaguely boat shaped, they lifted the woman into it, sat her up, stuck a poled road sign for a sail (the triangular warning that the road ahead sometimes had deer trotting across it). The men gave the Ark a little push and off it went, bobbing out of the room, Anne running ahead and opening the front door to let it out. Down the path it sailed and then it turned round the corner and was lost from sight. The men, the three Ark builders now excited back through the sofa, slamming the door behind them.

'There's still a lot of blood,' said Anne.

'Something happens to blood sometimes. We send to experiment...it'll follow her.'

'The blood will follow the woman?' And it did. It formed a soft red stream and sauntered off, the front edge testing the ground ahead of it as though following a scent.

Anne went back upstairs to check the girls. William followed. Then Anne followed William into the kitchen. He made a pot of tea.

'What did those Oracles say, William — you're going to be rich? I want rich. I want power. Why don't the Oracles promise me things. It's always you men. Blah blah you men can be kings and things. We just go with the flow.'

'What I get we share, love,' said William. 'That's how we roll.'

'And that cleaning fluid. Fludd. Don't just clean crime scenes with it. That's a total waste. It's a lot more potent than household or industrial cleaning chemicals. It's got like a...like a mythology with it. Who were those men? What was it with the floating hole. I thought they'd dug a grave for her and were going to leave her buried under our front room.'

'I've seen them before. I've travelled in one of the holes. They're called Arks. Look, if you're okay with the girls, I'll go back to Montgomery Square, to the house where I got his stuff, and ask them about it. Now we have a measure of its potency I can ask them what else it's capable of. I'd rather be told than have to experiment.'

'And are you going to ring Kit and tell him what's happened, or am I?'

'No, don't tell him anything just yet. Let me get more information.'

* * *

William drove through heavy traffic back to Montgomery Square. He found a place to parl. He got out. He turned full circle. The houses were different, as though they'd been shuffled. They were now recognisably present day. The vivid trees had gone. Smaller urban ash and cherry replaced the great, wavering willows. The railings had been swapped for squatter, rust nibbled ones. The park behind them was somehow less embellished, too. In the centre, near a noticeboard pinned full

of torn edges, a statue poked his arm into the air as though
changing a lightbulb. The gates were locked. Socks and gloves
clung to it like the adherent tendons from spiked heads. William
walked along the narrow footpath, past hedges hacked to their
kneecaps. Every detail had shifted pushed along the timeline to
the present. Shunted. They reminded William of Kit's needles
and thread in the mouth trick. The houses had a look of having
been slid rather craftily and dangled in front of him.

There was a steady pulse of older people on car crawlers
passing beneath the parked cars. None of these senior citizens
seemed to pay William any attention. William continued
walking. The gardens were full of large wheeled bins. Nature
had become angled and hard edged. Half a moon lit the sky
alongside a thin scum of stars that looked like petals skewered
on a damp pavement.

William followed several garden paths but when he reached
them, the doors were wrong. The rooms and windows were
brightly lit. Televisions sounded everywhere. Applause. Gun fire.
Dramatic music. Jingles jangled from every direction. No, this
wasn't the right square. The other had removed itself. Gone.
Left. Perhaps they had used their own fludd upon themselves.

* * *

Back home, Ruby was slowly descending, his feet were now only
millimetres off the ground. He was scrabbling anxiously, his
legs working and his wings flexing, just like he did when he was
being lowered to the ground by William or Anne, and he knew
the ground was approaching. His dung had floated behind him,
had slid about in the house's air currents, congregating in a grey
brown mash where the small domestic breezes abandoned them.
It was strange. These unattended few dungs were also slipping
to the floor, now being pooled and pulled by gravity. Then, as

the floor met the cockerel, the cockerel sank. The carpet, the house foundations were hollowing out to take him.

'Grab him, Anne, he's falling through the floor!'

Anne leaned over and lifted him. As she did, the cockerel's legs stretched like chewed gum. There were robin-thin, flamingo length legs on a bantam cockerel. Anne dropped him and his body snapped back and sank a little way and he began walking as though nothing impeded him. No solid floor. He was just half in and half out of the floor, his lower half as invisible as a swimming duck's. But what had hatched out of Mr Ruby's egg? What had hatched out?

☙ CHAPTER 11 ❧

ALL THE WORLD'S A CRIME SCENE

All the world's a crime scene and men and women merely suspects. They have their exit wounds and their entry wounds; and one man in his time has many alibis, thought William, looking at the new moon through the window. It was lying on its back like a lot of people would be in London, right now. Jacques was helping Death Nell set up the decontamination unit.

'Political assassination, eh?' said Death Nell. 'Whose?'

'This was hushed up. News embargo. But it kicked off in here, the constituency office.'

'Posh office.'

'They struck by that little indoor water feature. Quasi Buddhist self-effacing stone thing.'

'Oh, this? Looks like someone's tried carving stone bowling balls.'

'Opposite of water cooler. Not a place for gossip swap, more for karma calming.'

'The sound of water. Relaxing unless you have a troubled bladder.'

'The man was a very forceful figure,' said William. 'A soundbite phenomenon. Oratory styled on traditional leadership, leading from the front, sovereign. He was a slippery ship in a slithery sea. A man of principles and...'

'Oversized hands. He had elephantiasis of the hands, a circulatory problem. He was, however, impressively dextrous with them but for television, with people being people, he had a hand double,' said Jacques. 'He came to the hospital. I wheeled him down to theatre. Nice enough man in the flesh. His hand double stayed with him all the way to the anaesthetic prep bay.'

'What? So nobody outside his cronies or family ever saw his real hands?' said Death Nell. 'Odds bodkins.'

'They once tried a publicity experiment. Had him cradling a baby in the palm of his hand. Then they stood him in the goal at a Derby match before kick-off and kicked balls at him. Basically, nothing got through. And they got him to learn British Sign Language and work as an interpreter for signed performances of West End Shows. Upper circle had no visibility issues.'

'Bet he sustained defensive injuries to his hands, then, when they attacked? In fact, shouldn't they have acted as a pretty comprehensive shield?'

'You'd have thought so. Anyway, they killed him.' Rigged up, wellington booted and face masked they began to clean.

'It's not just in this room, though is it?'

'No, most of the stains are downstairs in the party museum.'

'What political party is this? They have a party museum?'

'They just bought a load of old and ancient stuff and stuck it in glass cases. Tried to give themselves a history. Anyway, when the assassins struck, his body was covered in talismans, medals, religious medals, key rings, all clipped there by his wife. They also deflected the blows. His wife's very superstitious. Had a bad dream the night before about blood flowing from a fountain. She was right.'

'Poor woman.'

'Anyhow, they stabbed him very neatly. They cared about what he looked like in death. It was an attack but one executed with sheer cold resolve with as much attention to detail as signing an international treaty — not that this lot will ever sign anything like that. Not now they've started murdering their own.'

'I vote,' said Death Nell. 'I always vote but I watch the results with the same feeling I watch the lottery draw.'

'The knives were the sort you can buy for carving out pumpkins. Serrated but easily manipulated and controlled. Yes they carved him like they would a pumpkin. He was a showman and an orator. He was respected but not very loved. Multiple assailants. Everyone in his team had turned against him. They threw a white sheet over him and stabbed him through it.'

'To stop his hands?'

'No, none of them were murders by nature but only by political persuasion,' said William. 'Politicians are a kind of portmanteau people. Truthfully duplicitous. They were heard to shout, 'here comes the Death Marquee' when they threw the sheet over him.'

They finished the small matter of spatterings and went down the plain, grey stairs and into the museum. The museum was a mixture of re-articulated animal bones, taxidermy, Victoriana and crumbly, carved oddments from Egyptian tombs.'

'When he was dead, they all stood in a circle round him and sang party songs. Someone had bought a small fortune in balloons and the entire party manifesto had been felt tipped onto them one phrase at a time and these were inflated and fed through a smashed window.

'Go on, they smashed a window?' said Death Nell, gliding her mob along a trail of haemoglobin polka dots.

'The still felt a bit violent. And they fed the balloons — blown up but not tied — in sequence. It got a bit garbled towards the end, the police sirens were approaching, evidently, and they were all spooked. So they were also prosecuted for the environmental menace of so many balloons. Almost a novel-worth. Some, despite having no air or helium in them, went over the Bering Straights and into Siberia.

'They live a different sort of life, don't they, these high end people,' said Death Nell.

'In their own world.'

'That's why they muck up our world, there's no point of contact,' said Jacques.

'Any more clues about the other stuff? This sounds like it's another closed loop. Everyone involved is known. All arrested.'

'Yes, there's been a development, actually. But let's make a start on this. It's congealed blood. People skidded about in it. They ended up looking like ice skaters by the time the police got here, skating. The blood spread across the entire floor, they were caught in vortices and spins.'

'Oh, how horrible, so they were falling and getting bloodied?'

'Yes, some of the more important aids pushed the minions down so their clothes would soak up the blood and allow them escape. Except they were all trapped by the blood, they couldn't get sufficient purchase on the floor to escape from the room. Some skidded into display cases and smashed them. Some ended in the display cases. That's something we have to clean as well.'

'Funny how many different stories spilt blood tells. How many situations it's an ingredient of.'

'Yes,' said William. Jacques was bent over a case reading the information card.

'Someone can't spell.'

'Let me see,' said Death Nell. 'Oh, is that even a word?'

'So when we've done, Bill, is Nell vaping or do you think this is a straightforward political assassination?'

'I'm undecided. I feel more and more certain something's connecting the murders we're cleaning up after. Look at the trail we've followed across London, each time there's a hub — maybe it's Southwark Cathedral, the old Clink land. I don't know. Sometimes it shifts across the river. Someone's zig zagging across London. They seem to have created a giant M. Or it might be a slightly Greek style epsilon.'

'Where the murder scenes are, they're not using London like a giant ouija board, are they?'

'I don't know. I hope not.'

'Not every murderer is good at spelling. It could just be random and we're the ones reading significance into it. Like seeing faces on the moon but's just shadow and rock formation.'

William realised there was a soft humming sound that wasn't the slick and slop of their mops easing the memory out of the room.

'Stop mopping for a moment. Listen. Can you hear that or is it just me?' William was hoping he wasn't in for a full-on crescendo of fairy commuting time again.

'Is that musical saws?'

'It's not some weird art thing is it?'

'Whatever it is and wherever it's coming from we can all hear it. We can all hear it.'

'Evidently,' said Death Nell.

'But are we all hearing the same thing? Hum it.'

They each hummed what they heard and it was something different.

'Sounds like counterparts,' said Death Nell. 'We're each hearing one part of it but it's supposed to be sung together. Shall we all hum what we can hear? Right. On the count of three... one, two, three...'

It was a complete melody. They grinned at each other.

'We should create a Crow Choir,' said Death Nell. 'We're bloody good.'

Three women's heads bobbed up in her bucket, among the fouled water and the suds. Three women's heads one rising another sinking. Bubbling in Death Nell's bucket.

'Fucking hell! Is this because I vape? Is it?' screamed Nell.

'What unearthly forces have we encroached upon? Who's the lady in the bucket, William?' said Jacques.

'I'm not sure.'

'You are sure, William Shakespeare, we've spoken before but behind locked doors. You couldn't see us. Time for a face to face, we thought. Time for a tête-à-tête. That's why we decided to visit you at work. There are fairies present.'

'Oh yes, where would they be, then?' said William. 'Terrific.'

'They've been sewn inside this sumo-fantasist fella here when he had your operation.'

'I had my appendix removed,' said Jacques.

'You had several fairies install themselves at the same time.'

'On purpose? I mean wittingly by surgeons?' said Jacques, gripping his scar.

'Oh no, nothing witting, they took advantage of the open door. They'll quite happily live inside you. '

'They sound like parasites,' said Nell. 'And are we really chatting with heads in our mop buckets? I mean... I'm not even vaping. This is a bit premature.'

'No, not quite parasites. They use your body as a base from which to organise themselves. To undertake their various enterprises. You're like free electricity, my lad.'

'We can all hear singing,' said William. 'Is that them?'

'No, no that's not them.'

'Do you know what it is then?'

'Yes, we know what it is and we're not going to say.'

'Is it a sign of something?' said William.

'Yes, it's a sign. An omen. A message. Everything is.'

'An omen?' said Jacques.

'Forewarned is forearmed.'

'When you have enough fairies inside you, you can transform. Shift shape. Alter. Each fairy alters the configuration of your particular bones. They rework what's there and add anything that keeps the system standing and stable. That's why transformation hurts. They're running about under your skin altering how you connect up, clicking you altogether. Werewolves and the like are due to an infestation of fairies. Hundreds of them. How you behave once you've been transformed is a matter for your own conscience.'

'Oh. That's a bit… don't know how I sit with that. So it's not a bite or a scratch that carries the werewolf into another body?' said Death Nell.

'Well, fairies can hop from one body to another via a bite or a scratch. Then it kicks off again.'

'Can we get back to this music. If it's a warning why isn't it being more explicit? This way we don't know what its's warning us about,' said William.

'You will in good enough time to take action against it. Whilst it remains at this distance it's an alert but not top level… not signifying anything imminent. The thing about danger is that it's not a constant quality. What it is right now may not be what it is when it presents itself. Like people, it can change.'

'I've heard this at home. At night,' said Death Nell. 'The wind blows and you catch a bit of it, like a wisp blown at you, like one of those money spiders on its parachute in the wind. Those are human voices. Well, they're voices, something on the edge of hearing. Doesn't get any louder if you stick your head outdoors. Doesn't lessen if you put the pillow over your head. Even when you flush the toilet you can still hear it, other sounds don't cover it, you can listen to the radio or watch TV and it's there underneath. Like a layer you can always hear. It's sort of a brighter sound than everything else. Lit. Tempo changes. Male and female voices all balanced out. Nothing soars above. Scary. It scares me. I don't know why it scares me.'

'The goosebumps are rising,' said Jacques.

'Yes, gooseflesh. Shivers like when someone walks over your grave.'

'Yeah, well, whatever,' said one of the women's heads. 'We're here for quite a different purpose, William Shakespeare.'

'How are they all fitting in the bucket?' said Jacques.

'There's one in each of the three buckets and we change and change about, we swap and switch and chop and change.'

'Isn't it a bit disgusting being in that filthy water?'

'Water's water. It keeps its distance from what attempts to soil it. We are where we need to be and that is where we must be.'

'Sell your knowledge, William. Time to show what you can do. Your bellybutton's going for good, and when your naval vanishes something will take its place. Your wife, Anne, must give us the third baby born this month. We will appear in the Simulacrum River alongside her and her patient, and we will take the newborn baby and then things will come to pass.'

'You can't have a newborn baby. You can't take somebody's child like that? How's my wife going to explain where it's gone?' said William.

'We'll leave a quality something in its place. The mummy won't know.'

'Like a changeling?' said Jacques.

'Not like a changeling. Changeling's are such old hat. Now, what we leave now is an entertaining thing. Something that is every bit as capable as the child that it's replacing but with one exception. They're little golems. Little waterproof golems. Tiny sorts fetched from a pool where they exist to be brought into the world. We can only use them to defend you if they're accepted and nursed by human mothers. They need to be fed human milk to work the magic. Without that they are inert and incapable of their one great task.'

'What task? Did you know about this, Billy?'

'I did, Nell. Except I thought I was imaging it.'

'Obviously you're not,' said Death Nell. 'Reality's fucked, isn't it, if this is part of it.'

'Ahem,' said one of the women's heads, the bobbing Oracles, 'if we could just trespass for a moment longer on your time.

Okay, These golems replace older golems who have had their hands and arms torn off in the Great Fight.'

'Painful,' said Death Nell.

'It is essential we have the child. The child will be returned unharmed. They will be nurtured in the heraldic forest by Innocents.'

'Who?' said Jacques. 'Innocence?'

'We may take you there, William Shakespeare, to see how this is done. An Ark will take you.'

'What's an ark? Like Noah's?'

'We do not address you, Nell D'eath except to warn you. There is danger in channelling the images of death. There is danger in allowing your body to exhume them from their rest. You are stealing from the store when you do so. You are stealing from the store and they will trace you track you down and you will lose what you cannot afford to lose.'

'Like what?' said Death Nell. When you get a threat you should at least know how much of a threat it is.'

Jacques knelt down and peered into the bucket. 'What are you, exactly? I mean, I know Japanese myths and all that and disembodied heads have their place. But what are you? Billy's wondering that too, aren't you?'

'I know what they are, Jacques,I think I have a handle on that.'

'Righto. And you'll tell us when you've time?'

'Yes. As they said they're Oracles.'

'Righto. Oracles. Consider me up to speed.'

'Something's coming this way and you'd better not shout I'm telling you why, Santa is coming to town.'

'He knows when you've been naughty.'

'How can I build up my business. I need to do that for all your efforts to amount to anything. Am I right?'

'Thought you'd never ask.'

'Well, I have asked. Please tell me.'

'Use the black then the white then the red, seven drops each and that is all. On the floor here. Inside a circle. Then you'll be brought fame and fortune and publicity. Do not watch what happens. You must never see how things and people are altered. Magic's a blindfolded art. Scrutiny impinges on its efficacy, as they say. You must close your eyes and wonders will work for you. People will come into your life with answers. Watch and pray and listen and obey. All will be well. '

'Your next reward is coming accept it with humility and use it with grace. Be alive to the moment be dead to temptation. Here is a man who died because people had reassessed his powers and found it was not sufficient for a warrior god. Where you root yourself should give you enough magic to contend with the robbing sky, and with the first hard lessons.'

The heads bobbed together. Blew out a few sudsy mouthfuls of filthy water and sank. Jacques followed them with his mop, pushing down into his bucket until he felt the floor, then wiping around at the sides, just to ensure they weren't lurking under the bit where he squeezed his mop.

'Gone.'

* * *

The next day, William was reconsidering his past. He remembered the Blood Experiment.

Midnight. Hail and well met, thought William, we were the Clandestine Four, come to do the blood path test, one that the Path lab never did. We were anonymous — unknown to each other, although we could have guessed if we wanted to — and we must have cut a freakish silhouette as we scurried to our secret rendezvous. Our headgear made us outlandish. That one lamp post shone like a sweet wrapper in a bag of coal. Darkness hid us, the hospital's moon shadow deepened the darkness. William had lead the way. He had the key. South followed behind with the mobile heater with the thermostat. East came next with

171

syringes, hypodermics, test tubes and medicated swabs. West fetched up last with the lipped, silicon tray, one metre square, and the blood pressure cuffs, the ones that now dangled on the telephone wires outside the house.

Inside the builder's site office there was give to the floor, a resonance and chime that bounced our footfalls. We hopped, skipped in the dark, gaffer taping the small windows with black cloth. South plugged in the heater with the thermostat turned to body temperature, we all slipped off our jackets to reveal short-sleeved hospital blues. West cleared a space on the desk and we arranged ourselves around the sterilised silicon tray having used a spirit level app to check that everything was level. Yes, everything was spirit level level. Next, by the light of our phones we wound the blood pressure cuffs round our arms, swabbed a patch of skin clean and slid the hypodermics into our raised veins. We drew off 20 mils of blood, un-cuffed, staunched, applied a plaster. We were serious and thorough. WE then switched on the office lights. Our faces and identities were hidden from each other — South's head was enveloped by a paper bag with eyeholes cut into it, and a bowler hat over a Tibetan bonnet, East wore a pink balaclava and sunglasses, West had face-painted himself to resemble Constable's Haywain, and William was behind a generic Hallowe'en mask. However, our medical histories had been shared and pored over. We were two men, two women. They called ourselves after compass points. William was North. Then they'd sat four square to each other and scribbled lines of blood like they were making one of those picture puzzles 'which fishing line has the old boot dangling from it' — they wove and interlaced, melded and puddled, swirled and curlicued the bloods, adding calligraphic flourishes. They had scroodled-out their blood, and when the syringes were empty they pricked their thumbs till a dot welled up and dunked that at the end of their own blood trail. Then they'd waited, keeping their thumbs pressed down into the blood skeins. They'd videoed it. Filmed it on their phones. Four hours passed. The blood slowly unscrambled into four equal slops and gathered round their thumbs. Four pools, four thumbs. They each sucked it back into the syringes and checked how mixed it was. They were four different blood groups. O, A positive, B negative, AB negative. Splosh, into the test tubes; simple reagents confirmed the blood was unmixed. Each type had isolated itself and returned towards the flesh it had been drawn from.

Had they chatted during the four hour wait? No. How did they come to meet to do such an experiment? William had advertised. William had sieved and selected from the anonymous responses. People who worked in hospitals tended towards the arcane. Blood replies to blood. Blood will have blood. Was that all part of the same magical mindset that William had exposed, he wondered? Had he been party to the superstition? Was he a hypocrite.

In a previous experiment their hands had been incarnadined as the blood climbed back onto them, clinging, dripping, there was a pulsed roll in the small puddles, like miniature bore-tides, as though they still moved when the four hearts pushed them. Once the bloods touched the flesh they had been sucked from, it died. It dried out, setting in vermillion crusts and coral, in umber slicks and blue-black pitted leaves.

If enough people said 'shush', thought William, it would deafen the world.

CHAPTER 12

ANNE SHAKESPEARE & JUST WILLIAM

FROM ANNE SHAKESPEARE'S POETRY CHAPBOOK ANGELS HELP ME WITH MY WASHING

WONDERCRAWLER

poor albert lear has gone away
they threw him on his back till he looked askew
and put the blame on you-know-who
police won't find a single clue
it seems unlikely that anyone
feels someone's got away

You are old, Albert Lear,
the young man said
and your companion wears nothing but white
and yet you incessantly slide under cars
do you think, at your age, it is right?

William, Nell and Jacques were in the Crow hatchback negotiating the traffic in Brentford. The street lamps gave everything the brassy yellow bloom of trophies handed out as consolation prizes at community sports days.

'Albert Lear had been found in the sub-basement level of a multi storey carpark. There was CCTV footage of him on his car crawler accompanied by a very reduced retinue. There they went, negotiating the ramps, gliding beneath the parked cars then down the ramps again, coming to settle at the farthest, darkest corner. Dead. Albert Lear's youngest daughter was also found with a tow rope around her neck, dead. She seemed to have been towing someone on the car crawler. The pathologist said that she had died of towing. She had been horizontally hung. Some friend of the Lear's had been friend blinded. Lear's closest crony, Hercule Pierrot, was missing, and thought to have hanged himself but no body had been found, just the dangling skein of rumour. A couple of sad corpses, father and daughter, left undiscovered for a week in an overpriced, barely used multi storey carpark in an economically stagnant patch of the metropolis. Seemed the old man's other daughters may have killed the youngest. He went into cardiac arrest — well, it's cold down there, and combined with the shock… So the murders left the bodies. Another closed loop. The police aren't looking for anyone else connected with it.

'Thought we were only doing high end crime scenes, Billy?'

'The crime scene might not be high end but the deceased were.'

'Grim place to die.'

'Grim place to park.'

'What's the thing about the car crawlers. I've seen them sliding under the traffic — even moving traffic when it's slowed in the centre of the city.'

'I don't know. It's a nifty. Keeps you fit.'

'They're getting a bit of a liability to be honest.'

William climbed out to release the police tape cordon, drove through the barrier, then climbed back out to replace the tape. The last thing William wanted was for that odd, tulle-veiled woman with the heavy arms to buzz round them whilst they worked.

'The car park's closed till further notice. Nobody's inconvenienced because nobody noticed. Couple of rough sleepers found the bodies,' said William as he coasted into the basement and parked up.

'Again, police aren't searching for anyone else. Closed loop.'

They changed into their gear, hoisted their paper hoods and snapped the face mask elastic round the back of their heads. Goggles on, buckets primed, mops swabbing, plunged and rung.

'We're not going to get those women's heads back in our buckets again are we, William?' said Death Nell.

'No, I shouldn't think so.'

'They asked a lot of you, didn't they?' said Jacques. 'I mean, asking Anne to steal babies.'

'Yes, stuff and nonsense. As if Anne would, under any circumstances.'

'You're okay. I've got bleeding fairyland sewn up in my abdomen,' said Jacques. 'I can feel them. Now I know they're there. I can feel them, especially when I lie down. When I lie down I make a better floor for them to cavort across.'

'I think she was having you on,' said Death Nell.

'Right. Three women's heads appear in a bucket — or buckets — and tell you stuff. You think they are, like, unreliable narrators?'

'Definitely. You don't know what they're agenda is. They might be other-worldly and freaky, but that doesn't mean they don't have agendas and ulterior motives,' said Death Nell.

'Yeah, you're right,' said Jacques.

'I don't know what to believe,' said William. 'Except I'm not about to lose my moral compass.'

'Well, on the other hand, business is bucking up, isn't it? You're doing really well. Jacques says you were buying another house. Up market. Hampstead Garden.'

'Yes, we are. You might have noticed larger salaries, too.'

'Yes, we did.'

'Yes, thanks, Bill.'

'Thing is, Nell, Jacques, we're working in a kind of limbo. Who knows what's what?'

William checked for further contamination with the UVA wand, and then did an unnecessary radial mop just for the hell of it.

'Just be sure,' he said. 'Just to round off the site. Like mopping up any spilled...'

'Auras,' said Death Nell. 'Could you get aura smudge? Do they decay or do they like, pop as soon as the source is switched off?'

'I don't know if I believe in auras,' said William. 'Remember, I went against the occult NHS. Auras are in the category of beast I fought against.'

'I've seen an aura,' said Jacques.

'I bet,' said William. 'When you were doing sumo.'

'No, it's the optical distortion you get with migraine's called. A crystalline aura. I have migraines. Just the optical bits, feel a bit nauseous but I don't get the walloping big headaches. Just I go a bit partially sighted for half an hour. Funny thing. Bad if it happens when I've got to cross busy roads. I don't drive cos they happen a lot. Unpredictable things.'

'Auras?' said Death Nell. 'Neurological tics. Not the radiance of a soul leaking from the body. Like microwaves from a faulty oven.'

'Nah, just a temporal lobe glitch. Had them since I was fifteen. In fact, the first one I couldn't see out of my left eye. Very strange. Told my dad but he just waved his hands at me. Told me he'd no time for that, enough on his plate. Packed me off to school.'

'Funny sort of dad.'

'Not really. Just not interested. Fair enough. Why should

parents be interested in their kids? He went odd after my mum disappeared into the sea. He used to tap his teeth. Get tunes out of them. Said he was playing sea shanties.'

They tidied round.

'Concrete's horrible, isn't it, when it's gone grey like this? Do you think sunlight'd mellow it or make it look even bleaker?'

'Bleaker.'

'So, let's get the lamps unrigged and then, if you're ready, what about a spot of vaping, Nell?'

'Yeah, that means you're not convinced everyone's rounded up, all's sorted and the crime scene accounts for all perpetrators?'

'Let's look at what's happened. Moneyed, powerful families either destroyed or a generation removed from the picture. Why? Why is it these families are sustaining the destruction of an entire bundle of relatives? New unrelated people are taking their place. You arrest Mr Lear's other daughters and sun in laws for murder and that's that family cleared from the playing board. These murders create opportunities, they are all about handing over power to people who would not have gained it otherwise. That priory also got two new fetish objects, they'll make bejewelled relics of the two deceased lovers.'

'They were an odd pair,' said Death Nell.

'You suspect that the friar is in league with a kind of master criminal, a serial killer?'

'I've not ruled it out.'

'Have you got more?'

'I've been doing some digging. The woman with the heavy hands. The one spelling out words. She's somehow connected. There was another woman — before we began doing this, my last day at the hospital — a woman orchestrated an attack on me.'

'What, she gave you a kicking?'

'No, no she didn't touch me but... this is going to sound weird. I didn't tell the police because it sounded... well...'

'Hurry up, anticipation's giving me hiccups.'

'It was a bear.'

'Go on with you.'

'I thought it was a horse box with a horse inside. She'd stopped ahead of me and flagged me down. I presumed she'd notice my doctor sticker on the car. Needed an emergency look-over — doctors, vets, you'd grab what you could if there was an emergency. But what loped out of the van was a bear. It ran at me.'

'What did the woman do?' They took off their soiled overalls, bagged them up, slipped off wellingtons, eased on boots, shoes and trainers.

'She seemed to be busy texting someone. I jumped over a hedge and it didn't bother coming after me. It just went back up the ramp and the woman drove off.'

'Did she say anything? Didn't she try and control the bear or say something threatening? I mean, if I was setting a bear on somebody I'd have a choice sentence to say about it. That kind of thing deserves some sort of announcement.'

'Nothing. Well, she seemed to be saying something but I couldn't hear her. I got out of my car to try and catch what she was saying. She was twirling a banana skin round her index finger. Like a gunslinger'd sling a gun. Looked like she'd put in a heap of practice?'

'A banana skin?'

'She stank like bananas left to fester.'

'So, shall I vape?'

'Yes, please, Nell. If you're okay?'

Death Nell took out her E-Cigarette. She puffed. Sucked. Shook the stem. Puffed again. 'Sorry, William, the battery's flat. I charged it before I came out but there's obviously no juice.'

CHAPTER 13

THE FOLLOWING WEEK

The very substance of the ambitious is merely the shadow of dream. How far that little candle throws his beams: so shines a good deed on a weary world. Out, out brief candle.

Life's but a walking shadow, a poor player that struts and frets his hour upon the stage and is heard no more. It is a tale told by an idiot, full of sound and fury, signifying nothing.

* * *

The hatchback turned left into a drive shaped like a jiggled circle. The surface flashed in the late afternoon sunlight.

'This is called Millionaire's Tarmac,' said William. Jacques slid on his sunglasses.

'Like synapses sparking randomly in a dream, my friend,' he said.

'It's quite pretty, actually,' said Death Nell.

'There's a ceremony attached to it. The tarmac's laid, then whilst it's still hot, young men and women in heat-resistant shoes walk across it, walk a kind of mandala made up of the coat of arms, and scatter the polished gemstones from baskets.

Then a prayer's said. It's always laid on the day of a full moon. There's a party to celebrate its first glittering night.'

'Like when you get a vajazzle,' said Death Nell, 'speaking personally.'

William slowed down. The flickers and surges of light looked like the ground received the fallout from every snapped necklace in the universe, the tarmac sentient to every bead apocalypse. William wound down his window to let in the warm, evening air. Birds sang. They climbed out.

William touched the stone of the castle, as though for luck. Jacques stretched, Death Nell walked to the low knot garden hedge. The shrubs were as tightly bunched as though gripped by teeth, by a herbivore who'd torn them loose and was thoughtfully masticating from below, winding them in with its incisors. Fountains juggled invisible clubs next to them, the water as silvery as saliva.

Hefting the bags of equipment from the hatchback's boot, William stopped to let a male grouse totter past like a collapsed golden harp, whilst two peacocks teased the cold end of the spectrum and moved it a little further out of reach.

'It just shouts 'POSH!' doesn't it?' said Death Nell.

'Peacocks put in lot of effort to look good,' said Jacques, 'and then they sing like cats on valium.'

The sun was setting and the castle had breathed out after holding in its stomach. Its walls extended further and its bloat spread, the girth emancipated. The west side of the castle was burdened by an external glass lift.

'Ouch. That's what I call an eyesore,' said William.

'I quite like it,' said Jacques. 'It's like a bumbag on a rugby player.'

William checked his notes. 'Evidently, a young woman went mad and lived in the glass lift for a week before plundering the herb garden and gifting sprigs to her relatives. Shall we go in?'

Really? There was a magician who lived in a suspended glass

box for a month and everyone threw sandwiches at him. Maybe that's where she got the idea?'

'I still think it looks like a bumbag on a rugby player.'

* * *

The great oak front door was open. 'We're to go in,' said William. The new owners are on the top floor until we've finished.

'Surprised they've stuck around after the murders.'

Well, distance wise, given the vastness of their living space, it's like they've moved across town.'

They set up the decontamination and changing unit and got into their gear just outside the great hall. A great chequerboard floor. Death Nell pushed the door open and looked in. Two great glass chairs on a raised dais. Behind them a map of the world with the rose compass needle as a fencing foil. The faces partially under gauzy net on a frame that looked like the face guard. Glass tables. Glass tables with little keys sealed into the centre and on the walls hundreds of little doors, doors of various sizes

'Bling bling that's my thing,' said Death Nell. 'In a kind of dynasty you'd have expected to find heirs and heiresses with hearts like funeral urns.'

We have a lobby to ourselves where we can set up the changing and decontamination area.'

'What's the story behind this, then, Bill?'

'They hosted the Annual Fencing Society Ball. Things got out of hand. The people who died are royal contenders — a lineage history sidelined into bad marriages and stupid behaviour. Evidently.'

'Ooh, there's vindictiveness,' said Death Nell.

William shuffled into his overalls and sniffed. Yes, the castle had a smell all of its own. It smelled like the ancestor of all barbecues, something soft and flayed dangled over fire by compact muscle and newly forged iron. The deer heads had been given human range glass eyes whilst the family portraits were all doe and buck-eyed. Soft brown eyes, animal brown, the whites hidden, gave a fierceness to death and a docility to the far from biddable temperaments of their sitters.

'Their eyes don't follow you around like other paintings do,' said Jaqcues. 'They stay fixed on what they're looking at. Yep, there's not a direct look among them.'

Yes, the paintings blanked you, thought William. They patently looked away. Ignored you. The Dead ignoring the Living. '

'Do they know about my thing when I vape? Do they know the Dead come out of me like watery play dough — and I just checked, the e-ciggy's functional?'

'No. But it's something we need to do. We've got to get more clues. This is a similar high-society, closed circuit murder. The police don't believe anyone else is involved. We know better. Never the same modus operandi but...'

'Always the same imagination. Yep, we mustn't be stifled by facts.'

'What's the damage?'

'This time it's blood. Vomit — there were several poisonings as well as blood lettings.'

'Must've been a pretty good annual dinner.'

'Yes. Because of the high rank of the attendees no photographs have been issued. No one wants to be associated with the events.'

A man scuffled in. He was booted in armour, the long toed sort, it crunched against the floor, and the spurs were cocked at his heel as daintily as little fingers behind a teacup. The man shrugged and blinked at them. His eyes were ringed and his nose was long and close to his face. He was whistling, the lips ruched even when the whistling stopped. The air answered him, a great gust came and ambled about him, twisting his clothes, corkscrewing them against his body, first one way then another.

'You'll not be cleaning here tonight, William Shakespeare. We're at the dance,' the man hissed.

'I guess your name in one: Rumpelstiltskin,' said William. Heard it before.'

'You're going to dance on blood?'

'It makes the finest and most magnificent of ballrooms. But follow me now, I have something to show you. Follow. Follow. No mortal has seen this before but.'

William waved at Nell and Jacques and pointed at the man to show he was just popping out with him. Nell and Jacques carried on setting up.

You're a fairy, I take it.

'I take it,' said the Fairy.

'Finding you in the ultrasound scan alongside a human foetus was a little trying.'

'We go where we must. No place is barred from us. We hold sport where it is good. Come now.'

The fairy, his feet echoing and his tail of bracken and bullrushes swished behind him.

'My tail? It's for ceremonial purposes. You might have swords, we have the ingredients of a spell. Each assortment of plants would give quite a different result. That's how we indicate who we are, what we intend. We can be read by them.'

'And what does your tail imply, sir,' said William.

'It's to blind the firstborn for fifteen generations. I do not like to be watched. I shan't use the spell but it speaks of my intentions in the coil of the ferns and fathom of the grass ears. Spells are plain speakers.'

The fairy man led William along a dark corridor, down steps, down more steps now rougher hewn and with greater wear so that each steps was sunken and held the feet like cupped hands.

'Down here, sir, are things that would overshoot the world and make us all change. The thing that hatched from your cockerel's egg has taken refuge down here but it won't remain in the darkness for much longer. Your pet cockerel has hatched your nemesis. Your nemesis. Your...

William looked up. He was holding the mop. The area was spotless.

'Oh, daydreaming there for a moment.'

'Okay, Billy, I'll start vaping. Jacques, you recording this?

'Yes, said Jacques. 'I'll catch everything. Bill's going to write it down. Get a transcript, in case technology gets fouled by the energy. Hey, we're a lot more organised than when we started!'

Death Nell began sucking the tiny metal-latticed pipe. Out came fragments.

'Like the cutting room floor,' said Death Nell. The bits we won't see in the greater picture.'

'I've got them on record,' said Jacques.

'I'm drawing them,' said William. Nothing'll be lost. Keep going, Nell.

A young man appeared. He wore a teeshirt that announced him as THE GREAT PROCRASTINATOR. Another young man appeared at his side.

'I'll tell you what happened,' said the young man. 'This is the truth or my name's not Hamlet. Okay, Laertes?'

'Go on, then. Explain yourself,'

'They told me you had been to her
and mentioned me to him
she gave me a good character
but said I could not swim

he sent them word I had not gone
we know it to be true
if she should push the matter on
what would become of you

I gave her one, they gave him two
You gave us three or more
they all returned from him to you
though they were mine before

if I or she should chance to be
involved in this affair
he trusts to you to set them free
exactly as we were

my notion was that you had been
before she had this fit
an obstacle that came between
him and you and it

Don't let him know she liked them best
for this must ever be
a secret kept from all the rest
between yourself and me
Oh here's that ghost...'
A ghost appeared.
Thou comest in such a questionable shape

like an ambulatory egg,' said Hamlet.
'That I will speak to thee: I'll call thee Hamlet,
King, father, royal Dane: O, answer me!'

The ghost just shook his head, pointed, then went out in the
direction he had indicated.

'Go on; I'll follow thee although it is not just the fog that
rolleth...'

[Exeunt Ghost and HAMLET]

However the egg only got large larger and more and more human. When he had come within a few yards of it Hamlet thought it had eyes and when he had come close to it he saw it was the King his father's ghost. It can't be anybody else Hamlet said to himself. I'm as certain of it as if the King my father's name were written all over his ghostly face.

It might have been written 100 times easily on that enormous face. Hamlet Senior was sitting with his legs crossed on the top of a battlement and such a narrow one that Hamlet Junior quite wondered how he could keep his balance and wondered, should the `king his Father's Ghost fall off, would he plunge directly back into hell; and that the King his father's ghostly eyes were steadily fixed in the opposite direction and he didn't take any notice of Hamlet Junior, he thought he must be a residual spectre after all. Hamlet noticed the way the King his Father's Ghost was sitting, ensconced in his armour, the moonlight giving it the look of a large white egg shell with the sulphurous vapours of hell enshrouding it.

'And how exactly like a boiled egg he is,' said Hamlet Junior aloud standing with his hands ready to catch him for he was every moment expecting him to fall. 'He even smells like a boiled egg.'

'It's very provoking,' the King his Father's Ghost said after a long silence looking away from Hamlet Junior as he spoke, 'to be called a boiled egg— very.'

'I said you look like a boiled egg' Hamlet Junior gently explained, 'and some boiled eggs are very regal you know,' he added hoping to turn his remark into the sort of compliment he thought the King his Father's Ghost might like.

'You,' said the King his Father's Ghost, looking away from Hamlet Junior as usual, 'have no more sense than a baby.'

'You're wrong,' said Hamlet junior. 'Twas brillig, and the slithy toves did gyre and gimble in the wabe: all mimsy were the borogroves and the mome wraiths outgrabe,' said Hamlet Junior. 'I am neither a baby nor mad.'

The King his Father's Ghost took out his pocket watch. 'But, soft! methinks I scent the morning air; Brief let me be. Sleeping within my orchard, My custom always of the afternoon, Upon my secure hour thy uncle stole, and tipped some poison in my hole. The leperous distil took effect and into hell I promptly checked

Thus was I, sleeping, by a brother's hand Of life, of crown, of queen trepanned Cut off even in the blossoms of my sin, my soul let out, all hell let in O, horrible! O, horrible! most horrible!

Adieu, adieu! Hamlet, remember me.'

'I'll just swap liquids. Just a mo,' said Death Nell. 'I'm trying cherry cola. Okay. We're off.'

Vapour slewed into the air around them. Shapes formed.

The king shouted, 'Fetch the stoup of wine! I'm putting something in it for Hamlet. A pearl. A big one. See. Bloody whopper gobstopper.' The king tied a label around the goblet. It said 'DRINK ME' in very fine print. The king pointed to Hamlet, then pointed to the goblet. He mouthed the words,

'Something in it for you,' and acted out glugging it back.

It was all very well to say 'DRINK ME,' but the wise little Hamlet was not going to do that in a hurry.

'No, I'll look first,' he said, 'and see whether it's marked *'poison'* or not'; for he had read several nice little stories about people who had got tricked into going abroad with so-called friends who intended to have him murdered, and about others eaten up by bears, and other unpleasant things, all because they would not remember the simple rules their Dead Father had taught them such as, that a red-hot poker inserted into the anus will kill without leaving any outward marks (other than soot on the drawers), and that, if you cut your finger very deeply with a knife, it usually bleeds; and he had never forgotten that, if you drink from a bottle marked 'poison' it is almost certain to disagree with you, sooner or later.

However, the king had not added any warnings to the label so Hamlet put out his hand to sip but Gertrude grabbed the goblet first —

'Don't drink it, Gerty!' shouted the king — but she ventured to taste it, and, finding it very nice (it had, in fact, a sort of mixed flavour of rue, rosemary, dead men's fingers, long purples, cherry tart, custard, pine-apple, roast turkey, toffy, and hot buttered toast), she drank half straight off. It wasn't a crisp Chianti. In fact, she couldn't place the variety or vintage.

'What a curious feeling!' said Gertrude. 'I must be shutting up like a telescope drunk!'

And so it was indeed: she was now only ten inches high. Nobody seemed to have noticed, not even Hamlet who'd been prodded in the back by his opponent, Laertes. For safety, Gertrude shuffled under the glass table she'd been sat at. She waited for a few minutes to see if she was going to shrink any further: she felt a little nervous about this; 'for it might end, you know,' said Gertrude to herself, 'in my going out altogether, like a candle. I wonder what I should be like then?' And she tried to fancy what the flame of a candle looks like after the candle is blown out, for she could not remember having seen such a thing.

'Out, out, brief candle! Life's but a walking shadow, a poor player that struts and frets his hour upon the stage and is heard no more. It is a tale told by an idiot, full of sound and fury, signifying nothing,' Gertrude said, frightening herself a little.

After a while, finding that nothing more happened, she stepped back out where she might be seen. Hamlet saw her.

'Look to the queen!' Hamlet yelled.

'Where is she?' the courtiers asked.

'There! Ouch, a palpable hit!' Laertes had poked Hamlet in the back.

And they were off again, fencing fit to bust. Gertrude had a little cry. She felt odd. She was tiny. Fortunately, her clothes had also shrunk, otherwise she would have had to run down her sleeve to keep decent and poke her head out of the frills.

Soon Gertrude's eyes fell on a little glass box that was lying under the table; she opened it, and found in it a very small cake, on which the words 'EAT ME' were beautifully marked in currents. 'Well, I'll eat it,' said Gertrude, 'and if it makes me grow larger, good!'

She ate a little bit and said anxiously to herself 'which way? Which way?', holding her hand on the top of her head to feel which way it was growing and she was quite surprised to find that she remained the same size. To be sure, this is generally what happens when one eats cake — there is a sideways embellishment of girth; but Gertrude had so much into the way of expecting nothing but out-of-the-way things to happen, that it seemed quite dull for life to go on in the common way.

'Curioser and curioser!' cried Gertrude (she was so much surprised, that for the moment, she quite forgot how to speak good English), 'Now I'm opening out like the largest telescope there ever was! Goodbye, feet! (for when she looked down at her feet, they seemed to be almost out of sight, they were getting so far off). 'Oh my poor little feet, I wonder who will put on your shoes and stockings for you now, dears?'

Hamlet stared up at his towering mother.

'Look to the queen!' he said. This time it was impossible for anyone not to look to the queen. She was nine feet tall and growing.

'The wine,' Gertrude said. 'And this cake. They've done for me!'

Hamlet grabbed the goblet, drank and shrank to the floor.

'Well, pimp my stature!' Hamlet cried.

'Me, too! Pimp mine!' said Laertes and swallowed the last mouthfuls and shrank. Gertrude leaned over them. The cake will make you tall again,' she said. 'It has me!'

'What have I done,' said the king. 'Oh, fie, look to the queen!'

Gertrude, Hamlet and Laertes shot up and down, towering over the guests one moment, their hair mussed by the ceiling one minute and then by the backs of their own shoes the next. And they continued to vary. At times they seemed to stall, stay, and the king and the court tried to embrace them, but after a minute or two they were growing or shrinking again. Sometimes so quickly that they blurred.

'Treachery!' shouted Hamlet.

Gertrude's head sat on her feet and she chewed the buckle of her shoe. Up and down Laertes, Hamlet and Gertrude shot, snatching a mouthful of cake as they fought the effects of the wine. Chins thudding into shoes, necks bending as their heads struck the ceiling's bosses and drew plaster dust around them. They all wept.

'I die, I die!' said Hamlet.

'I am dead,' said Laertes.

'I'm done for,' said Gertrude. 'It is all up with me.' The light from the table lamps stayed at their chins and their great, high-up heads were balls of spectral hollows. Up and down they shot, weeping, their bodies beginning to collapse under them, their necks writhing as they fell, then bodies snapping shut so their heads were back on their feet and their feet were kicking in the throes of death, and their heads shot in every direction, coming to rest at the king's feet. He lifted his feet off the floor.

'Aye me,' he said, 'and drank what was left in the goblet. He grew. He shrank. He shrank more and went out like a candle.

Then a boney hand appeared, holding a handful of teeth which it carefully arranged in the air above the tragedy. Then it sang.

'how doth the serial killer improve their body count?
they pass unseen like air through air
and make the pressure mount

how cheerfully they seem to grin,
how neatly spread their hate
and welcome every victim in
Like Saint Peter at the Gate'

'Blimey,' said Death Nell, pulling the e-cigarette from her lips. 'This time it was like a joint.'

❧ CHAPTER 14 ❧

THE FOLLOWING WEEK–ANOTHER ONE

The Spillages and Spurts trade journal Annual Dinner was always held in a giant, converted Elizabethan dovecot in the gardens of Thebes Manor, a building close enough to New Scotland Yard to hear the desk sergeant's phone ring. William, Anne, Nell and Jacques were seated together beneath diaphanous awnings painted with assorted cloud formations — the one above them was a towering cumulonimbus. Lit from within by storms, it resembled a corkscrewed castle with lights shining through myriad archers' windows.

On a small raised dais the MC, Hermione Falstaff, editor of Spillages and Spurts, pressed the button to set the ceiling mounted glitter ball spinning. Applause greeted its ignition. This glitter ball was the equivalent of trophy and accolade. The glitter-ball had been technically enhanced, the light beam hitting its rotating mirrors creating a sequence of luminal-effect blood spatter patterns that swept across the diners. It was always a matter of great rivalry whose crime scene blood spatters revolved around the dovecote. Every crime scene cleaning business recorded the stains during pre-clean documentation. They were uploaded onto the Spillages and Spurts website along with the 'after' photos. The stains that had been removed best of all were the ones that were returned ephemerally, the way mediums returned spirits into the company of those who saw them depart. William's eyes were tracking the dazzling flight with an unmistakable look of recognition and triumph.

'That's ours,' said Death Nell to Anne. 'A lot of ours are like spray-painted stencils. One of them was saucepans. We also got fencing foils, and a car crawler. Our spray always seems to have hit things.'

'Well done, Nell, Jacques,' said William.

'That's just ever so slightly wrong,' said Anne as the pattern glittered over her. 'Ever so, ever so slightly disturbing. Hey but well done you three,' Anne raised her glass to them as food was waitered to their tables and drinks refreshed.

The cuisine was always vegetarian, few people in the trade had the stomach to eat meat. Then it was cabaret time. The MC vacated the dais after announcing the singing sensation that was Chacun a son Gout. Nine fuchsia gowned people crowded onto the platform, their hair coiffed to look like ornate plaster mouldings. William shuddered. He could feel the cold air rolling off them as they began to sing torch songs a cappella. He knew who they were. He grasped Anne's hand. 'It's them. It's the bulimic cannibals, the people who gave me the cleaning fludd!'

'My, aren't they a talented family. I wonder if they're related to the Von Trapps?' said Anne. 'Creating cleaning fludds that wipe out all trace of death, and singing pitch-perfect harmonies, they ought to be bottled for posterity.' William noticed how uneasy his fellow crime scene cleaners seemed as the Nine flowed through the immaculate heartache of their repertoire. Someone tapped him on his shoulder but, when he turned round, there was no one there. He grimaced at his fellow tradesmen. How childish. Just because his spatter patterns, not theirs, were rolling across the cloud-painted awnings like a fleet of UFOs.

Desserts cleared, coffee served, the bulimic cannibal torch singers applauded and dispatched, the DJ took over. It was as though pins and needles had crept into the air in the room and it was now being chaffed back into comfort. Anne led William to the dance floor and shook him around a bit in time to the music whilst Nell and Jacques watched. Another of their splatter patterns circled the room.

'Do you think William told Anne about what's been happening? You know, the heads in the buckets?'

'The heads in the buckets demanding Anne does a spot of baby trafficking?'

'Do you think she has any idea?'

'They're close, aren't they? Look at them. Do you think Bill doesn't talk about work?'

'It's not the kind of work you offer up as family banter, is it? I don't mention it to my kith and kin, do you?'

'I have no kith and kin. Just Matt. The friend I flat share with.'

'Oh, I didn't know you were an orphan.'

'It's not really something I think about,' said Matt. 'My mum died when I was a toddler. Vanished into the sea. My dad died three years ago. Then this doctor came up to me on the ward and said dad'd donated his body to medical science.'

'Your dad never told you?'

'No. They just whisked his body from the morgue and into the prep room. Embalmed him and all the rest and then he went off to the medical students. Never left the hospital he died in. That's why I went and worked there as a porter. I used to bob into the dissection room — don't know whether it's called that — but where the students worked on their bodies. I tried to see if I could find him. Just to, you know, say it was okay. I was okay with what he'd done. I presume he never told me his intentions because he thought I'd try and stop him. Anyway, I had a decko at a few of the bodies, didn't see him among them, and came out. When I thought about it afterwards it made me think of Advent Calendars. The bodies were advent calendars but ones where you had to cut out your windows.'

'Bloody hell. And you're sure your dad was in there somewhere?'

'He must have been. But I thought, what would I do if I saw

him like that?'

'It's all done respectfully. It's all done with a view to maintaining the person's dignity.'

'I know. But it's still my dad. I've got memories of us. He was a sad man but, you know…. Anyway, working with Bill, I thought how funny if my dad had been given to Bill.'

'Double bloody hell. How would you feel if he had been?'

'Odd.'

'Yeah. I bet.'

'No, really odd because… I'm going to whisper. Bill took his designated cadaver home with him.'

'No!'

'Like they were both ending their medical career together. He wanted to have him cremated, scattered somewhere peaceful, or interred.'

'Decent bloke, our Billy.'

'I hoped it was my dad. I boxed up the remains for him and the man looked a bit like my dad so I hugged him and gave him a kiss, but I couldn't be sure.'

The dovecot was now very hot. Condensation had formed into droplets on the cloud awnings. They fell in a gentle rain. Anne and William returned to their seats, flushed and grinning. William's CROW company's blood spatter patterns continued to spin around the room in twinkles. Then William noticed something. A smokiness just below the cumulonimbus. A bony hand hovered in it. Teeth came tip-tapping through the gaps and the hand lined them up in two rows, each tooth correctly placed. Anne, Jacques and Nell presumed William was watching the spatter pattern circulate and didn't bother following his gaze. William raised his glass and toasted the hands and teeth. It was obviously a night for reunions. 'Here's to you, my dear friend.' The teeth responded with a smile. Then the hand slid between the teeth and the teeth bit down on it and a crackling voice said things. William strained his ears to listen but the fairyland baffles impeded him. Small parks flew off those teeth with fillings as they struck the hand bone. They acted like flints. One spark flew. Zip. Another spark took flight. The effect was that of a sparkler made of mindfulness. One spark landed in Anne's vodka and flames irrupted, the glass shattered, and fire flowed all over the table, igniting the tablecloth and the crumpled paper napkins.

'Fire!' shouted William, grabbing Anne's hand and pushing Nell and Jacques ahead of him. Everyone fled. The bones and teeth went about biting down on the flames, chomping and swatting them but the fire took hold despite their efforts, and that was the end of the Elizabethan dovecote that not even the Great Fire of London had even so much as sooted.

* * *

William placed his fiftieth advertisement feature in the paper and online editions of the crime scene cleaners' trade journal, Spillages and Spurts. He'd got the hang of it now. His successful, discreet and nocturnal crime scene cleaning prowess had won CROW a slew of recommendations. He was a wealthy man.

He wondered how hospital doctors, consultants' and GPs would fair listing their successes, showing before and after photographs of their patients. Here's Goneral Nim presenting at A&E with a cracked patella. Here she is after a course of prescribed pain relief and physiotherapy sessions.

He was crime scene cleaning behind the VIP cordoned area, the set-aside hang-out for the monied, the elite in all their manifestations, their paddock, their stall, their turf, their manicured killing green. To help him further his business William had booked for elocution lessons, deportment lessons, Mandarin and Russian, too. His clientele were international. They were whatever the stupidly wealthy called themselves these days. Non Doms. Tax dodgers. CEOs. Whatever name their tribe coalesced around, he would be defined by it as well.

CHAPTER 15

JACQUE'S STORY

J acques lived with Matt Tuttle. They'd started university together. Matt was a friend who'd had all his teeth knocked out in a car accident when he was twelve. The final adult tooth had emerged fully from Matt's gums the day before the crash. The full set had flown out of his mouth on impact, like a berserking travel chess set, and embedded themselves in his parents and younger brother, killing them outright. Matt believed that dentists used his name as a swearword to curse each other. Orphaned by the good strong teeth he had inherited and that his parents had nurtured through strict diet and comprehensive oral hygiene. His parents had bought him a new electric toothbrush the day before the crash and it remained untouched, trapped in its box, Time's dandruff, dust, covering it. Time's floss, cobwebs, poised as though stretched between the index fingers of two ghostly hands.

'Those teeth need a stronger mouth than yours,' his dad had said through the rear view mirror.

'Those teeth of yours are going to be the ones dictating to you,' said Matt's mother, 'like a strong-willed horse.'

Whilst Matt had fallen into confessional stand-up comedy, Jacques had become obsessed with sumo wrestling, despite having the wrong physique, temperament, nationality, lack of co-ordination, weak ankles and little information to stoke his obsession — other than stock images of a sumo wrestler, occasional television footage showing them grapple each other, thudding flesh against flesh, demolition balls with an invisible city between them, trying to hoist each other by their loincloth belts. Those belts fringed with beads. Big barefoot men. Hair in a knot. Huge, voluptuous males. Soft fleshed but with muscles hidden beneath them like a plates beneath mounds of sandwiches.

Jacques' sumo obsession had been a slow secretion (a slim sumo gradually pearling up into great girth and great worth) ever since his mother had had vanished into the sea when he was three years old. She'd been paddling, no deeper than her shins, standing alongside other women with skirts lofted clear of the waves. Skirts huddled around her, bent forwards, grinning into his dad's stalking camera one moment and gone the next, thrown backwards, like a magician's trick gone wrong. Sumo was, perhaps, his way of reinstating an accommodating body to comfort all his little hurts against but, like Richard Dadds (confined to a male only asylum after killing his father) he had begun to forget what women were really like.

'Your dad, what is his sorrow?' Matt had asked Jacques when they met as they moved into student halls of residence at the start of their academic career. Hugh had just carried a box of bedding and a reading lamp into Jacques' room. They could hear him sighing as though his heart was carved out of the north wind.

'Is he crying?'

'Yes.'

'He is upset at you leaving the nest? Where's your mum, then?'

'Dead. She's dead.'

'Oh, so he'll be on his tod at home. Um, tough for him. I live with my Uncle Nick, he's a carpenter. Into am dram. Always rehearsing. You think that's hilarious when you're a kid but then you hit adolescence and you're so embarrassed.'

'I can imagine.'

'Know what he made me for my birthday. These...' Matt dragged out a heavy pair of headphones. They looked as though they'd been carved out of wood.

'Wooden headphones. Slightly better than the year before.' Matt dragged out a very heavy bag and tipped out...'Wooden trainers.'

'What? Like clogs but shaped like trainers?'

'Got it in one, sir,' said Matt. 'Wooden trainers. Bought some of the little sample pots you can get from DIY stores and painted them, too. Really accurate imitations. Hinged them as well. Copied the way armoured boots work. I mean, they're a labour of love but a gift you don't want to be seen dead in. I had to bring them with me or he'd have been hurt.'

'Your Uncle Nick sounds like my dad.'

'Could be they're both emotionally dented men. I tell you what, he made me some wooden teeth. There's a history of wooden teeth out in the world. Abraham Lincoln had wooden teeth. Carved from the cherry tree he chopped down and was reprimanded for, but was honest about. Mine's from the orchard where Newton was supposed to have been struck by an apple. From one of the old trees. He goes the whole hog does my Uncle Nick.'

'He must care a lot about you.'

Matt nodded. 'Your dad, he's not stopped weeping yet, has he?'

'I've got used to him. He's been like this for fifteen years. It's just how he is.'

'Depression. Nasty.'

'Sorrow. Not depression. Similar shade of blue but half-a-metre deeper.'

'He may recover now you've gone. Maybe you reminded him of her. Do you look like her?'

'Identical, evidently. Except she was a woman. '

'Right. Your face is your mum's. I can kind of see her in you.'

'Yes, he talks to me like I'm her sometimes. Disquieting.

Sometimes he gives me the wrong kind of kisses. '

'Ugh! No way. The wrong kind of kisses… like…?' and Matt kissed the back of his hand very juicily.

'Shush. Don't. He's only in the next room.' They listened. Jacques' father was huffy with sobs.

'You all right in there, dad?' said Jacques.

'Yes,' said Hugh.

'Shall I make us a cup of tea with this nice kettle you've bought me?'

'No, thank you,' Hugh said between sobs. 'You know me. This'll pass in a moment. It's just when circumstances change. I shall be fine. You know me.'

Jacques took hold of Matt's arm and guided him back outside where more parents were busy bedding their offspring into the soft loam of the Outside World.

'Once, I was a real father,' shouted Hugh so they could hear him.

'You're still a real father,' Jacques shouted back. 'Dad. You're a real dad. Genuine. Bonafide.'

'No, Jacques. I was swept out to sea along with your mother.'

'You weren't dad.'

'I was.'

'Aren't you going to contradict him?' whispered Matt.

'No. He won't budge. He always says this.'

'I'm a fish,' said Hugh. 'Out in the deep, marking where your mother is. A fish stopping other fishes feeding on her.'

'Gross,' said Matt.

'It gets grosser. He'll go home in a minute.'

'I learned what it was to be a husband in the sea. The sea taught me.'

'Yes dad.'

'The sea. Nothing mixes, everything is always isolated. You swim in a shoal but there's still space around you which nothing ever fills. Nothing at all.'

CHAPTER 16

THE DISSECTED CADAVER'S TALE

Hugh Mercutio Oatcake loved a good jigsaw puzzle. Lid off, fingers in among the tiles like feet treading the margins of the deep, deceptive sea. Such waves! The tessellated. The interlocking. Thirty eight pieces by twenty seven, twenty seven pieces by nineteen. How fragmented things could be and yet they could come together again. Find each other. Call and answer. Jigsaw puzzles. One image cut into shuffled quantities and humans could clip them back into their rightful place. The old sort of puzzles created by seven hundred tons of force wielding the apportioning and precise knives. Like a bank of synchronised surgeons making incisions. The newer jigsaw puzzle was cut by light.

Jigsaw puzzles were Hugh Oatcake's icons. He bought them from charity shops irrespective of the fact that they weren't always complete, and some were adulterated by pieces from other puzzles, and some were whole but didn't match the image on the box. And now there were three dimensional jigsaws. Hugh Oatcake rejoiced. He purchased one, a globe. Straight away he had an idea. He saw what he could do. He would create a life-size, three dimensional jigsaw puzzle of his dead wife. Presumed dead. In his imagination his wife rose from the flat sea of memory. She took up space again rather than being consumed by it. Oh yes, three dimensional jigsaw puzzles enabled his wife to pop up from the seabed, his wife, there she was, set adrift in an eggshell, or on a scollop, her thirty-years-grown hair needing a headwind to carry its weight, her clothes worked from her by the abrasion of the tides. Her neck as sinuous as a conger eel. Her eyes rolled blank of their astonishing brown irises. Her lips a coral ridge that would cut his flesh like jigsaw knives.

Her body was never found. Into the sea, waving, up to her ankles, waving, skirt held above her knees so she could no longer wave. Then she tumbled backwards and was gone. Sucked out by a rip tide. Evidently. He couldn't swim. He didn't know if his wife could swim. She had never mentioned it in their discussions. Sucked out to sea and never fetched back. He holidayed there every year and kept vigil. The beach had won a blue flag, since, for the cleanliness of the water and the spotlessness of the sand. Oh but his wife would scour and scour and scour. That was her doing. Her soft brain clumped in her hands for a cloth. That would be her.

Hugh Oatcake had thousands of snaps of his wife, Miranda Mercutio Oatcake. Boxfuls. Sprawls. Drawsworths. Shedloads. Albums jammed open. She was effusive. He had photos from every angle of her, posed ones and accidental ones when the analogue camera went off in his fingers whilst he was trying to turn the spool to latch onto the next unexposed frame. Or in the new digital ones where the focus drifted, everything converging and then dispersing as though caught in the drag of an expanding universe as he battled with the jut and contraction of the lens, and his large fingers diddled uselessly against the buttons and knobs. The buttons and knobs made for firmer hands, finer fingers.

His marriage had happened through the camera. The golden lens he'd threaded onto her ring finger in the church. His Miranda eating an ice lolly against the whole spangled sea, tin foil twinkles, the trillion dabbled diamonds and the refracting salt in the air. Then at home in winter in the iced garden, holding one of his frozen shirts, her frozen bra, her frozen nightdress, locked and posed and placed on the hurriedly assembled deckchair like a person, like an invisible snowman. Photos of Miranda Oatcake in the summer on a tartan throw, sifting through autumn with a spade, walking the dog. Hugh Oatcake persisted until he found images of Miranda Oatcake from every angle. Here she was. Then he had the images brought to life-size. Initially it was hit and miss with his draughtsmanship. He found it hard to gauge her and three years to engineer her carapace, to fathom her posture and her grace. She rose slowly from the bedrock of her back and clustered and cluttered, Eastman and Kodak bright, until she lay supine on the living room floor. Exactly right. The correct expanse. Her typical look. Her usual expression. Here she was, Miranda Mercutio Oatcake. Hugh Mercutio Oatcake lay on his back next to her and watched daylight probe the ceiling and the bric-a-brac on the window ledge, and then he watched night sprout from their kernels. Then he broke her, boxed her, carried her upstairs and remade her on the top sheet of their bed and drew the duvet over her, ever so gently. Good night, dear. What do you see, dear? Then he removed the pieces up to her hips and wriggled gently inside her, his face inside hers, popping out her eyes and staring up out of her face.

Afterwards, Hugh Mercutio Oatcake took her apart and put her in a jigsaw puzzle box with her photo on all of the sides. So she might be reassembled when the Last Trumpet sounded. And Hugh Mercutio Oatcake sent off for the forms and filled them in so his body, at death, would be donated to science. To be cut and sliced and sawn into fragments and placed in a plastic sack in a flip topped bin and reduced from connection into portions, resilient against reconfiguring. A human confetti to rain down when we are called to Judgement, to be assembled alongside Miranda Mercutio Oatcake by the Good Lord for whom nothing and no one is a puzzle.

❧ CHAPTER 17 ❧

THE JABBERWOCK

Night time and Kit Marlowe was loitering in his workroom, that Savile Row stitcheroo was busy tacking a paper pattern onto cloth. Then he set that aside and began to make a pommel out of the plectrum shaped lumps of tailors' chalk, binding them together with a vintage linen measuring tape he'd picked off an overhanging tree as he walked past Regents Park.

It was a fine pommel and gave like finger bones when firmly gripped. Kit was sitting crosslegged on his work table with all the pins and needles pointing at him, giving him away. Kit had pulled on a pair of white cotton gloves, gloves his father had sewn for him, as was the tradition going back seven generations, of father's always sewing white gloves for their sons, seven pairs, each different from the preceding pair to varying degrees. For example, the first pair were merely little mittens with satin ties.

The gloves explained how their family divided up their lives. Newborn, toddler, child, adolescent, man, man, man. The 'toddler' held the infinite and the final 'man' held the absolute. The discarding of one pair and the taking up of another was always celebrated, even if only privately. Kit was in his first man's pair, and he wore them now because he had taken out the large, old book from its glass case. The book bound in a hanged murder's skin. Kit didn't want to touch human leather.

It was plump and had the finger-sinking quality that only the best leathers had. The tanner had done an excellent job tanning this pound of flesh.

Philip Spivey the Third was at home creating a series of felt crowns for a fashion show. He had shut himself in their basement with his hat blocks. It wasn't worth going home before Philip had lost his antagonism towards anything that wasn't a hat.

Kit opened the book and stroked diagonally across the pages. The book closed on his hand and held it very firmly, three notches down from hurting him. Leather glove held cotton glove. And somebody was coming up the stairs.

Somebody was coming up the stairs. Somebody who sounded like something was coming up the stairs.

Something stepped through the doorway. Something with as jagged an outline as the window through which it had escaped. Something that had dabs of dried yellow yolk adhering to it. Something cradling an armful of loose pins and needles as tenderly as it might cradle an infant of its own kind. It curled and unrolled and snaffled the sheers from the table whilst Kit sat holding the biggest of his needles to ward it off. Its head was very sea horse-ish. It moved at a tilt like a cloth shopping trolley being drawn along the street. It cut at the air, a sword sort of shape, and dropped the pins and needles it was holding into it. They dropped in and stayed where they were. A sharp shape. Long and very, very pointed. Then it took the tailors' chalk and vintage linen tape measure pommel and clipped the two together. The sword immediately curled into a corkscrew. It was a vorpal sword. Kit had read about them long ago and his memory was running its finger down all the pages of every book he had ever read to find out what he knew.

They are very sharp. They give you pins and needles all over. They are the worst sort of sleep. They enter and the pins and needles disperse inside and go about the business of pinning the heart to the brain, the lungs to the kneecaps, the kidneys to the tongue. Kit would have liked to have screamed. He thought it was probably the most opportune moment of his life to scream. He opened his mouth and the vorpal sword went in.

Snicker snack.

Snicker snack.

* * *

At the same time, across London, Kit's half-brother couldn't sleep. He went into the kitchen of his big new home and drew a glass of water from a tap as large as a boxing glove. William looked out of the window. A moon was leaping rapidly up the sky. It was shooting up from the shrubbery, its sudden movement triggering the intruder light. Then the moon steadied itself against the Evening Star and was still. Beneath its light stood the three ark builders. They were awake and staring in at him. William went out to them, locking the door behind him. As soon as William's foot struck the lawn the men began digging, forking, raking, and an ark was formed in the emerald turf where they worked. William tried not to fret about the damage to the expensive lawn. The man with the spade plunged in the pole of a GIVE WAY road sign. The three men stepped back, took off their bracken fangled hats and bowed, and William climbed down into the hole. As always, the soil beneath William's feet was firm but the hole rocked as though he was in an open boat on a sea. The road sign rattled as the wind gusted, the sign turning in its pole to catch the shifting wind. Off he sailed.

William bobbed through night-emptied side roads, fetched up alongside houses, peering through the windows as he slipped past them, underlining them with a streak of breath, then he scudded past areas of deep shadow, the moon shining through the buildings as though the moon was more real than they were.

William couldn't be certain but he thought he glimpsed other solitary sailors passing by in their shallow grave-like arks, bobbing in the currents of London's hidden soil. Along they gadded. If William leant over one side the hole tilted as though his weight altered its balance. He dropped his hand against the passing soil and felt his palm slapped and fingers emptied as though the soil was indeed some kind of water. 'I wonder what would happen if I capsized?' William said aloud. A cat watched him, the wake of his passing toppling it onto its side. It recovered and sprang away, its fur clamped shut, shrieking.

'Sorry about that, oh cat,' William called after it. Now he was travelling by the Thames, skidding the Embankment. How was he going to cross the river? A hole was something that water filled. Then he wondered how many apparent road works were actually abandoned arks? That would explain the profusion of roadworks and the lack of workmen in attendance, and that the road works always looked exactly the same for weeks on end. They were Arks awaiting their next voyage or whose magic had failed to reclaim them when their voyage was over.

William looked up at a series of glitters above him that weren't stars or civil aircraft lights. They hung at cloud height as though hung across an invisible rig. Like theatre lights. They were differently hued, from white glimmers to red, golden to green and others twinkled a pale sapphire blue. Beautiful beneath the clouds. The Ark crossed the Thames, cutting through the current as though William was standing in a hollowed out floating island, the GIVE WAY sign clanging as the river winds struck it. Then William was on top of Saint Paul's cathedral, bobbing over the great dome and around the masonry. He glanced up and saw that the lights above him made a spectral map of London before dispersing. He floated back over the dome which became transparent and let the light pass from the vault below. William felt the skin of his naval tighten, the snapback of his belly button, and he felt the tiny earplug spat out into his shirt. He undid several buttons over his stomach and fished the plug out, warily prodding where his naval had been. It had gone. Here was St Paul's cathedral with its naval, its inny from below, its outy from above. And as William coasted the dome again in his ark the dome slowly lost its volume until William scudded on a level disc, as flat and mottled and bright as the moon seen through a telescope, a wan whitewash moon.

Then the Ark was off over the darkness between buildings and down through the underground and through the walls until he was in an underground river, floating with a brick sky above him.

There was a bank on which enormous figures crouched, their bodies folded into their legs and arms and torsos, but each with their hands raised, catching at something, with the soft clop of a cupped pair of hands, the swish of a closed fist.

His Ark skirted around them, the first obstacles not to give way or vanish as he approached. Their hands were grasping at something in the air. When they caught whatever it was, the closed fist squeezed down hard and the hands dropped into the river and floated off into the darkness upstream not down. William slid on into the darkness, towards a light somewhere ahead of him and the glimmer of the same stars now glinting in the tunnel sloped tunnel ceiling, just as small and twinkly and just as distant-looking despite the fact that William could brush the ceiling with his fingertips.

Then William was on an underground river bank, by a pebbled beach. He shivered and drew his dressing gown close. A light formed in the tips of his fingers and coated his hands so his hands looked like flaming torches but there was no heat, the flames were thick and moving so fast his hands were invisible under them. He would have screamed if something hadn't covered his mouth from behind.

'Don't scream. They will startle and release their prisoner. That will be bad for you. Don't speak. I can speak but they can't hear me. Your voice is the most audible sound in the world to them. They have heard everything you've said however quietly or far away you were when you spoke,' the voice said. 'They have heard every word. They have memorised it all.'

William felt something push him in the back and, prompted,

he began to climb the figures although they were coated in damp mud and his feet sank into them. The one beneath his hands and feet was shivering with the strain of containing something, it was leant as far back as it could and was folded deeply into itself, braced against the ground. Both its arms were wound round something like a thick sheet that had thinned against the stress it was exerting to free itself. The creature's hands had stretched with the tug. Innumerable grey folded people were bound to the struggling entity which roared and clamoured against the low roof and seemed to pass partly through it. This strange thing was thin but also had great depth, a wavering deep.

The battle was like people holding the edges of an ocean to keep it from moving away.

'Who are they? What's fighting them?'

'They are golems. They are holding back a day. One day that tried to begin but was stopped in its first few seconds. They're holding back one day. The day that would have changed how things will be. They are doing it for you.'

'How is that even possible? Why should I believe you? How does anyone know what's going to happen on a day before it happens? Answer any of those questions and I'll be a happier man,' said William.

'You will change everything William Shakespeare. You are the exception that proves the rule. You are the accident of birth. You should never have been born.'

'You could say that about anyone. It's all pretty random.'

'No, this isn't random. You were not intended for birth. You were not intended to inhabit the earth. You were not supposed to come here and draw breath.'

'My mother wanted me. My father wanted me. Even if they didn't when I was conceived, well, they sorted it out in their minds either before I was born or after.'

'These golems fight your war. '

'What are the others doing further downstream. With their hands. Catching things then their hands dropping off and floating up against the current? What's that about?'

'They're catching seconds. They're stealing moments out of every day and keeping them safe. In case any of the day escapes we can patch it up. It's like a jigsaw. The edges are all sky. We can patch sky with sky. It might not match in colour and weather and cloud but sky will mesh with sky. How many times have you seen a sky that was all over the one smooth colour? Now, to help us and to help yourself you must begin to use the fludd given to you by the Nine. Use it. It will self-replenish when it is used for the right reasons. If it's squandered it will drain away quickly. Use it. Cleanse the world with it. Wash away the sins. Memory is the last blood spatter.'

The light in his hands went out and William was back home, holding a GIVE WAY sign in his right hand like a spear bearer in a play.

'Up to a spot of vandalism, then, William?' said Anne who was standing in the kitchen sipping the glass of water he had drawn for himself and abandoned.

'What? Oh. It'd…it'd been knocked over by a car. Some, er, kids were waving it at passing cyclists. I took it off them. I'll ring the Highways Agency tomorrow and tell them where it is.'

'The youth of today, eh? We wouldn't have done that. Not tried knocking cyclist down.'

'There's a lot of anger.'

'And a lot more cyclists marked up as bright and obvious as targets.'

'Hi vis isn't about making yourself a target.'

'Nature camouflages everything till it's time for mating and everything steps out of its khakis and duns and parades like spilt petrol.'

'I'm not arguing.'

'Has something happened?'

'Why do you ask?'

'Your bum's all muddy.'

CHAPTER 18

ANNE'S DAY
FLASHBACK

Anne smiled as she suckled the twins and Odette. The twins on her own breasts, Odette hugging a cushion and latched onto Shirley's nipple on the crook of her elbow. Anne could feel the milk bristle beneath her forearm, the same packed pressure she had in her breasts, the milk swelling all the spaces and spurting at the draw of the little mouth. 'Thanks, Shirley,' Anne said. Shirley was a great help during water births. Anne drew the new born up through the water, caught on the crook of her elbow by Shirley, a lure no newborn babe ever resisted.

William looked down at Anne nursing their three children. The twins at her breasts, Odette snugged around a cushion and latched onto Anne's elbow.

'Shirley helps. She's helped rear these three,' said Anne.

'It actually gives milk, then, that supernumerary pip?'

'She actually gives milk. Shirley's a god send.'

'You've fed our babies that way? All of them?'

'Yes.'

'You never said.'

'You didn't take an interest. And she's better than a baby monitor,' Anne said, using her nose to point to her supernumerary ears.

'You can't possibly hear through those,' said William. 'I'm a doctor. Ex doctor, I know.'

'Well, Shirley's in my body and I know. I can hear better. Especially the children. She's very good. Selective with what she listens to. Or lets me hear.' William watched Odette feeding with great relish and saw the bulb of milk flow to the outer edges of her lips and be sucked in again. He couldn't deny there was milk.

* * *

Anne worked at the specialist Simulacrum River kept immaculately clean by solar panels and guarded day and night by specialist lifeguards. A series of small, fast punts patrolled throughout the night, lit, light and agile, each punt holding a watcher and a punter, as deft and sprightly as a mayfly. They worked to keep the water free from swimmers and dumpers. The bathing machines were patrolled, too, each having a guard occupying them, sleep overs since the births also happened at night these had to be accommodated, too. The patrols would slip by camouflaged a large dark curtain shielding them from view, the punter delicately prising the barque along the water. Several people had attempted, unsuccessfully, to dump terrapins and an alligator, but they had been caught. Anne was on duty at night, her costume and kit being phosphorescent, wearing a light strapped to her forehead and the mother to be enveloped in a special light kit that didn't share its light further than the immediate work and birthing area. The women floated, their bellies making little islands, so many sometimes that the water looked like bubblewrap from the sky when Inspector Benedicke Othello and Sergeant Iago McDuff flew over them in their police helicopter, the downdraft scooping the buoyant women along and gently knocking them against the bank where they bounced several times before the pulsating muscles of birth propelled them slightly upstream and mid river.

'Here come the next generation,' said Inspector Benedicke Othello. I wonder how many of them will grow up to be arrested?'

'Isn't it a bit indecent to be hovering over naked women?'

'No, it is part of our remit to ensure that they are safe. We see bodies we must protect but not women we might ogle. We can watch and the sight doesn't ignite passion in our loins. My loin is insensible.'

The police helicopter rose, jinked and vanished.

Anne knocked on Bathing Machine number 13 and was shown in by a man she'd never met before. He was immaculately groomed and impeccably dressed.

'I'm the birth buddy,' he said.

'Good,' said Anne. I'm Mrs Shakespeare, the water birth specialist midwife. Let's get everything up and running and slide this bathing machine into the river.

'I didn't know about the river,' said the Escort. 'I have never heard of your company until Mrs Macbeth mentioned you.'

'We're a well-kept secret. We don't advertise, we rely on word of mouth. Is our mum-to-be ready?'

'She's installed in the changing room. I've done everything that's on the list you sent.'

'You're very poshed up,' said Anne. 'For a birth. Most attending men incline towards stubble and casual and awry and dishevelled.'

'Ah, I will gravitate towards those states I am sure. Just one moment, please, Mrs Shakespeare,' The Paid Escort turned towards the inner door. 'You're beautiful, mmm, you're delicious. You're very desirable.' Mrs Macbeth screamed, swore loudly than moaned. 'Shall I massage your shoulders, petal-cleft?'

'Bleeding get this bastard out of my crotch!'

'We all respond to labour differently. Swear words work as a natural anaesthetic,' said Anne.

'Isn't Nature wonderful? Perhaps the Oxford English dictionary ought to have the words organised into their physical efficacy. Their effects on the speaker and the listener.'

'Such a book exists. It was written by my husband's mother.'

'Can I purchase a copy?'

'You can indeed. When the baby's arrived I'll get you one. They're in my kit bag. Cash or card?'

'Card.'

'Fine. Now, let's pluck a soul out of heaven through the tradesman's entrance. Lovey, roll your sleeves up, eh?' How well do you know Mrs McB?'

'Ah, intimately.'

'Good, because this is about as intimate as it gets. It's the equivalent and opposite of a post mortem. The body opens of its own accord and hands you its contents. Mind you, some scientists have dicked about and created the self-post-mortem kit. Using electrical and chemical stimulation of the neurones they can get a corpse to open itself up and hand out the necessary. It's supposed to be a terrifying thing to witness, although very efficient. The product of a disturbed pathologist.'

'I bet.'

'So, let's get the lady into the water and make her more comfortable. Are you coming in or staying dry?'

'No, I'm going to, ah, literally immerse myself in the situation.'

'Off we go.'

Anne manouevred the bathing machine down the gentle slope and into the Simulacrum River. Fish nudged her back and hips and slid between her legs. Once the water was level with the interior platform, Anne opened the door and partially swam over to Mrs Macbeth who was crouching hands and knees on the waterproof bed, panting and swaying, her long hair over her pain-contorted face.

'In you come, lovey,' said Anne, and gently toppled the woman into the balmy river.

'This is really weird for me,' said the Paid Escort.

'Really weird for all of us,' said Anne. Mrs Macbeth made a raspy noise followed by several squeaks. 'This is where we get to know a person's full vocal range. It's always an illuminating experience.'

'I thought my vocation was the only one to draw forth the full vocal range, but I'm willing to be contradicted.'

'So Mrs Macbeth had no one — and had to hire an escort to accompany her through childbirth?'

'Apparently.'

'How come?'

'She, ah, she was behind bars. Life sentence. Came out. A friend donated the, ah... and she, ah, to herself. Administered it. Administered the spoonful of sugar and... before it was too late. She didn't want to waste time dating. All that palaver. So, and then the first attempt was successful so she needed somebody to be there. Prefers paying. I said I'd do this free. Have this on the house but, no, she's a proud woman'. Bubbles broke the river's placid surface. 'She'll have her family now. She was married. Maybe still is. Co accused. No contact. This is her answer to life's loneliness. Something, ah, innocent. Unblemished. Hers.'

The Paid Escort birth buddy, his broad chest puckered with muscles, ducked beneath the water and then rose out of it like a torso in a perfume commercial. Oh his thrusting buoyancy, oh his hair plush with water, oh the whip of spray created by his tossed head shucking its watery payload. Anne struck him on the buttock with the prow of her miniature submersible scooter anchored in her working patch of river, the ride that allowed her to visit multiple cervixes during the busiest weeks, and he doggy paddled over to Mrs Macbeth.

Twenty metres downstream another bathing and birthing machine was being lowered into the water as yet another full term belly was launched into the artificial river. Several punts went past, the sun glittered on the water.

Anne felt her conscience vomit. There it was, standing on a

high watchtower platform, like a beach lifeguard up on their eyrie, their crow's nest, staring down at her, vomiting a cloud-white curd, her conscience unable to stall Anne's intentions. She had to take the baby or forfeit her future. The woman seemed like the best bet, the most appropriate victim. She wasn't someone Anne was warming to. The woman was abrupt and bereft of social graces. Ambitious for a baby but angered by the process. Surrounded by paid support. Friendless. The baby would only be borrowed. Anne's conscience jumped and swam down the still wuffling vomit like a backtracking salmon, the hands into fists as it hurtled itself at Anne's heart. A midwife prepared to use a baby to buy her fortune. Lend. Fate the Pawnbroker. The child would be back with its mother, the pledge redeemed, the fortune garnered and all would be well with the world.

The sun continued tickling the river.

Anne felt something nudging her back.

'I'm bobbing back down, Mrs McB. Remember, I can stay under for almost nine minutes so don't think I've drowned or swum away. I'm observing rather than switching to manual for the latter part of the labour. All right?'

'Yeah, go and have a squint. I'll try and get my money's worth from my birth buddy.'

'I feel redundant, actually,' said the Escort.

'Yeah, you guys forget that your place of work sometimes gets hired out for other uses. You mess about at the entrance to the world. Sheesh, it should be guarded by angels. This is the portal to life.'

Ann took a deep breath, a very deep breath. She carried on inhaling because her longs were trained to capacity, she continued inhaling. Mrs McB and the Escort stopped their banter and watched her.

'You got balloon in your chest?'

'That's be a great invention, instead of silicone implants, compressed oxygen or air so in an emergency people could keep themselves alive by latching on - save lives. In men too, use moobs as storage.'

'You should be a novelist the ideas you come out with.'

'I am writing a novel, actually,' said the Escort. It's my route out of Escorting.'

'Don't you enjoy your work, then?'

'Yes, yes I do but I'd like a change of career at some point. I mean, it can be a lonely and isolating existence. Most men don't like me because of what I do. The women I see want a temporary fix and nothing long term. I have no time to socialise.'

Ann was underwater, the river water like swimming in liquid glass, clear and sparkly and under lit, the river bed phosphoresced naturally, and tiny cleaning fish scattered hither and thither, travelling in their silvery clumps. Mrs McB was dilated seven centimetres and the baby's crown visible. Hairy headed as though the hairs that had been shaved had returned by a slightly different door. Anne grinned. The fish swam at her in a hub and dispersed around her leaving three floating women's heads. Anne exhaled with shock, almost emptying her lungs. The heads weren't severed, just detached, alive. They blinked, the fish dallied around them and when they spoke they spoke as clearly as they would in air.

'Give us the baby. We have one to give to the mother. You know we have to take it. WE have to take the baby to keep the day held back to ensure you and your husband's fortunes. We borrow we do not steal. It is a pledge that shall be redeemed. Here is a perfectly acceptable baby, a well made replacement.'

A newborn-looking baby floated in a voluminous and almost transparent sac towards her. Its eyes were shut but the irises could be seen through its eyelids. It was perfectly formed although Anne was pretty certain she could see the imprint of hands and fingerprints across its skin. It had a clay placenta attached to it on which words were written but Anne was unable to read them since she obviously didn't wear reading glasses underwater. The heads nodded encouragingly and Anne caught the baby's soft containers and held it between her knees against the river's slow flow. Then she bent to assist the baby from Mrs McB. She gently tugged and guided and the baby latched onto Shirley and the three heads caught the baby in their teeth and swam away in a snap. Anne's breath was running out. She could see Mrs McB trying to see what she was up to, the fish having shielded the heads from sight. Anne ripped the sac to extract the baby and its eyes sprang open. It eyeballed her as she raised it out of the water and into Mrs Macbeth's arms.

'So this is the little fucker?' said Mrs Macbeth. 'Quite a decent looking thing anyway. What happens now? Do we climb out and stuff? Do I need stitches or anything?'

'Yes, let's get you and your baby back into the bathing machine so's I can check you both over and ensure all's hunky dory.'

'There's a lot of fish abut in this river. Do you never have problems with fishermen? Anglers?'

'They try but we have continual surveillance. The fish eat all the birthing matter and tidy it all up. They keep the river hygienically clean. We need the fish more than the fishermen need the fish.'

'This birth River's a wild idea but it's okay. And this is my baby, then?'

'Yes it is.' *You liar, Anne thought. You absolute liar.*

'Does it look like me?'

'No baby looks like anybody at first. They just look roadworthy. They've just been assembled. They get customised once they're out in the world. You'll see.'

'Do you have children?'

'Three.'

'Born in this river?'

'Yes.'

'Do they swim better than other kids?'

'Yes, I suppose they do.'

'Did you like your kids from the get go?'

'More or less.'

'Only I'm not feeling the glow here.'

'It'll come.'

'Gradually or a snap on?'

'Could be either. Where's your birth buddy.'

'I've sent him off. I guessed the length of my labour and paid him for that, but we're into extra time. Anyway, he was a distraction.'

'Did you see him leave?'

'No. But he knew I wasn't paying him anymore.'

'When did he leave?'

'Just after you went bobbing for baby.'

Anne looked at the baby. It was delicate. Not like the usual sorts whose heads rested on their chests like the top of a spade where it kinked into the handle. And the hair on this little one's head was long and wavy. The eyes perfect rounds. The belly button with its knot now wrapped in surgical tape a perfect squiggle. Such a sweet, warm baby. Was it really made of clay? She pinched it and it slapped her hand away.

CHAPTER 19

A CLUE, A HINT, AN UNDERSTANDING

William had gone to watch Anne's aquatic ballet team (Titania and the Titanics) rehearse in the Simulacrum River when a man on a car crawler approached him.

'My name is Hercule Pierrot,' said the man.

'I'd guessed,' said William.

'I want to help you. I believe I can help. I know something.'

'I'm sure you do.'

'You can't drift about London at street level and not spot what's going on. That's why we Car Crawler Cavalry chose to go about like this. Public transport with its free passes? No thank you. State allowing us to go where we liked as long as it was after 9:30am — no, not when each time we used our pass the computer registered it. We were being tracked, trailed, followed. We were being monitored. And through CCTV. Now we can slip along almost unseen beneath the low tunnel of cars. Go where we want, where we like. Quicker, safer. On an Odyssey. A great adventure.

'Why do you wear the Pierrot costume?'

'Because it's my fate. One each generation. I am tuned to the moon.'

'Sounds painful.

'It has its consequences. However, we Car Crawler Cavalry

have become aware of something inexplicably awry. There have been a lot of murders amongst influential families. And the police believe that every perpetrator is accounted for.'

'Closed loops.'

'Exactly. No one else being sought. We think that they're being a little premature, a tad presumptive.'

'I'd come to that conclusion, too.'

'It's someone who doesn't bear the traces of their deeds. Not physically.'

'Right,' said William.

Hercule Pierrot stood up, flipping the car crawler under his arm, as deft as a skateboarder, his moon white costume billowing around him, the black pompoms rising majestically like the sky's view of ascending birds. He was much taller than William expected, and he seemed to unfold out of himself like an escalator's steps. Yes, William thought 'the human escalator' — there was something in the way his muscles moved. Hercule Pierrot's silken white moustache, waxed and immaculate and his silk grey curls twisting from the black swim cap lent him a courtly and other worldly grace. He looked younger too, there was speed and dexterity in his gestures, a precision to his speech as though he had memorised lines to fit every occasion. His tattoos were of the moon, the dark side and the light and they sat on his wrists like watches.

Hercule Pierrot took William by the hand and walked him towards the river where they watched Anne's legs held proud of the river alongside the lower limbs of the other water midwives in their aquatic ballet repertoire.

'Hypnotic, isn't it?' said Hercule Pierrot. 'And they can all remain submerged for so long you begin to wonder if you're watching water nymphs. Genuine undines. Has that thought ever crossed your mind, William?'

'No it hasn't, but...' said William slightly uneasy now. Perhaps he had married the Uncanny.

'Could she hold her breath for so long when you first wed or has this been a continuously developing skill?'

'She held her breath for five minutes when we first met. Apple bobbing. Hallowe'en. She'd eaten half the apples by the time she re-emerged.'

'We all bring different skills to our marriages — if we marry. I never married. I have been engaged fifteen times, though, none have taken me into that happy estate. I was never the one to break off the engagement. My devotion to the moon and the Lunar Assuaged Curiosity Agency I established, well, nobody likes to believe everything can be solved by a short spread of the Tarot beneath the moon, whatever her phase.'

'You're speaking to the wrong man,' said William, watching five pairs of muscular legs engage in numerous geometric patterns, the water around them swirling gently, a moorhen hiding in their midst and a gillie netting it so it could be removed to another river. 'I don't believe superstition has a place in the modern world.'

'It's not superstition. I use the cards to help me to think. I have a dialogue with them. It's like they each notice something slightly differently from their fellows. Each have their own interests and observances and observations. Each spots a moment and a nuanced expression that links with their family. See how this one is irked at the moment. And this one descries a traitor to his own self and morality. I know not whom they are observing but they are people watchers. I have seven packs and they each watch a different person. Their attention spans are significant.

'Do you think we could go into one of the bathing machines, most seem to be empty on this stretch?'

'Yes,' said William watching the legs continue to angle and flex, waxed with warm sunlight.'

'Were you always this tall?' said William.

'No, I don't believe I was. Lying down, well, that lets the spine stretch. Perhaps all of us would be taller if we lived horizontally — not like Les Grandes Horizontales, mind. The courtesans of France. But as a kind of age and gravity deterrent.'

'Interesting,' said William. 'At the moment they seem to be advocating everyone standing up.'

'Good gracious. A vertical world. Not to my liking. How will you keep watch on the sky?'

'So, what do you know? My own observations have been more about a slowly awakened sense that something isn't right. Hard to say what exactly's working at the edges of my suspicion.'

'Let me do a tarot spread.'

'I'd rather you didn't. I whistle-blew about tarot being used instead of empirically-based diagnostics.'

'Ethics aside, do you believe in the Imagination?'

'That's a very vague question,' said William sitting crosslegged on the bathing machine birthing bed.

'This tarot's different. Look.'

William stared at a pack that consisted of maps — of terrains, sea, sky and political affiliations, product and history. It also included pictures of Anne, Odile, Odette and Odear. 'That's not tarot. It's maps and, well, stalking.'

These cards interfere and interact rather than comment or describe.'

'What? They're cards. How can they interfere? And these are photos of my family.'

'Family always interferes. And the other cards, well, there are armed forces whose personnel consist of maps. Soldiers, sailors, pilots that are ambulatory, sentient and war-inclined maps.'

'That's impossible. That's sci fi.'

'You can explain it away as much as you like, Doctor Shakespeare, but all I ask is that you allow me to demonstrate their efficacy.'

'Cards only have efficacy in a game where they're part of a system of play underpinned by rules.'

'These are, too, but the game is broadened to incorporate real shifts in geography. In place. In people.'

'I'm sorry but I'll have to go. I've got to prep my team for our next cleaning job. And you've made me miss Anne's rehearsal.'

'And I have to prep you, Dr Shakespeare. You must understand there is something untoward in what you're doing. The abilities you believe were endowed, caused, by the fludd, well, perhaps the fludd isn't the thing with the power round here. Perhaps the origin and the source of the power is being masked. It's a Wizard of Oz situation. The power for change lies elsewhere. We're in the realm of the red herring. The Plumber in the Sea is what I call it. Noah's Fludd.

The Nine who gave you this were once Ten. When the umbilical cord is cut, the Grave takes the place of the nourishing placenta. From the first breath we are nourished by the Grave. What did you think when you first saw the three men dig an Ark for you?'

'I thought they were digging my grave.'

'They were.'

Hercule Pierrot sank back onto his car crawler and disappeared beneath the sun-glinting cars in the Simulacrum River's carpark.

* * *

William lay in bed with his hands all over his belly. He hoped that, under the cover of darkness, his missing naval would sneak from its hideout and revisit its former home. When it did, he'd cup his hand over it or sink his finger in and pin it down. Yes, it could pull away as fearsomely as it liked but he wasn't going to let it go. Not even if it meant he'd have to insert medical staples to nail it into place.

William did another broad sweep, searching round his back and under his groin (what if his anus and bellybutton had lined up like Venus and Mars sometimes did in the night sky?) Had riding in the Ark finally ended his ownership of a naval? Had the dome of St Paul's vanished in sympathy? Were William's belly button and the dome of St Paul's Cathedral sort of, well, quantum conflations of each other? Mirror images? Was it that old black magic, quantum strings — St Paul's dome and William Shakespeare's naval as its end stops, or transmitter and receiver? It was no good, sleep had changed the subject. William slunk out of bed, Anne muttering something into his departing back — 'mind how you go...' was that Shirley's voice?

William went to the cupboard where the fludds were kept. It was a high cupboard with a small led light in its rustic green ceiling. William pressed it and the jars shone. The white liquid looked like bottled snow or bones ground to powder or heroin or one of those other illegal, powdered drugs in their purest intensity. The red was oxygenated blood, obviously, and the black was the black of a nourished shadow. William flicked each bottle with his thumb nail and they chimed. Three sweet notes. William played a little tune on them and, when he stopped, the normal things of his expensive kitchen rang with the notes. Even the apples in the fruit bowl. Even the shaggy cactus on the window ledge, its needles like molten glass pips ready to be blown into lightbulbs. William wondered what would happen if he dripped some of each fludd onto his belly, onto the spot where his naval ought to be? Would fludd bring it back? Why did he cleave to his naval? What was it about his belly button that made him desperate to retrieve it? It wasn't an active part of his body. It was like an external appendix, or the flanges and sockets on a space rocket left when the boosters were shed, lost after they'd shoved the rocket where the sun never shone (other suns, further off, took its place). Why was he so attached to his belly button?

William wasn't going to bother himself with a definitive answer other than it was part of him, had been since birth, it defined him as a mammal, and he felt conspicuous, marked, without it.

William lifted the jars onto the work surface and popped each glass plug. Then he rummaged in a draw and found two rubber-bulbed glass droppers, and an old syringe from the vet's (used to measure medication doses for poor Mr Ruby who had now sunk beneath the ground, occasionally visible as a flat, raspberry beret comb gliding across the floor). William extracted a small amount from each flask and then he got a hand mirror out of the bathroom, a ball point pen from his study and, returning to the kitchen, William lay down on the floor. Lifting his pyjama top William drew a circle where he thought his belly button had once lived. With the droppers and syringe hovering over the target he counted down from three and squirted. Boom. William's clothes flew off, and he was as naked and visible as a glass shrimp. Light hummed a ditty. William was proofreading fanfares. William was swimming through the adipose tissue of religion, William was a blue ceramic teapot in which all the seas were brewing and he was playing mother and pouring them into their cups, gluglglglgugle into Atlantic's large, grey cup, glushglugglegliss into the Pacific's steel blue cup, and so on and so on... That job done, William was beneath the earth among the denizens of purgatory, among the remote flickering of souls in limbo, and he drifted through them on a horse made of bread. Here were coins having post mortems, their soft metal skins flipped open and the contents of their stomachs tipped into a dish — a mingled blag of men and women in various stages of digestion.

William could see out of every part of his body. He was still arms legs head torso but light entered and made sense on every bit of his surface. And what rose out of his touch was violets, a whole footprint of violets grew when he walked, great swathes of violets grew as he lifted his hands. And the perfume was like Winter's alibi for absent Summer, and William felt a cold wind punch his head and realised someone was knocking on the door. Knocking on the real door. William waved goodbye to the agitated Dead. Someone was knocking with great urgency. William sat up, stuffed the stoppers back into the flasks and carried the flasks back to the cupboard like lulled babies into their cots. A baby was upside down in the vacuum cleaner — he threw a tea towel over it — and dragged the vacuum cleaner onto its side beneath the kitchen table. All the while the door kept being hammered.

'Knock, knock knock,' William muttered, and padded down the hall to answer it. Two figures were visible through the glass panel, lit by the intruder light.

'Who is it?' said William.

'The Police,' said one of the two figures. 'Please open the door, we need to speak to you, Dr Shakespeare.'

William unbolted and unlocked the door, keeping the security chain in place and peering at the callers through the gap.

'You're police officers.'

'Yes.'

William noticed a helicopter parked behind them. 'Is that your helicopter on my lawn?'

'Yes. Yes it is.'

'Why didn't you drive here in a patrol car? Isn't that the convention?'

'We wanted to reach you quickly and your grounds are big enough for us to land the entire national fleet of police helicopters so, yes, we landed our solitary craft — scuffing the sward a little, but that's all. I am Detective Inspector Benedicke Othello and this is my colleague, Detective Sergeant Iago McDuff. Please may we come in? We have some bad news, I'm afraid.'

In the front room, William placed his slippered foot over Mr Ruby's comb as it emerged from the wood flooring and coasted along, William letting his fuchsia slipper glide as the little fellow strutted off. Strangers had always made the bantam nervous.

'What's happened?' said William.

'It's your step brother, Kit Marlowe. He's been murdered.'

'What?! No, no, he can't have been. He's a well-known tailor, he's the stitcheroo from Savile Row!'

'He's definitely dead,' said Detective Sergeant Iago McDuff. 'I am very sorry for your loss.'

'Me, too,' said Detective Inspector Benedicke Othello.

'I...that's...'

'Yes, Death is a great conversation killer.'

'I only saw him... recently.'

'How recently?'

'Three months ago.'

'Is that recently? People's time scales differ, sir. We find that people who don't like other people operate on a grander timescale. It's the ring-fence they erect to keep them at bay.'

'What, no, I like people...'

'Of course you do. You clean up after them,' said Detective Inspector Benedicke Othello.

'I'm a crime scene cleaner,' said William. 'I used to be a doctor but...it didn't work out.'

'It's all right sir, we know the reason for your change of career,' said Detective Sergeant Iago McDuff.

'We also have to fight superstition in both rank and file. One section of the Yard has been given funding for remote viewing, you walk in and there's a swathe of officers in loose-fitting civvies wearing noise excluding headphones and staring intently at maps of London and trying not just to preempt crime but to drop their souls into the places, as doppelgangers, soft crates of self-parachuting into moments of transgression and parting the victim from the assailant like sweet Jesus subject dividers, as my good friend here says it.'

'But who found Kit? What happened, do you know?'

'Here you are, Dr Shakespeare, a crime scene cleaner and used to the slops of violent murder, and a medical man to boot. Not like the common lot whose brushes with the body are normally of either the carnal, the lavatorial or the ablutionary kind. So...'

'Please, tell me, I'm imagining all sorts...'

'He was sort of cut out and reassembled. What people in the handicraft world might call upcycled. His head has been reorganised.'

What? What do you mean?'

'He's been sewn into something resembling a man with a horse's head. Very cleverly stitched.

'A man with a horse's head?'

'It's...horrible, yes, because it involved death but, aesthetically speaking, it is one of the most beautiful...ah...atrocities I have ever seen. It makes you doubly sad that he didn't survive the procedure. He is exceedingly beautiful in death. He is, probably to one who knows him so well, enhanced...'

'Death reinterprets us all,' said Detective Sergeant Iago McDuff. 'Shows us that, underneath, we are all the same silly grinning billies.'

Two things happened. The dissection cadaver began to form above the police officers' heads and several other golem babies appeared, ready to be swapped for human infants. Their number always matched the babies due to be delivered by Anne next day. She took them to work in her bag. Easy to pack. Top and tail them like you would a pair of shoes and they fitted flush. One was in the fruit bowl, rising up with the apples balanced on it, another golem's feet were visible, kicking above the sink. A third (or fourth, if you included the one in the vacuum cleaner) was peering out of the dishwasher, nonchalantly waving a dirty fork around. William was torn between the wild grief he felt for his beloved step brother, and the sheer sweep of his ascension into power represented by these little clay creatures.

'Can I ask you where you were this evening at around midnight, sir?'

William thought he had probably been circulating above St Paul's cathedral. But he hadn't been wearing a watch and he hadn't notice any clocks. He also wondered if St Paul's cathedral had lost its dome and, if it had, if anyone had noticed. 'I, ah, was

F.J. McQUEEN

either asleep or down here getting myself a glass of water.' The glass was still on the sink top — Anne had left it there. 'Thirsty work, insomnia,' said William.

'Can anyone vouch for your whereabouts?'

'Well, my wife was with me until I came down for a glass of water but…my hatchback's not been out for two days.'

'We need you to come and identify the body.'

'Have you told Kit's partner, Richard? Richard Spivey the Third?'

'We did call round, sir, but it was a double mission. We told him of the death and we served him with deportation papers. He said he was disinclined to accompany us to identify the body in case it was a trap to hike him onto a plane.'

'Oh, poor man. And who found the body?'

'Somebody saw what might have been the assailant jumping out of the window and leaving a trail of bloodied footprints.'

'His upcycling hasn't destroyed the original, just reworked it. There are photos of him on the walls.'

'Are there? They're new. He normally had nothing but cloth swatches. He wasn't overly keen on displaying his likeness, not in his shop. I don't know why.'

'Well, one wall is all over photos. Well, the one photograph.'

'I believe the word for that is 'simulacra'. Copies.'

'It won't be Kit's doing.'

'So, come with us… but not as Nature intended.'

'I'll go and get dressed,' said William blushing. 'I, ah, probably… should I wake my wife, Anne? I ought to tell her what's happened. Where I'm going.'

'Ah, wives,' said Detective Inspector Benedicke Othello, 'in my experience, Dr Shakespeare, wives my lie abed forever more.'

Five minutes later, William was back in the front room, dressed. 'No, I couldn't wake Anne,' said William. 'That's quite usual.'

'Ah, sir. Mine won't wake either,' said Detective Inspector

Benedicke Othello. Detective Sergeant Iago McDuff clapped his superior on the back and smiled knowingly.

They set off.

* * *

When they arrived at New Scotland Yard the helipad had gone.

'There seems to be an amount of tarmacadam. If I wasn't afraid of sounding an idiot I'd say that looks like a carefully folded road on top of New Scotland Yard.'

'It extends to other buildings, sir. Look'

William and the police officers looked down on a huge heap of road. Great loops of it were dropping over the tops of the tallest buildings.

'Is it an artist intervention? You know, these days they let them escape form the confines of galleries. I mean, here we are, gentlemen, intervened.'

William recalled his first trip in the Ark, how he'd sailed past the giggling telemons and the laughing, conspiratorial caryatids. This is what they said they would do with the M25, the London Orbital. Had they achieved their ambition? Was this the London Orbital stowed neatly enough across an assortment of London's skyscrapers?

'We'll have to take you back home, Mr Shakespeare and then we'd better phone for a patrol car or...'

'I could give us all a lift.'

Two hours later William was at the mortuary behind the glass screen as Kit's body was wheeled in front of him. Kit's face beneath the cloth seemed very tall. Very muzzle-y. William nodded to the mortuary attendant. The two police officers gripped his shoulders, one either side, and the cloth was drawn back — a thick, muscular cotton probably third or fourth rate and anathema to Kit. William stared at this horse-headed demigod in front of him. Kit had been a most beautiful man, with something feminine in the grace of his features. And here was Kit like a prize, fine-boned filly. Whoever had done this to him had a finesse and facility the equal of Kit's. It was, William thought, as though Kit had done it to himself. Created his own totem. Somebody down the corridor behind the glass screen was making whinneying sounds. Somebody else was kicking them for doing it.

* * *

William took Anne a cup of tea. The girls had gone off to boarding school, driven there by the Shakespeares' chauffeur, and wouldn't be home for three months, driven there by the chauffeur. William had given the rest of the staff a day off.

William drew the blinds. Sunlight entered like an admirer fetching daffodils, leaving once he'd struck his beloved's outline with the entire bunch. Clouds of indifference took his place.

'Anne, love, are you awake?'

'Someone is,' said a small voice. Anne snored.

'Is that you, Shirley?' said William.

'Could be,' said the voice, 'But isn't…!' a head came rolling out from under the bed.

'Oh,' said William. 'The Oracle. How long have you been there?'

'Long enough to chat-up your dust bunnies. Now listen carefully, William Shakespeare. Kit's murder has something to do with the fairies.'

'Oh yes?'

'Be sure of it. They have a jabberwock, a barguest, an avenging beast. It's under their control. They choose the victim and the time.'

'But why my step brother?'

'They were trying the beast out. They wanted to make sure

it worked. Like buying a pen. Kit's death was the test scribble.'

'That's indefensible.'

'They're not going to try and defend what they did, are they? They just wanted to try it before they made any sort of commitment. It works. Now it's poised ready to come into play again.'

'When, against whom?'

You, of course...' and the Oracle vanished inside the pale wicker waste basket filled with Anne's used, aloe vera suffused, Shrewds brand face-wipes.

'Anne, love, please wake up. Something's happened.'

'Day off, buster,' said Anne. 'This is my time to snoozle like a slob.'

'Please, Anne. Kit's dead.'

'Mmmmm?'

'Kit's been murdered.'

Anne's eyes hoovered William up. William crouched inside Anne's head and stared out at himself. He looked appallingly sad.

CHAPTER 20

PORTIA PEASE THE BOTANICALIST

Portia Pease with her white hair as composite as a blob of poster paint. Portia Pease with her fanatical experiments with banana plants. Portia Pease with her gunnysack full of banana plant hybrids, hybrids acclimatised to temperate British weather, hybrids whose sideways slithering, their yearly sixty centimetre sidestep as their roots hauled them through the soil had been sped up to sixty centimetre continual canter through the year; faster during the growing season, and a sweet paced trot during dormancy and rest. Off she slid beneath the cars ready to stab the soil and slide a seedling in. Dot dot dot all over London, in all the little places weeds engineered their way through concrete, tarmacadam and stone. Then there were the bears, all being reared for pace and stamina, bears able to keep up with the forest of banana plants criss-crossing London, converging from the four cardinal points, passing through each other's groves and continuing on to their diagonal counterpart, bears exeunt-ing London suburbs at a continual sprint. Portia Pease laughed. Her prosthetic plaster hands (cast from the moulds made by her own severed ones) with their lovely weight and the middle finger raised in a perpetual dibber on the right hand, on the left, the index and the middle finger raised to dig the hole in which to plant the seedlings. Such egress of form and purpose! And in her mouth, all a-fluttering, the tongue the fairies had returned to her. A sweet tongue capable of flight and with its own bird legs to jaunt on.

* * *

William visited Richard Spivey the Third, Kit's partner. He knocked and, when Philip failed to come to the door, William let himself in.

Philip was sitting on the floor among hundreds of hats. He was dressed in a shell-like puffa jacket and had on his outdoor shoes, nimble slim things that forced the feet to walk on their sides. Made the wearer proceed like a car tipped on two wheels and displaying the fine craft of unnecessary balance. The gait made the walker bow legged like Norman arches.

Hat boxes stood in ramshackle pillars around him. Richard had shut his eyes and, by the look on his face, he could not envisage a time when he would ever open them again. William made him a pot of tea and placed it on a tray along with a cup, milk jug and sugar bowl. He lifted one of the perkier felt hats over the teapot to act as a cosy. William glanced at the deportation order and then left.

A week later the police, having processed the murder site, allowed William to clean it. He went alone. He went with the fludd and no other cleaning equipment or mops. He went having poured more of the fludd on his abdomen in lieu of his belly button. The sweet violet scent drifted from him. The room gained grace from it.

The room was broken up, like a badly chopped log. The table was scratched. There was blood but it wasn't laid in any particular track. It looked like it had been randomly appointed not spilt by his beloved step brother as his life ended.

William shut the door. He looked out of the one window at the traffic fading into the dusk and the slither of car crawlers peeping between parked cars. A moon was gaining confidence in the sky.

William went to the glass case and looked at the book bound in murderer's skin. There was a hole smashed in the glass above it, a fist shaped gash, and William dropped some of the fludd in through it and onto the book. The black, the white and the red dripped down, three spots each. Out of the book came a great steaming eruption of human organs and the skin caught them all like a baseball glove catching an exploded baseball. The skin swam around them and up stood a great living tube in shape very much like an Egyptian mummy, everything bound, held in, swaddled. The shape had marks around the neck, a great squeezing, lengthening it, bruises, rope burns but these faded. A face appeared. Rudimentary and with the proportions of a baby's face, not an adult's. It was weeping profusely and very soon the carpet at its base was sodden. Shortly after that the room was floating in a depth of water quite out of proportion to the amount of tears. It seemed that every tear shed increased in volume. Each had the capacity of a full water cooler. The blood lifted from the floor in floating plates.

* * *

William arrived home from cleaning the room in which his step-brother, the Savile Row stitcheroo, had been murdered and upcycled. He went to find Anne. She was still in bed. William sat on the bed and sang to her.

Anne wept under the duvet and fell asleep with the grief still shaking her. Shirley's nipple softened and retracted, burrowed into its aureole with sadness. Shirley's ears were rigid with shock and the one on her back stood up beneath the soft billow of bedclothes.

❧ CHAPTER 21 ❧

OTHELLO

One month later, the Crow team turned up at a beautiful detached house in Chelsea. Inside, every household thing sat foursquare as though inside a sermon advancing virtue.

'The woman who was murdered was the heiress to a paper handkerchief and wipes empire. The Shrewds lent their name to their most successful brand,' said William. 'Brand my wife, Anne, uses.'

'Not impregnated with artificial saliva, though, eh?'

'No, aloe vera.'

'The husband …actually, I met her husband….'

'Did he kill his wife?'

'Thinking back to what he said, my guess is that he'd just murdered her before he came to tell me about Kit.'

'Oh, that's horrible,' said Death Nell. 'Chilling.'

'Did he seem remorseful?' said Jacques.

'He mentioned about wives never waking up. Then he and his deputy took me to identify Kit.'

'Jumping joss sticks,' said Death Nell.

'People, eh? You never know the day,' said Jacques.

William brought out the equipment. Three tiny phials containing fludd. No mops, no buckets, no swabs. No luminal no UV wand no reagents, nothing but fludds.

'Is this that stuff? Have we gone all minimal? Does this work?' said Jacques.

'I'm going to feel a fraud if I don't mop and scrub then bag up at the end,' said Death Nell. 'Do we need our protective gear? Or a decontamination area?'

'Best follow health and safety, Nell, Jacques. I've used it at home and, although it does some funny stuff, it's not seemed to be dangerous at all. Just very, very effective.'

William, Death Nell and Jacques went into the master bedroom and looked at the blood. At the rumpled, torn bed sheets. At more blood. At a pillow rising in its middle as though somebody's head lay beneath it. Or the pillow itself was diaphragm breathing.

'What happened here?'

'Domestic violence — honour killing. Detective Inspector and pilot in the police helicopter fleet. Led to believe his wife was being unfaithful by a fellow officer. I met him, too. Devoted couple. Who knows what goes on in a marriage. The closed loop again. Simplistic scenario. The whole thing awash with controversy. Very different cultural backgrounds. Families against the union. Class difference. Age difference — massive age difference. They eloped, married secretly.'

'What a shame. So romantic, except for the murder.'

'Before I use the fludd…'

'Is it 'fluid' or 'fludd'? said Jacques.

'The people who make it call it 'fludd'.'

Righto.'

'The bedlinen needs to be bagged up for disposal. Nobody wants to sleep on the sheets where a woman's been smothered. The actual pillow used to smother her has been removed by SOCO. So, let's strip down to the mattress. They want to keep the mattress because it was new. Expensive. Made by Shaolin monks.'

'You're joking!' said Death Nell.

'What about?' said William.

'The mattress being made by Shaolin monks.'

'No, I'm not. We've got one at home and they're great.'

'Kung fu kips!'

William unstoppered the phials. 'It's a bit spectacular,' said William. 'What this stuff does. Unpredictable.'

'But it works.'

'It works. I've added a drop or two to other crime scene cleans but not in the sequence you're supposed to. And I've never used all three types together. So, here goes.'

The black, the white and the red dripped down.

'The room expanded. Morris Men came dancing slowly forward. A great chessboard that spread across London with a Morris Men chess set making their way across it. White moved, then Red. Then Black. Three armies shifting towards each other, taking turns to move their pieces. The ankle bells jingling as they did. All Morris Men, no Morris Women, and a great bag of air, the East wind, was being winched down by the Three Kings. 'The East wind is the corpse wind,' said a Morris pawn as he raised and shook his handkerchief and the bells around his ankles jingled. Several hobbyhorses swayed their way towards each other, a small steeplechase circuit erected for them by the chess board itself spitting out poles and hedges. Three players, each hanging from helicopter winches, were dipping down and moving the pieces by kicking them along. The Ark builders walked into the central squares and began digging a very large Ark. When it was ready, the man with the rake walked along and slid every Morris Men chess piece he could reach and shoved them into the hole. The three men skirted round and round each other, driving the Morris Men chess pieces into the hole. Down they tumbled, dragging the chess board with them as though it had been a great chequered tablecloth. Everything disappeared into the Ark, as into a sinkhole, and when everything was done the Ark builders planted a road sign on a pole (a circular speed warning — 30). The Ark builders began hitting the great linen bag containing the East wind with their fork, their spade and their rake, as though the bag of East wind was a pinata filled with treats. The East wind fell out in streamers and glitches and the Ark sped off into the night. Then William, Jacques and Death Nell looked at the sweet bedroom they were standing in, a room filled with vases of violets, the curtains with the moon soaking through them like honey through bread. And in the bed, beneath the hand sewn coverlet with its intricate Escher-like pattern of helicopters turning into flamingoes and croquet hoops, beneath the vellum-like Irish linen sheets, lay two bodies curled together.

'Spoons in a draw,' said Death Nell.

On one bedside table were police cufflinks, a crocheted truncheon cover, a book on cloud formation and one on DIY helicopter maintenance. On the other was a great wavering stack of seed catalogues and a clock in which the plain dial had been replaced by an ultrasound scan of an almost full-term litter of puppies.

They stood and watched. They wept tears with the loveliness of the pair. And the peace of their matrimonial bed.

'We've come to the wrong house,' said Death Nell.

'This'll take some explaining if they wake up,' said Jacques.

As they watched, the bed clothes slowly deflated until it was clear that no one lay in bed.

William turned and went down the stairs. Death Nell and Jacques followed him.

William took drove them both home.

'We'll get home at a decent hour,' said Death Nell. 'I bet my mum and dad are still up.'

'You ought to move out of your parents' house, Nell,' said Jacques.

Yeah. That's my plan. Last time I tried my mum hid behind the curtains and wept.'

'What? She hid in the curtains and wept?' Like hide and seek?' said William.

'Something a bit off there,' said Jacques. That way it's like,

like 'it's all about me. Poor me!' Selfish.'

'Yeh, she's like that.'

'Get out as soon as you can. Look, me and Matt have a spare room. It's not ideal but it's, yeah, comfortable. And it'll be your own. Time for striking out on your own. I mean, you can afford to now. Billy pays well.'

'Yes, Billy does, doesn't he?' said William grinning.

'Bill, can I ask you something?' said Jacques.

'Of course, Jacques.'

'You know that, er, dissection cadaver you took home with you...'

'Oh, yeah. It, well, I had an accident with it.'

'Oh, right.'

'What were you going to say, Jacques?'

'I said to Nell that I thought it might be my dad.'

The hatchback began to slide across the road and towards oncoming traffic as William turned to stare at Jacques.

'Billy!' cried Death Nell as William spun the steering wheel as the car continued its trajectory and careered into a willow tree whose soft canopy was spinning in the wind like a carousel.

* * *

William was awake. The Nine bulimic cannibals were gathered round the hatchback all hidden by the willow. The Nine faces had lost their dreaminess. The Nine faces were those of minks. Of slinking ferrets. Their teeth were bared and moisture pooled at the sides of their thin, quivering mouths.

'The cards you carried showed us you had crashed your father's hatchback. But William, you aren't dead. Neither are your companions. We will go hungry tonight. However, one night we will be summoned by the cards you carry in payment for your great good fortune, and on that night my siblings and I shall dine and dine and dine…' The Nine stepped back, their diaphanous grey shifts and their thick, colourless hair cut square at the shoulder made them look as though they were the children of stonemasons got upon the highest ramparts of medieval cathedrals — that they were things of flesh and sky and cut, dressed stone.

* * *

A week later and something happened to Vatican City. Three work men had appeared as dusk fell. Dressed like Commedia del' Arte figures, they had begun digging all around the city, working assiduously as the stars filled the sky like wildly swung golfballs. People came to see what the men were doing. Some fetched torches and lanterns the better to see. Others assisted by moving piles of displaced soil and broken flagstones. Towards three o'clock in the morning the three men had completed their task. Somehow, climbing to the very tip of the topmost building as though simply climbing a short flight of steps, the man with the spade planted an Italian traffic sign on the roof of the basilica. The wind caught it straight away and Vatican City sailed away over Italy. It entered the sea, slid majestically along the sea bed and rose up along the Thames estuary, floating into London City, making land in the City of London, its walls chiming against Canary Wharf's great conglomeration of glass. Then it slid seamlessly over Buckingham Palace and the two structures fused.

People weren't certain if they'd seen what they'd seen. They decided they hadn't, and no more was said about it.

The Pope was found by a cruise ship. He was bobbing about in the Mediterranean Sea, befriended by a pod of dolphins. The Queen was found among the rooftop bee hives of London, a queen among queens.

And William was walking in Highgate Cemetery. In his pocket

were three little phials of fludd. How much Death would remain behind if he was to sprinkle it here. Was it morally right to pour this strange alchemical liquid onto consecrated ground? Was it wrong to wipe out all the traces of Death? What happened to memories? How did the Dead fare when their deaths had been vanquished. What did that entail.

Dusk and the midges were rising. A fox peered out of some sorrel at him. Should William read the headstones and work out which of the plentiful Dead had died violently? The ones whose lives had been considerably shorter than they ought to have been. Or would the fludd find them out?

William decided to walk along and allow the droplets to fall where they may.

Done. William watched as people floated to the surface of the graveyard. They sat up, their graves were like Arks. A road sign appeared in each one. The wind blew and caught them and the Arks coasted off, a convoy of bewildered faces. The ground where their graves had been now glittered with violets.

'Ah ha!' said William Shakespeare. 'I get it. The Ark I've travelled in is the grave.'

CHAPTER 22

A WEEK LATER

J acques and Death Nell were in the back of William's new
car. William's father's old hatchback was a right off. Now
they had a customised van. It was roomy and comfortable
and smelled of sweet romance. The fluffy dice filled with
William's mother's ashes were no longer depending from the
rear view mirror.

'You're different, said Death Nell. Billy, you've changed a bit
since I first met you.'

'Well, I wasn't Pope back then,' said William.

'How's your wife taking it?' said Jacques. 'Popes don't have
a 'first lady'. That would render their papacy null and void.'

'She's deciding how to make the most of the opportunities
her husband's papacy affords,' said William. 'She can't be 'the
first lady' but she has power.'

'How come they made you Pope, though,' said Jacques. 'Isn't
there a sort of protocol involving cardinals and a vote? White
smoke going up a chimney?'

'Yes, normally. But the thing that swung it is the fact that
I have no naval. I'm like Adam in the Garden of Eden. I am
prelapsarian. I look as though I was born before the first sin of
disobedience was committed.'

'Blimey,' said Death Nell. 'You never know the day.'

'I've also been able to wipe death from the world. Death is a result of original sin.'

'Theology's never been my strong point,' said Jacques. 'There's like a fistful of assertions that, if you don't buy into them, you're lost.'

'You can't half smell the violets now. They've become really pronounced,' said Death Nell. 'Amazing. The smell of sanctity — that's you.'

Let's just clean the scene. Don't worry about the way I'm dressed or smell.'

'You'll never get your overalls over your papal frock, Billy.'

I have a paper frock overall.'

'Funny how things have turned out, isn't it?'

'Is being Pope the opposite of all the hospital's superstition?' said Jacques.

'Oddly enough, no. They're joined. What religion calls faith — belief without proof, can also be called superstition.'

'C'est la vie,' said Jacques.

'And are we doing the fludd thing, Billy? No mops and slops?' said Death Nell.

'Correct. So, Nell, can you vape before we begin? I'm still concerned there is one mind directing all these deaths. One perpetrator. Before I wipe Death — and, with it, sin — from the face of the earth, I would like to know who's responsible. I want to know why thy killed my step brother. I don't believe it was the fairies, unless the fairies were acting under instruction.'

William, Nell and Jacques entered a large mansion. The decor was tartan and heather colours. The Saltire hung, framed, in every room. A copy of the Stone of Scone in reconstituted stone was placed beneath a large, carved chair.

'I want to know what happened,' said William.

Nell began to vape.

* * *

There was a table set out under a tree and Macbeth, wearing a crown as tall as a top hat, and Lady Macbeth in rabbit-ear deely boppers, were having afternoon tea at it. Duncan was sitting between them, apparently fast asleep, and the other two were using him as a cushion, resting their elbows on him, and talking over his head.

Banquo lowered himself from the branches above the table and landed, softly, as any freshly-made ghost should, on the periphery of their vision.

'Hae some tea,' said Macbeth.

'I dinnae see ony tea,' said Banquo.

'Thas because there isnae any tea, mon,' said Macbeth.

'Then it wasnae very civil of ye tae offer it,' said Banquo angrily.

'It wasnae very civil of ye tae sit down wi'out being invited,' said Macbeth.

'I didnae know it was your table,' said Banquo: 'it's laid fer a great mony more than three.'

'Who cut your hair?' said Macbeth. 'Only they seem to hae snippet your throat and face and the rest o' ye along wi' it.'

'That'll be yoursel',' said Banquo.

'Fuck's sake, who said the time is out of joint' — was it me?' said Macbeth.

'Nae, you ne'er said that. I ken it was some foreign guy.'

'I caution ye not tae make personal remarks,' said Banquo with some severity. 'It's mickle rude.'

Macbeth opened his eyes very wide on hearing this; but all he said was, 'What the fuck's up wi the local ravens? Someone did tell tae me but I forget. I ken that it involved writing desks.'

'Come, we shall have some fun fun now!' said Banquo. 'I'm glad you've a mind to call up memories. Now we're gettin' somewhere,'

'Do you mean that yersel' thinks ye can find out what's wha'?' said Macbeth.

'That's it, aye, exactly,' said Banquo.

'Then you should say whit ye mean,' said Macbeth went on.

'I dae,' Banquo hastily replied; 'at least, wull, I mean what I say and that's the selfsame thing!'

'Isnae, isnae one little bit,' said Macbeth. 'Why, ye might just as well say that, 'I see what I eat' is the selfsame as 'I eat what I see'!'

'Ye might just as well say,' added Lady Macbeth, her ears swishing, 'that I like what I get' is identical tae 'I get what I like' and it isnae!'

'Nae room, nae room, ye cannae sit there!' said Macbeth as Banquo coasted towards a chair. 'Ye must hover a little way off. Duncan here is 180 degrees prone upon the table. Should the guy awake, weel, he'll not like the intrusion. Ourself will tinkle the teaspoon upon the cup, and play the humble host but do not mention 'jam'.'

'For fuck's sake what's up wi' the jam?' said Banquo.

'Unavailable. No substitute provided at your request,' said Lady Macbeth.

* * *

After an hour of this, William signalled to Nell and she put away her E-Cigarette.

'They were a bickering lot,' said Jacques.

'Too true,' said William. 'Fludd time.'

William scattered the three fludds, spun on his heel and left.

* * *

A month later and two days short of William taking up the papacy full time, instead of fitting it in with his crime scene cleaning business, he was driving to a former diplomatic residency, the home of an exiled Russian oligarch (deceased).

'It's been a wild ride, Billy,' said Death Nell.

'The business will be defunct when I start up full time,' said William.

'Can't imagine a world without sin. Without violent death,' said Death Nell. 'It's going to take a lot of getting used to.'

'Your fludds have affected gaming. Some people aren't happy.'

'Give them time, they'll adapt.'

'Never thought the video gaming industry'd have its trade in graphic violence thwarted by you coming along and cleansing the world of sin.'

They entered a very Russian world. Human sized snowdomes lined the walls. Samovars were set into alcoves in the walls. There were priceless, gold leafed icons framed on the wall. There was an exercise treadmill created using the great caterpillar tread of a Soviet tank. There were photographs of internationally famous footballers strapped to giant wooden poles across a football pitch which the oligarch and his family manipulated at professional derbies.

'I'll vape,' said Death Nell.

Hectorevski sat in the corner on a beanbag shaped like a babushka. He sat curled like a fern frond. Cressidaya entered the room, her long dark hair in a plait that was coming undone, her ears like tweaked rosebuds. Her face like an icon painted by a man who had forgotten what women looked like. He had remembered their roundness but not their particulars. She looked like a frumpy fertility figure.

Hectorevski got up and walked over to Cressidaya, offering her a sweet from a crumpled paper bag. She dipped in her hand and he held it inside the bag, she punched him in the stomach, took a sweet and popped it into her mouth. Then she switched on the enormous television.

It showed a group of elderly Cossacks doing their Cossack dance, the bent knee, foot out thing, but from a convoy of car crawlers. They were bobbing beneath the great displays of munitions and weaponry in Red Square, the swarm-like rigid patterns of machine and men with the aged Cossacks in a kind of slipstream of nostalgia, flexing and flicking their legs in a marvellously coordinated glide between the great and heavy wheels of the Armed Forces' major weaponry.

'Oh, oh, look, Friar' Laurence's weapons — look, in that launcher on those great carriers!' said William.

Even in the soft vapidness and muted tones from Death Nell's ectoplasmic outpourings, William could see the tell-tale illuminated weapon shells, the soft vellum, the illustrated manuscripts surrounding the nuclear-level violence of these hybrid poltergeists. William was almost weeping as he registered what this meant. 'The Americans have them, too. Friar Laurence, being of an ecumenical mind, is happily supplying the levels of poltergeist weaponry to everyone. If they have equal amounts then war is unlikely. The balance of power game is a very dangerous ambit. Friar Laurence for all his wiles, may not have done the world a good deed.'

Death Nell coughed. 'Some awkward bugger…' she gasped, as something spluttered and rose from her lips like an inflating speech bubble.

'This is new,' said Jacques, busily filming.' This is very new — is it to do with the crime scene or is it because Death Nell's getting very adept and, or, very tired?'

'I don't know,' William said, trying to watch to see what was happening with Nell and focus on what the ectoplasm vapour was doing. It was the woman with the white blob of hair and the bear. She had emerged in a great ball, her arms grasping her bent feet. She drifted over the Russian convoys and the bear emerged out of her mouth.

'Russian bear Russian bear!' said Jacques.

'No, no that's not it. The Russian Bear was something the West invented. It first appeared in political cartoons. The bear means something else. That woman there, she was the one twirling banana skins.'

'Like pratfalls, like comedy pratfalls?' said Death Nell.

'Could be. I don't know. I really don't know. You okay Nell?'

'Yeah. A bit fidgety on the old nicotine but okay, I'll keep going.'

Then William felt a pull from his abdomen. A great surge where his belly button used to be, and that's when he noticed the fairies. They appeared, thousands of them, riding on taps. Plumbing taps. They clicked and galloped across the floor as William, realising what they were trying to do, trickled the black then the white then the red cleaning drops across the courtyard and into the rooms of the great house, the icons staring down from the walls, the little coves for quiet veneration, the statuary, in he went, carefully dripping the liquid and after him came a screaming horde of seelie and unseelie court all riding on bathroom and kitchen taps. A tap cavalry. They rang and clanked against the marble floor and thudded across the thick carpet. They followed him as he sprinkled the fludd, the great sweep of images still attached to his abdomen. Above him Hugh Mercutio Oatcake appeared, Jacques's father, his teeth placed in correct order by the spectral boney had. Arranged and thrown into the air and rearranged as the hand guided and placed them. The fairies clattered and once they were in position on the taps (each tap seemed to carry the reflection of a horse seen from some distance — the horse shone from brass and steel and chrome and gold and silver) and then the taps began to pour. They were fighting the inevitable trying to douse William's ability to wipe death from the place, they were trying to dilute his work. He kicked out at them. He poured the drops onto their heads and some of them popped and lay like burst bladders. Death vanished. The fairies fled, leaving the rubble of their taps behind. The woman with the bear retracted and strained against him, dragging his belly forwards then was pinged back into him. He fell to the floor. Waited a moment. Stood.

'You all right Nell, Jacques?' There was no reply. William

ran outside. Nell's and Jacques's inert bodies were being carried off in an Ark, the soil rocking around them. The air knocking its head, butting the road sign (BENDS FOR HALF A MILE) William retrieved the phials from the great hallway and continued to drip the fludd onto everything. There was peace. There was a great and sweet peace. William could smell the Parma Violet sweets exuding their lovely scent around him. He could feel it buffet his feet. He walked on the scent, he strolled off the ground and climbed a little way into the sky before descending. This was his purpose. This was his calling. Pope. The Oracles had said he would be Pope. He would move into the architectural and spiritual fusion of Buckingham Palace and Vatican City. He thought that he's better go home and tell Anne.

When he got home, he wasn't concerned about Nell and Jacques. He was sure they were being cared for. Anne was suckling three new golems.

CHAPTER 23

THINGS COME TO PASS

'As for me, William, I'll breastfeed as many golems as it takes. What do you think that the stalled day held?'

'My death.' said William.

'We don't know what conditions will attend the State of Grace. It's not very particular. What are the specifics. A feeling of warmth and well-being is all very well but what is the physical manifestation outside the body? What will the political map look like? And the cultural map and the historical map? Things will be redacted for all time.'

'It's a gamble but we've come this far. My naval has gone for good. I have the beatific perfume of violets surrounding me and I never have to use deodorants of any sort.'

'Yeah, that Parma Violet habit of yours has paid off big time.'

'I think I was drawn to them because I had this coming, this…specialness. This… I am the Blessed Zeitgeist.'

'You heard it here first, folks,' Anne said, to the golems whose little mouths were gaily suckling. 'They're nice little things. You could get attached to them,' said Anne, smoothing the top of one of their smooth heads. 'They're creating out lives. They're our body guards. I keep imagining the great Chinese clay army. Only ours aren't just standing down, ours are engaged in a perpetual struggle. I can't help wondering what was supposed to happen on that day. Why and how it was restrained.'

'Although I still don't hold with medical diagnoses being made through occult and extremely silly means, I think the Oracles are somehow able to predict. Unless they control everything so it's not prediction, simply the route they're travelling, the options they've chosen, the decisions they've made.'

I sometimes enjoy thinking I do what I have been placed on the road to do, my strings are being pulled, my feet travel one before the other at someone else's bidding. It can't be a sin if you're a puppet.'

'We're not puppets, love. I still think there's free will but free will still has to negotiate conditions and occurrences. Free will is still reactive and responsive. But the Oracle means that Free Will is the instigator and not just like the emergency responsive services. Free Will is apart from that. It's the arch creator. The problem is — and it's why we tend towards totalitarianism, everyone's free will causes snarl ups because most people are in opposition. TO capture everyone and launch free will in the one described, clearly outlined direction, that means we achieve more as a species. It's a strange thing but we do more as a collective but dream more as individuals.'

'You're becoming a right old boring fart now you're nearly Pope. And a married Pope. Has the other Pope said anything about it?'

'He's seen my vanished naval. He's seen how goodness follows me, he's woken up and smelled the violets. '

Hugh Mercutio Oatcake began to form above the television. 'Look out, he's here again.' William watched the bony hand attempt to line up the teeth. They were all over the place, floating in from strange points, always in a particular constellation, the hands lined them into two rows, swapping one with the other until they floated in a grimace, the hand tapping each in turn. A strange tattoo. The hand scooped up the teeth, rattled them in its boney palms and threw them back into the air. Out of each tooth fountained a hiss.

'Is this Hugh Oatcake's version of the 140 character thing?'

'I think so.' They listened. 'I didn't get any of that, did you, William?'

'No. Sorry Hugh. Try again.' The boney hand clawed the teeth back into its palm and flung them with — as William thought, unnecessary violence. 'Temper, my friend.'

'Perhaps this is more like the I Ching or Runes?'

'Perhaps.'

'How reliable has Hugh's information been?'

'Useless. I'm wondering if he's installed himself as our conscience. Or as a kind of killjoy.'

'Killjoy.'

'No, I don't think he'd do that. He's having problems explaining things to us but that might be because we have problems accepting what he's trying to say. We may be psychologically rebutting him.'

'He's been obsessed with the sea. He's been very nautical at times. Perhaps it's to do with the sea again?'

The teeth gathered in pairs and applauded.

'It's like fucking charades. I never thought the spiritual stuff was a major game of charades. Not because the one with the information is attempting to keep it all to themselves so they win whatever stakes are going but because there is a fundamental dissonance in basic communication. Oh, I squeezed this little gollem. I've lengthened its arm. I'd better roll the other one out a bit more so they match.'

'I didn't think they were still malleable.'

'Only when they're feeding. Probably so they can grow. If they kept rigid they'd probably burst, so their substance, clay, whatever, allows them to take on the extra bulk and then redistributes it accordingly before they go back to being form enough not to show handprints and fingermarks.'

'There's one major flaw in my getting rid of sin, and Death. I won't find out who's been killing all these powerful families. Whoever's been doing it will be forgiven. The Deaths will be lost. The murdered won't come back. That confirms Death again. Their absence confirms the fact that Death happened. No, I really don't know the outcome for the murdered will be.'

'Hugh Oatcake's teeth were very agitated. The boney hand was chasing after them like an incensed sheepdog after an errant flock.

'What also bothers me is that Hugh is a bit of a fire freak.'

'That might come in handy.'

'You were thinking of a spot of arson were you?'

'Not arson, no, but the Burning Bush, fire as sign and portent. The pure flame of love. Hugh's could be understood as that. That he literally carries the flame for someone. That's his power. Love.'

'Now who sounds the sentimentalist?'

'I do but then Love is a tough subject if you're trying to avoid soft centres. Hugh has a story. He was something to do with the sea.'

The teeth applauded then did their own take on the billowing waves. 'He's getting adept at pictograms.'

'I don't think so.'

'The Oracles. We need to speak to the Oracles.'

'Can't you sort of summon them?'

'No. No, I've never summoned them. They seem to be aware of what we're doing.'

'But perhaps an Ark could take you there.'

'That's another thing you can't summon. You just have to wait till they decide to send you one. I suppose we could try digging our own. Drop some of the Fluid into it. That seems to have its own properties, how do we know that the Arks are also a condition of this Fluid's powers?'

William and Anne went out into the garden. Their three girls, Odile, Odette and Odear were audible, their voices floating to and fro as they called from the swings as their Nannies' pushed them. The sky was flecked with scudding clouds with the density of upholsterers' rubber foam. The sun was a glossy, finger-painted yellow. William always carried three crystal phials with him, held in a padded gold case lined with Mr Ruby's moulted feathers. Each phial had a tiny glass stopper that fitted so perfectly nothing leaked even if the filters remained upended for hours. William sat Anne on the grass, her three golems still latched onto her and carried in slings, the one feeding from Shirley carried in a blanketed trug. Anne rested with her back to an ancient oak. Hugh's teeth stood on the two branches above them, top teeth on the higher branch. The bone hand draped itself longitudinally. William lifted the spade from its mount in the shed and put it over his shoulder, just like the Ark Builder. Did he need the fork and the rake? Yes, he lifted those down and slung them up on his shoulder than sauntered back into the sunlight. The world around him seemed so peaceful. The sound of the sea away to his right. The sea always sounded lie leaves rustling and the trees always sounded like the sea. His fringe flapped against his forehead like an injured bird. 'I'll dig here. In the freshly dug bed. He started with the fork, loosened the soil, Dug, raked. A hole deepened which he circled until he needed to step into it to continue work. He flung spadefuls out. The Golems opened their dust coloured eyes and stared at him. Perhaps they felt the draw of their old womb. The clay beds from which they had been formed. Each of their clay was a slightly different hue. The sunlight shaded them, showed their differences. One golem baby looked marbled like Odear's plasticene, all colours mixed into a ball that gradually melded, but left light and dark behind.

'It's looking good, William,' said Anne, lying the golems down at her feet and covering them up completely with her shawl so they could rest. She undid the sling from her arm and the carriers from her breast, buttoned up, lifted sunglasses from her pocket and slid them on. Then she came over to watch. 'Wonder why I've never been offered an Ark? You'd have thought there would have been a time or a reason to send me off to witness something. Hah. Everything happens to you men.

'Well, if this works we can both go off in it — or you can

go alone.'

'There's expressed milk in the fridge if I'm gone when the Collective need feeding again.'

'Let's see if this works. Are there destinations waiting for us throughout the day and night, changing as circumstances change?'

'That's quite a thought. Crime Scene Cleaning's changed the way you think, my love. You're a lot more philosophical. You should write a book.'

'On top of the seven books I'm already signed up to write? Yes, well, maybe I will. I can see levels of connections I never saw before.'

'Like fairies.'

'What would happen to a human if they were given fairy eyeballs?'

'You'd have to find a fairy with big enough eyes.

'Not necessarily. I've been designing new operations, new technologies…if fairy eyeballs were slotted into human eyes, the way they currently implant lenses and corneas, well, my guess is that we might learn something. We don't know the full scope of the fairy world.'

'They're a bit reactionary, though, aren't they? Won't push themselves to new discoveries.'

'Perhaps there's a reason and if we could see through their eyes we'd know why they're stuck as they are and so fearful of change.'

'If you dig any deeper you'll have a bore hole, love. Come out.' William scrambled to the side. 'Now for the experiment.' He took out the black phial and unstoppered it. He dropped a little into the pit. Then the white. Then the red. Three tiny drops. They peered into the hole to see if anything was visible. Nothing.

'It's not worked, William.'

'I don't know. Not everything is obvious at first. It seems to differ from thing to thing. It never behaves the same twice. I've an idea. Watch.' William walked to the edge and put his right foot against it and pressed down. The hole rocked like a boat. 'It's an Ark. It is an Ark, Anne. This must be how they're made. Come on, let's climb in.'

'What about the golems?'

'They'll shufty into the tree if they wake. They're not like human babies, they'll go somewhere safe and wait.' The Ark set off, Anne and William were thrown together by the movement and by the hole's sloped sides sloped creating a small space where two adults could remain upright by standing very close together.

'This is weird,' said Anne. 'Can you steer it?'

'I haven't been able to. What we're lacking is a road sign. They seem to serve as sails. I don't know whether we'll get where we might learn something or do something because we haven't got a sail.'

'How about if we use my jumper. I'll hold it up.'

'You can try. I have no idea what works and what doesn't.'

They drifted out, under hedges that caught Anne's hair and left strands torn and dangling.

'Did it do this before?' said Anne, rubbing her scalp.

'No. The Ark always bobbed away from obstacles. I wonder if this is just a random trip, then. Perhaps there's nowhere for us to be.' He decided not to mention that the Ark was, in fact, a grave.

'You, Mr William Shakespeare, the next Pope? You're joking. There's always somewhere you're supposed to be.'

'But the Ark's different. I go into places that don't behave like normal everyday geography. It's changed. It's metaphorical.'

'Oh. Right. It's getting dark.'

'Yes, that can happen. Time's different or the Ark goes to different Time Zones. Or parts of a story.' They looked out and noticed that the horizon was rising and dragging everything up with it. No optical illusion. They bobbed about, under cars, almost had some of the car crawler cavalry in with them,

pushing them back to stop them falling in,' sorry, sorry there.'
And then they were by the sea, sending the sand up, displacing
it as they tore along. 'We're not going into the sea are we? Will
we float?'

'This has never happened before, love, I don't know. This
new.'

'Hugh was saying something about the sea.'

'He's always saying something about the sea. There's some
nautical fascination there.'

They skimmed along a little more, churning up shells and
lugworms then they went into the water. They curled and sloped
and sank below the waves. The Ark kept the air in right up to
the top, the deeper ocean towering above them.

'There's not much air in here, William.'

'I was thinking that. '

'I took a deep breath. I'll hold it in. You get gaspy I'll breathe
some into you. Quiet now.'

They could feel the vast squeeze of the ocean around them.
The hole edges, the soil they stood on, was rippling with the
pressure. The light faded and an immense grey blue took its
place, sometimes a shaft of light gave them a faded green with
oval fish flickering like thrown coins. After a while William felt
light headed. For the next moments however long they were,
William shared the breath from his Anne's body. Then something
dark a light disc, the moon and dark shapes thronging across
it, one huge dark shape filling the moonlit water. Up the Ark
shot, the air dented a deep concave as they blasted towards the
surface. The pressure made their ears pop. For one moment
William felt the whole jarring screech of The Noise, he heard it
distort into chaos then, as his ears popped, he felt it physically
shatter in his ears. He twirled a finger into his earhole and a fine,
glittering debris came out, some sliding down his fingernail.
Then they were out on the surface, level with the waves and
always missing the higher wave leaning into it. Miraculously, no
water got in. They had emerged next to tree roots that grasped

each other as close as rung hands. Anne and William looked up. They had bobbed alongside a huge galleon made from a forest.

'What the...?' said William.

Ann lifted her hand to the bow of the great ship. Things were fastened and shifting against it. 'What 's that? What are all those?' she asked. They made a sound. 'Ludlum ludlum.'

'Oh dear god, said William. 'Anne, can you hear that?'

'Yes. It's loud.'

'I know what that is.'

'So do I. You're not the only one familiar with anatomy and the sounds made by a living body. I usually hear at least two of them when I listen to my patients. Are those hearts pinned to this galleon?'

'Yes. Small hearts. Human hearts.'

'Small people's hearts?

'Children's hearts, Anne. The ship bow is covered in beating children's hearts.'

'Okay, right, why are we seeing this? What's this about? Who would do this. It's horrific. '

'I'm going to see if I can find out what or who's aboard this floating forest.

'Is it a fairy domain?'

'I'd have thought so. Nobody else could keep a whole forest alive in sea water.

'Go forth, doctor, Pope, and investigate.'

William hauled himself out of the Ark which remained where it was despite the push of the tides. He climbed steadily, the roots affording him foot holds and hand holds and he eased himself past the hearts. There were a lot fresh pink beating hearts but pitted around them were blackened ones, dead and preserved by the seawater.

On top of the ship William stared into a dark, deep forest and in the top of the trees there were lots of beautiful tree houses, each lit from within. William hunkered down, creeping from trunk to trunk as the forest dipped and rose with the sea. A stag walked out from the undergrowth. Beautiful, unnaturally regular, regal and smooth. Then a unicorn strolled out, walking on its hind legs, its head's central horn glittering with gold leaf, its fur as white and undifferentiated as milk. The unicorn strolled slowly through the gloom. Great bears angled after it, and slender greyhounds and a rampant lion. It was as though all the beasts of heraldry lived here — an heraldic forest in which nothing of real flesh and blood existed. Then he saw the children. Children grasping the tree trunks, face forwards, the trees' softest green boughs slid into their small chests and their chests falling and rising as the tree breathed for them. The children's eyes danced beneath their closed lids. Dreaming. They reminded William of coma patients who, when woken, recounted dreams rich and oddly appropriate to their circumstance, yet all allegorical and as vivid and memorable as life. Small children, none older than five or six years old, were all gently held by the trees. Heartless children that the trees kept alive. Heraldic beasts and innocents. A man appeared from a treehouse and gestured to William. William began climbing. The man held out his hand and hauled William up the last few metres. The man was tall and tonsured. William immediately knew he belonged to Friar Laurence's priory. The friar took William by the hand and held his hand to his chest.

'This is the cost,' said the Friar. 'This is the cost. There is always a cost and the cost is always specific to the ends.' William looked into the forest and saw small children nestled against trees, each lost to childhood. An eagle and a phoenix twirled in the air above him. 'This where all the beasts from heraldry live?'

'Yes. The children's hearts keep chivalry alive. Ideas are always kept at the cost of beating hearts. At the expense of a generation. No idea has ever appeared without a dark shadow trailing it. Chivalry. Justice. Democracy. Humanity. These are the price for those. We spend our future on maintaining them. Their presence among us costs us dear. If Death goes, what becomes of these children? Your own children will join me here. See, I have three silver birches ready to ween them of their hearts.' William saw three slender, silver trunked trees with their small soft foliage, each band of bark so beautiful and silken. 'The softest bark of all the trees, such sweet dreamers, too. The silver birch is the first tree of the tree alphabet. Your children will be safe here in the arms of Mother Holle. This must happen if you continue, if you wipe away Death and Sin from the world.'

'No, you can't have my children. No. What do I have to do so they're not fetched her. I don't want to lose them.'

Then you must understand the consequences. Sin is a great battle to win. Death is a great foe to overcome. But loss is the cost of doing so. Great loss.'

William scrambled away back down the tree and ran to the first child attached to the bark. He tried to ease the child clear but the child was being absorbed into the tree. The child seemed happy. There was a smile on her face. Her dress was soft and leafy and her skin warm and dappled by moonlight. She twitched and smiled. There was some great joy in her sleep.

It was helpless. Tears welled and he scrambled back over the side of the great forest ship. As soon as his feet touched the base of the Ark, Anne embraced him and they sank back beneath the sea.

Then home. Then home with a terrible knowledge.

⚜ CHAPTER 24 ⚜

FINALLY

William walked into the Houses Of Parliament. 'Hats off strangers, I'm the Pope he said. Hats off strangers.' William walked into the Commons and the parliamentarians fled before him. 'Very biblical,' The Palace of Westminster emptied. The House of Lords spilled its peers into the Thames where a fleet of little boats and packets and river taxies pulled them out of the water.

'I am the Pope and all is forgiven I am cleansing the sins of the world and the Palace of Westminster is filled with the root of many deaths.' The fludd followed them all like a million fuses and the Houses of Parliament stood as sweetly unencumbered as the sky.

Hugh Oatcake appeared,

'If there was ever a time for friendly fire, my friend, this is it,' said William. Hugh's teeth flinted up and sent their fire into the wood and upholstery.

The Houses of Parliament burned but their burning was a transformation, a metamorphosis and the great buildings became a thunder cloud, an earth-anchored cumulonimbus that William closed his fist around and walked to Buckingham Palace.

'This is the Papal State, said William. 'This is the start of the end of all sorrows. This is Death's final fling, its hen party, its stag do before it marries its Fate.'

Inside the cloud there were the sweetly released Dead and they wandered the perfect rendition of the Westminster Palace. They moved among the benches and the galleries and into the rooms and the chapel and the star chamber (in which real stars shone) and the dormant thunderstorms lay beneath their soft insubstantial feet. And laws were passed and floated off and rained down their fair justice where the laws were needed. No sin. No death. The sins of the world gone. Memory is the last blood spatter.

Out of the three-hundred peeled-to-the-gullet chimneys of Buckingham Palace, white smoke irrupted. The new Pope had been chosen. It was William, of course.

Crowds had gathered. Among the crowd stood a number of caryatids, many wearing hats made entirely of keys. Several young men and young women clung to their heads and had the best view of everything that happened. Flotillas of car crawler cavalry swept along the grounds, replacing the Household Cavalry. The horses could be heard proclaiming their liberty in Regents Park. Free of harness and rider.

'I shall call myself Pope Innocents the First,' said William. And Pope Innocents the First strode onto the balcony of the fused Vatican City and Buckingham Palace and the crowds cheered. Above him the masons shifted the cloud chambers into their correct order — overseen by Hugh Mercutio Oatcake, the phenomenal jigsawist, capable of reassembling a trillion shards, of putting back an entire universe from its atoms. His was such power!

The sun and the moon shone brightly in the sky. William's wife, touched by fludd, was now two persons in one, indivisible, by his side, Shirley and Anne.

William, Pope Innocents the First, held out his hand to quieten the crowds, someone slid a microphone in front of him. Now was the time when sin would be taken away from the world and with it, Death.